THE GINGERBREAD QUEEN

CARRIE ANNE NOBLE

Cover art by Dar Albert at Wicked Smart Designs

Published by Oliver-Heber Books

0 9 8 7 6 5 4 3 2 1

One

ESCHLINSDORF, GERMANY, OCTOBER 1825

Long ago and not so long ago, in a small town in Germany, there lived a sister and brother. As children, she'd been called Gretel and he'd been called Hansel, and they'd had a horrific experience with a witch and a house made of gingerbread. So horrific, in fact, that the girl had grown to hate being addressed as Gretel. The nickname, however, was easier to shed than the memories of the witch's atrocities.

Thirteen years had passed since the girl, her brother, and their father had moved from the woodcutter's cottage to a big brick house on the edge of Eschlinsdorf. From that day, she'd insisted on being called Margarethe, or Marga. It mattered little, for she'd kept no company apart from Hansel and Papa.

She'd been polite, pious, and fashionably garbed, yet no one had offered her an ounce of friendship, for the townsfolk had heard things about the Holzfällers Tales that painted Hansel as a victim and Marga as a willing accomplice to the evil witch of the wood. Their neighbors enjoyed embellishing the stories with lurid details. It was an amusing way to pass the time as they lingered among the produce stalls on slow market days or hung out clothes in adjacent gardens.

Two days after Marga's twenty-first birthday, she hurried along Friedrich Strasse, careful to stay in the shadows.

A fat cloud skidded across the pale-yellow moon. With a loud click, the hands of the clock on the church's bell tower shifted closer to twelve. Midnight had crept up on her. She'd meant to be home by now, and would have been, had she not been forced to take a detour to avoid being seen by the town's busybody midwife. If Frau Mueller or any of the other town gossips caught sight of her visiting the graveyard at this hour…well, the stories of deviltry they'd spin would make their current gossip seem like nursery tales. But before Papa had died, she'd promised him she'd visit his grave every day, and she wasn't one to break a promise.

A gust of wind too cold for autumn pressed against her back, urging her along the tree-lined, cobbled street.

"Alms," muttered a mound of dark fabric next to the churchyard gate.

"Frau Bernhard," Marga said, recognizing the crouched shape of the old woman who sometimes begged there. "You startled me."

A withered hand poked out from the mound and a gaunt face peered up. "Alms?"

"Sorry, I have no coins with me tonight." Marga stooped down beside the woman and held her cold, bony hand for a moment. "Come by the house in the morning and I'll have something for you. Sausages, at least."

The wind whipped around them. Frau Bernhard coughed and wheezed. Marga removed her heavy woolen cape and wrapped it around the woman's quaking shoulders. "You've forgotten your cloak again, I see. Borrow mine until tomorrow."

"Bless you, *Liebling*." Recognition sparked in the old woman's filmy eyes. She smiled toothlessly. "Ah, you're that little witch. Well, if all witches are as kind as you, I don't see what the fuss is about."

Marga didn't bother to insist that she was just an ordinary young woman. It wasn't right to argue with one's elders, and besides, Frau Bernhard would probably forget the chance meeting before morning. She helped the Frau to her feet. "You should go home. It's late."

"*Ja, ja*. Might as well, might as well." The old woman hobbled and mumbled her way down the street while Marga opened the wrought-iron gate.

With the wind at her back, she followed the path toward her father's final resting place. Six months had passed, but it still felt wrong that Papa was gone. She still expected him to meet her at the door when she got home, to chide her for wandering the alleyways with tomcats and drunkards as he had too many times to count. What she would have given to be scolded by Papa once more.

The gate creaked shut far behind her. Soon, it creaked and banged again. She blamed the wind and quickened her footsteps. But then the faint scent of fresh bread and cinnamon drifted into her nose—scents unbefitting an autumnal graveyard. Panic made her heart pound hard and fast.

Someone else was in the churchyard. Someone large, if the volume of their footsteps on the gravel was a true indication. She glanced over her shoulder and recognized Lukas Beckmann, the eldest son in the town's family of bakers. Perhaps in the darkness the young man wouldn't notice her, dressed all in black as she was. In truth, he probably wanted to see her as little as she wanted to see him. Wilted funeral flowers still adorned the grave of his grandmother. A man who came to grieve in the dead of night wouldn't be prone to idle conversation, especially not with an alleged witch.

Marga fell to her knees at her father's headstone. She closed her eyes and bowed her head as Lukas's footsteps grew closer. The dampness of the ground seeped through her skirt and petticoats. She pretended to pray, hoping he'd be too polite to interrupt a dialog with the Almighty. As he moved closer still, she stopped pretending and prayed in earnest.

Please let the man pass by. Please. And if I must speak with him, dear Gott im Himmel, *let him not be covered in crumbs, I beseech you!*

Crumbs.

The mere thought of crumbs made her shiver from head to foot. She bit down hard on her lower lip as images flashed in her mind: her older brother Hansel strewing bits of bread on a pine-needled path. Blackbirds swirling like a band of demons and devouring every morsel of the hope she'd had of returning home.

"Forgive me, Fraulein." Herr Beckmann spoke in a quiet, friendly tone. He'd stopped within a few feet of her, judging from the sound of his voice, but perhaps he didn't recognize her. "Are you unwell? You're trembling so. Would you accept my cloak?"

Head still bowed, she opened her eyes and beheld his flour-dusted boots. She forced her gaze upward, inch by inch, praying *Please* Gott, *spare me the sight of crumbs*, taking in the sight of his dark trousers, the heavy woolen cloak held out to her by sturdy hands, a knotted scarf of brown wool, a clean-shaven chin, a strong nose, and eyes so blue their blueness showed even in the weak moonlight. He was older than she, twenty-three or so, but his rounded face had retained its boyishness. The wind tousled his thick, blond hair.

Not one crumb besmirched him, thank *Himmel*. Surely that was a miracle.

She staggered to her feet. Her straightforward gaze fell on his lower chest, and she cursed her shortness. How could she appear capable of caring for herself when she'd never surpassed the height of most twelve-year-old girls? She tipped her head back to look into his face again and found another miracle. He surely must have recognized her by now, yet his countenance was full of kindness, not contempt.

With both hands, Herr Beckmann pushed the cloak toward her. "Will you take it? You should be mindful of your health, Fraulein. The chill of these October nights brings fevers, my *Mutti* says." He opened the garment with a flick of his wrists and draped it around her shoulders. Its hem pooled on the ground at her feet. "There now. Better?"

She met his gaze and crossed her arms over her middle. "I'm fine, thank you. Not as weak as you think."

He blinked as if surprised by her bold speech. A moment passed before he offered a morsel of a smile. "I wouldn't dare to assume a woman was weak. Every woman in my family is formidable." His smile faltered, probably at the thought of the grandmother he'd lost recently.

"Sorry." Marga offered the simple word as both an apology and an expression of sympathy, and hoped he understood. She stopped shivering under the weight of his cloak. The garment's immediate effect seemed almost magical. But far be it from her to mention magic. It would be stupid to remind the baker of the rumors, nonsensical to provoke from him the townsfolk's usual questions: "Where did your family's riches come from? Did you steal them from the witch of the wood, or did she reward you with them for being an excellent pupil? Do you plan to eat the town's children to renew your beauty when your hair goes gray and your bones turn brittle?"

Although Lukas Beckmann gave the impression of graciousness, she couldn't trust him not to run to the town council or Pastor Günter to falsely report that he'd caught her performing foul rituals in the midnight graveyard. If he did, and anyone fell ill or died within the next month, she would probably be blamed. She pictured a stake erected in the town square, imagined scratchy rope binding her fast as eager tongues of flame lapped at her shins.

The baker's hand settled on her arm, light as the brush of a butterfly's wing, disrupting her nightmarish thoughts. "Fraulein Holzfäller? May I see you home? I do not think you are altogether well. Your face is pale, and you're shivering again."

Marga saw it then: a single bread crumb stuck to the front of his jacket. She covered her mouth as she gagged, wriggled free of his cloak, sidestepped his body, and ran for the iron gates and the path home.

* * *

"Where have you been, *Schwester* Gretel?" Hansel's huge form blocked the doorway of the three-storied Holzfäller family home. He was a giant of a man, a fearsome sight to strangers with his tree-trunk torso, muscular arms, and bushy, black beard. But while he towered over most men physically, he fell short in common sense and courtesy. A hundred times she had asked him not to call her Gretel as the witch had, yet he appeared to derive pleasure from using the name to torment her.

"What does it matter to you, Hansel?" Marga rested her fists on her hips. She didn't need to be reminded again of the dangers of solitary moonlit strolls. Sometimes one had to put aside fear and rules and do what was in one's heart. If one had a heart.

He continued to block the doorway and glare down at her.

She scowled and barely resisted the urge to kick her brother in the shin. Mostly because it would hurt her more than it hurt him. "I went to visit Papa's grave, if you must know."

He pulled her inside the house and bolted the door. "Traipsing about the graveyard at midnight! And people call me *Dummkopf*!" He swore, then swiped his rumpled linen sleeve over his mouth. "Get your things. A warm cloak, sturdy shoes for walking. We must leave quickly." He stepped to the window and peered through a gap between the heavy velvet curtains.

"Don't be ridiculous, Hansel. No one saw me," she said. *Well, no one other than Lukas Beckmann.*

Hansel turned to face her, his broad forehead creased with worry. That was unusual. "They're coming for me, not you. But if I leave you here, they'll tear you to shreds like wild dogs on a fox."

The scent of cigars, alcohol, and perfume wafted off his body. She narrowed her eyes in accusation. "*Ach*! You've been gambling again. And losing! After you promised Papa on his deathbed that you'd stop."

He shrugged. "Papa is beyond caring. But yes, *Schwester*. I lost everything we had left." He smiled and patted her head as if his mistake was negligible. "Now, do not fret, little Gretel. I know where to get enough riches to repay all my debts. One simple trip into the forest, and we will have ample wealth to keep us like kings for the rest of our days."

It took less than a second for her to grasp his meaning. Hansel wanted to return to the witch's gingerbread cottage in the Igelwald Forest. He wanted to stuff his pockets full of gems and coins from the witch's coffers, as they had just after the witch's death.

"No. No! We can never go back. How can you suggest such a terrible thing?"

He slid his shirtsleeve up his arm to reveal a thin band of dark metal encircling his wrist. "You may not be a real witch, but Frau Grüber is. This shackle will tighten bit by bit until I pay what I owe for calling on one of her girls—or until it severs my hand. Look. Already it digs into my flesh."

"Whores, too, Hansel?" Whenever she thought he could behave no worse...

The sound of fists pummeling the front door echoed through the receiving room.

"Holzfäller! We're here to collect!" a man shouted.

"Come now, open up quickly and we'll only take the furniture and silver and leave your sister!" another man said.

"Speak for yourself, Conrad," said a third man. "It's high time we dealt with the little witch. I'll have her repenting of her sorcery before the cock crows."

Marga's stomach threatened to expel her supper. She stared into Hansel's face with disgust and astonishment—although she ought not to have been surprised by any of this. Everyone knew Hansel was a scoundrel.

Hansel raised one fat eyebrow. "You still want to stay? Take your chances with Jorgen or Karl?"

Seething, she grabbed a black woolen shawl from a hook near the door. "Hurry. The old root cellar. There's an underground passageway there that leads to the edge of the forest."

"Clever girl. I'd forgotten it." He took his own cloak from its hook and balled it under his arm.

The crunch of an axe splintering the front door sent them both scrambling toward the back of the house.

The trap door to the root cellar lay concealed beneath a braided rug in the pantry. As she ran toward it, Marga pictured lifting the door and descending the wooden ladder, remembered the shelves of pickling crocks and preserves, and saw in her mind the little door behind the shelves that led to a tunnel. The tunnel would take them to the outskirts of the Igelwald. They could hide in the woods until...Until what? Until the men fetched hunting dogs to sniff them out?

Hansel was right.

They'd have to return to the witch's cottage—not only to fetch treasure, but to take shelter until the angry mob dispersed. Hansel spoke often of his friends, so she knew they worshiped gold and enjoyed hunting wild game in the Mertenwald—the "safe" forest south of town. They'd not give up easily on prey that owed them money. On the other hand, like the other townsfolk, they were a superstitious lot. If they did dare to enter the Igelwald, and then somehow discovered the well-hidden cottage, they'd never venture into the house of a child-eating witch—no matter how long the hag had been dead.

Or so Marga hoped.

A shout of victory echoed from the other room, and the tromping of heavy boots followed.

"Hurry," Hansel said.

Two

The white duck glided across the lake in the heart of the forest. The night was fair but cool, the water as smooth as the starry sky. Rarely did the inhabitants of the lake cease wrinkling the surface with waves, for they were wild things, fond of sparring and splashing no matter the hour.

On most nights, the duck slept in his well-hidden nest along the shore, but tonight, fierce hunger had driven him onto the water. He always felt hungry of late, even after eating dozens of minnows or swallowing down the fattest of frogs. It was more than a bodily hunger. He wanted something he could not name. Something he could not touch.

A memory flitted through his mind. He saw himself not as a duck, but as a man. A wizard standing beside a beautiful woman. His arm draped around her shoulders as she stirred a pot over a fire. The mixture bubbled and sparked. She laughed. He kissed her cheek, inhaling the scent of her skin and the aroma of the house they shared: spices and honey, herbs and wood smoke.

A breeze rumpled the water and ruffled his feathers. His vision broke up and blew away like the fluff of a dandelion. Not one seed of it remained.

He was hungry. He paddled his webbed feet and steered his body toward the place where the young trout lingered.

* * *

Marga grabbed a candle from a shelf as she scrambled through the narrow pantry. She tried to ignore the fear that gnawed at her guts, focusing instead on practicalities. Hansel would have matches; he always carried them for his pipe. With her foot, she shoved the rug aside. She lifted the wooden hatch, then stumbled down the ladder and into the dark cellar. Her free hand sought and found a few small apples and pears. She stuffed them into the pockets of her skirt as the trap door shut with a thud. Seconds later, Hansel collided with her, swore, and grabbed her by the shoulder to steady himself.

"Dark as sin down here," he muttered.

"Well, you would know about that." She took his hand from her shoulder and pressed the candle into his palm. "Light that and follow me."

A moment later, candlelight danced upon the shelves and dirt floor. Marga moved quickly toward the tunnel opening. Cobwebs stuck to her face and tickled her nose. The damp air smelled of old turnips and over-ripened apples. She stopped when she came to a four-foot-high wooden panel.

Hansel stepped around her. "Let me get that." He set the panel aside and they both stared into the hole it had concealed.

"It will be a tight squeeze for you," Marga said.

"Curse that witch," Hansel said. "And whatever she spelled us with to make me so big and you so small. We might have turned out the size of normal folk if—"

"Hush, Hansel, or those men will follow the sound of your big mouth and catch us."

Hansel obeyed. For once. Silently, he motioned for her to enter the tunnel first. Once they were both inside, he put the panel back into place without being reminded.

Marga had to bend almost double inside the passageway, but tall Hansel was forced to pass her the candle so he could fall to his knees and crawl. They inched along over bits of sharp stone and hard earth, sucking mildewed air into their lungs. It was as if they were once again children lost in the wilderness, Marga thought, as if thirteen long years had not passed. Unified by fear, although Hansel would never admit to being afraid.

The passage ended abruptly at a fungus-encrusted wooden door. A lick of moonlight and the eager tendrils of creeping vines poked through the decaying wood along its hinges. Marga passed the candle back to her brother.

Still bent at the waist, she yanked hard on the rusted handle. She pried and grunted. Cold sweat beaded on her forehead. The door yielded by inches, then a foot. Finally, it gave way enough to reveal a wall of thorny bushes. Marga tore at them, earning a dozen deep scratches on her hands.

She shimmied through the opening and out of the tunnel. Grunting and blaspheming, Hansel followed.

Just ahead, moonlight brushed a narrow road with silver-white beams. Flanked by old pines, the road led uphill before disappearing into dense and sinister woodlands.

The Igelwald.

Hansel took a few steps and stopped. His breathing was louder and faster than their exertions warranted. An effect of the strange wristband, perhaps? Marga turned to see him blow out the candle and then toss it to the ground. He bent and rested his hands on his thighs, above the torn and dirtied knees of his trousers. In between labored breaths, he grumbled profanities.

He glanced at her, grimacing. "I swore I'd never set foot in that cursed forest again."

Marga snatched the candle from the ground and pocketed it. "Do not forget whose folly forced us here."

Hansel glared. "Oh, so it's my fault alone, is it? Sooner or later the money would have run out, or someone would have decided not to tolerate 'the Holzfäller witch' any longer. You are as much to blame as I am, *Schwester*. Your oddness, your refusal to fit into society. How you slink about back alleys, haunt the graveyard, and barely speak to anyone but stray cats. I'd think you a witch myself if I didn't know how powerless you truly are."

Marga's anger boiled but she held her tongue. This was not the time for an argument. This was the time to flee as if a pack of ravenous wolves was in pursuit. Hansel's former friends were probably more dangerous than wolves, armed as they were with fists, weapons, and foolhardiness.

She started walking, quickly. Decades of disuse and weather had worn all smoothness off the road and unearthed big, jagged stones. The moon illuminated the ground just enough for her to make out safe places to set her feet. She spoke to Hansel without looking back at him. "This road leads to the grandfather oak. The road divides into two there. Do you remember which way to go after that?"

Hansel, with his long legs to carry him, caught up to her in a few brisk steps. Out of the corner of her eye, Marga saw him rotate the band encircling his wrist.

"I remember. Papa always used that path to bring us back and forth from town when we lived in the woodcutter's cottage. There was a boulder shaped like a bear's head after the oak. A mile or two on, the path forks again. One of those paths leads to where our little house once stood; the other leads straight to the lake." He reached inside his jacket and pulled out a scrap of paper. "Perhaps this will help. I made a map soon after we escaped the witch. Just in case."

Marga reached over to take the map but Hansel clutched it to his chest, saying, "You see, while you nursed your many fears, I had just one: the fear of poverty, of slowly starving as we once did. You scorn me because I am a gambler, but gambling helped me fill the family coffers when our savings dwindled."

Hansel's story had holes large enough to ride a pony through. He'd only been gambling with the townsmen for a handful of years. How could he have lost all of their wealth so quickly if he'd been good at it? The amount of gems and coins they'd taken from the witch's cottage ought to have lasted them two lifetimes.

He sidestepped a rock and continued, "So much money I handed over to Papa, keeping us in our fine house, providing our fine meals and our fine clothes—until the day I lost the alabaster cat I'd kept for luck, the one I took from the witch's mantelpiece when we fled."

Marga remembered the two-inch-high, pink alabaster figurine and its sharp-edged garnet eyes. She'd never liked the thing. Never trusted it. The witch had spoken to it sometimes, as sweetly as one might address a living pet. *Ortrun, my dearest. Ortrun, my love.* It might indeed have brought Hansel luck. In which case, Hansel had been using a form of magic for years—while the townsfolk imagined she was the guilty sibling.

They stopped for a moment. The ancient grandfather oak loomed overhead, its branches like a leafy umbrella blocking the star-speckled sky from view. Something inside her stirred as she stood in the shelter of the tree. For a moment, her fear was replaced by wonderment—and then a funny tingling feeling that warmed her like a good cup of tea but also made the world seem to tilt. She braced herself by resting one hand on the rough bark of the trunk.

"We go left there," Hansel said, pointing out a bear-shaped boulder shrouded in shadows.

The odd sensation ceased as if Hansel had blown it away with his breath. Marga caught the echo of voices somewhere behind them, or so she thought. It might have only been the wind playing in the trees. Nevertheless, it stoked the embers of her fear. "Hansel. We must walk faster. Run, if your knees will allow it."

"They will, if they must." He took her hand in his and set

off as if competing in a footrace, dragging her along beside him. His odd, loping gait bore witness to the constant pain he suffered in his knees. His height had not come without costs, and crawling through the tunnel surely hadn't helped his condition.

The forest pathway wound uphill and down, around the trunks of old trees, along trickling brooks, and through grassy meadows, before it split into two again. Bedeviled by shadows, they tripped and fell a few times, got up, and ran again. Hansel chose the right-hand path when the road split into two.

They rushed along until they could rush no more. After that, they walked, stumbling with weariness as the first hints of daylight glowed above them.

Hansel mopped his brow with a green silk handkerchief. He leaned against a pine tree, his breathing labored. "I must rest or die," he said.

Marga listened hard, but heard nothing but wind rustling the leaves, the calls of a few birds, and Hansel's panting. She was tired, but her brother looked ready to faint with exhaustion. So much for being a big, strong man. "A few minutes of rest, then," she said. She extended her open hand. "Let me see the map while you recover."

With a groan of effort, Hansel handed over the map. She walked to a nearby stump and sat.

In the pink light of dawn, she squinted at Hansel's boyhood scrawling. Some of the pencil marks had smeared, and the paper itself had turned blotchy and yellow. With one finger, she traced the path to the cottage. It looked short and easy on paper, but of course it was neither.

Her fingertip touched a rough oval filled with wavy lines. The lake, they'd called it when they'd still spoken of it as children. It might have been only a pond, but they were small, scared, and desperate when they'd found themselves stuck at the water's edge after escaping the witch.

She glanced at Hansel. "Do you suppose the white duck is still there?"

Hansel snorted. "How could it be? What duck could have survived until now?"

"It was big and strong enough to bear us across the water on its back. It was no ordinary duck, Hansel. It must have had a kind of magic."

"No, it was a stronger-than-usual duck, one that probably became the dinner of a stronger-than-usual wolf. Now, let me rest, for *Himmel's* sake." He slid his back down the tree trunk until his rump rested on its roots, closed his eyes, and crossed his arms over his barrel of a chest.

While her brother napped, Marga surveyed their surroundings. As far as she could see in every direction were trees and more trees, ferns and moss, thorn bushes and fallen branches. Crows cawed in the canopy of leaves. Nearby, a mourning dove cooed a sorrowful song.

In the space between these sounds, faintly, faintly, she heard the rustle of water lapping a shoreline.

She dismissed her own feelings of exhaustion and tracked the sound through a stand of scraggy pines. The lake appeared before her, its greenish-black waters stretching wide and far. Insects hummed and chattered warnings in the surrounding trees and bushes. Frogs belched.

Marga shuddered as memories gushed through her mind

like water escaping from a burst pipe. On the far side of the lake, past a grove of slick, black-barked trees, through a copse of firs, beyond a broad brook, the witch's cottage waited for them. A house built not only of cake and candy, but of nightmares and suffering and everything she'd worked hard to forget.

Her stomach lurched. Her throat burned with bile.

This was a mistake, venturing back into this terrible place. They could not—she *could not* return to the gingerbread cottage. Not ever. Neither could they go back to Eschlinsdorf. They'd simply have to move far away and take new names to throw off Hansel's enemies. They'd find jobs and earn money for rent and food. They were the children of a woodcutter after all, fully capable of hard work.

She turned to rejoin Hansel, her steps hastened by the sudden volume of his moaning. She was used to his exaggerations, but this time his expressions of pain sounded far too genuine.

Pale and glistening with sweat, he still sat against the tree. He clutched his banded wrist. A trickle of blood slithered down his arm. "Help me up. We must hurry," he said through gritted teeth. "My fingers. I cannot feel them."

All thoughts of avoiding the cottage evaporated. They needed the funds to pay off Frau Grüber. Now.

Marga reached down for Hansel's good arm to help him to his feet. "I found the lake," she said, still nauseated by memories and dread. "Come with me."

If she'd learned one thing over the years, it was this: sometimes one had no choice but to act bravely and hope for the impossible.

Three

The scents of mud, algae, and decay filled Marga's nostrils as she stood at the edge of the lake. Beside her, Hansel cradled his oozing wrist against his chest. Small, dark waves tickled the muddy shoreline. Further out, large bubbles rose to the surface and popped, hints that something enormous lurked below the surface.

"Where's your blasted duck, eh?" Hansel asked, sneering. "We bloody well can't swim to the other side." Pain never improved Hansel's demeanor.

"Perhaps we must call out for it."

"You do that. I'll just sit here and wait for my hand to fall off, or for Karl's dogs to come tear us to pieces." He sat gingerly on a wedge of stone speckled with bird droppings and continued complaining.

Marga stepped close to the water. A dragonfly flitted past her ear and skimmed over the surface of the lake. So, how did one go about summoning a magical duck? When they were children, the duck had swum to them of its own volition, a white cloud of feathers drifting across the water. They'd watched its approach as they clung together on the shore, trembling with the thrill of escape and the fear of being recaptured. The witch was supposed to be dead—but after all they'd suffered, they didn't trust even a dead witch.

Behind her, Hansel gasped, then groaned. His wristband had likely tightened again. Although it seemed unwise to shout when being pursued, she had to try it.

She cupped her hands around her mouth and called, "White duck! We beg for the aid of the white duck that ferried us across the lake thirteen years ago!"

A frog croaked and leapt off a lily pad, entering the water with a plunk. Innumerable insects skated across the lake. A crane waded out of the bulrushes at the lake's edge and eyed Marga with all the haughtiness of the town gossips. Minutes passed. Her hopes sank.

She tried again. "We beseech the white duck to help us. Perhaps we can offer something in return. Please. We are desperate."

Marga looked back at Hansel. He lifted his swollen, purple and red wrist for her appraisal. "I do not think 'desperate' even begins to describe the situation." He took a deep breath and shouted, "Ho, there, giant duck! If you can hear me, hurry your white backside and get over here, dash it all!"

"Have you no manners, Hansel? Do you want to have to swim across? Why should the duck come to help someone so boorish?"

He shrugged and then pointed to a far-off, pale shape gliding toward them. "Ask him yourself, Schwester."

* * *

The instant he saw the children, the white duck remembered them.

It was like being struck by lightning. Like dying and coming to life again. His head throbbed as his mind rearranged itself. He blinked, and blinked again.

He remembered the children who stood on the shore, and the stories he'd heard of them from the other forest creatures. Ducks were not good at remembering tales, and had little use for them. But now, he recalled the stories, and so much more.

Of course, they were not children anymore—although the girl's short stature might cause one to believe otherwise at first glance. Evidently, nibbling at the witch's enchanted cottage had affected the siblings in opposite ways. In contrast to his diminutive sister, the boy resembled a young giant, with absurdly long legs and wide shoulders. The duck had a vague recollection of knowing giants long ago and in another place, before he'd become little more than a feather-bedecked ornament for the forested landscape.

Before he'd fallen prey to a powerful enchantment.

More memories unfurled. He'd not entertained un-duck-like thoughts in years. He'd floated and preened, sought and consumed grubs. He'd sired his share of ducklings, as any respectable drake would have done. But now...now, as if the spell had loosened its grip, he remembered who he was and who he might once more become.

Long ago, he'd helped these siblings to cross the water, and he would help them presently. Thus, he would unlock one of the invisible chains of bondage that kept him a duck.

Like a bud breaking into blossom, the spell's details unfolded inside his plumed head. This was no simple curse to be undone with a word and a flick of the wrist. The one who had crafted this enchantment had been wily, spiteful, and determined to make him work hard to earn his freedom. The forest had added its own stipulations, to complicate matters.

Firstly, he was to deliver the brother and sister back to the gingerbread cottage they'd fled as children. Sometime thereafter, he'd need to carry the girl across the water for a third time. His final task would be to inaugurate the new witch-queen of the forest. Wretched magic and its fondness for doing things in threes.

Once the third water crossing was completed, the magic would release him from the part of the spell that confined him to the body of a duck. He would shed his feathers and become the man he'd been. In possession of the full measure of his mental and physical prowess, he could use all his wits and charm to get the girl to accede to the proverbial throne. Only then would he be free to leave the confines of the Igelwald.

It was a simple list of difficult tasks. Almost impossible tasks for a duck. Yet he was not daunted. He believed that he'd done harder things in the past. Almost, almost he could remember them.

His past might be a puzzle, but he knew this with absolute certainty: once he'd reacquired his manly form, he'd never let it be taken from him again. He arched his white neck and made a vow to the skies—with a resounding quack that frightened a dozen frogs and sent them leaping into the blue-green depths of the lake.

Four

The sound of a single duck quacking echoed over the water. "There," Hansel said, pointing again with his good hand. "See? Near that dead willow tree."

A ghostly form glided toward them. The closer it came, the more solid it appeared—and the more certain Marga became that the thing approaching was indeed a white duck.

Not just any duck, but one with a small patch of black feathers between its eyes—identical to the duck that had helped them thirteen years ago. Marga hoped the creature was still as kind and helpful as she remembered—for without its assistance, the townsfolk might soon catch up with her and Hansel. But was it the same duck after all? The one they'd known had been large enough to carry two children. This bird looked no bigger than a tomcat.

"Here, duck. Here, *Dummkopf*," Hansel said in a sing-song voice.

"Must you be so rude?" Marga said. "Think for a moment. If you offend the duck, it might refuse to help us."

Hansel ought to have learned to respect magical things after the brothel owner clapped an enchanted shackle onto his wrist, even if he had somehow managed to forget their experiences with the gingerbread house witch.

The white duck waddled onto the shore and bobbed its head as if to say hello. Her earlier estimation of its size had been correct. It was no bigger than the ducks that swam in the pond near their home in Eschlinsdorf. Marga's faith wavered. This puny bird could never carry her across the water, let alone a grown man like Hansel. True, it had answered her call and greeted them, but what if that were the extent of its talents? If Hansel were right and this particular duck had no magic...

Marga whispered aside to her brother. "It cannot be the same duck, Hansel."

"Now you doubt? You're the one who insisted the thing was magical." Hansel swore. "I'll be deuced if I'll die here without trying." He moved a step closer to the duck. "You there. I demand your assistance. We'll pay you to get us across the lake. In worms, or fish eggs, or whatever your sort likes."

The duck quacked and spread its wings wide. And then it began to grow larger and larger, until its back was as broad as a young pony's. Finally, the creature ambled back into the water and appeared to wait.

Marga felt dizzy again. She stared at the big duck. It was one thing to say you believed in magic, or to remember what had seemed to be magical when you were a child, but witnessing the workings of enchantment firsthand shocked her in a way she had not expected. There was Hansel's strange shackle, of course, but this struck her in a deeper, more personal way.

"We should go," she said as firmly as she could. There would be time later to reflect on the magic and its implications.

"You ride across first," Hansel said, giving her a little shove toward the duck. *The milksop.* Marga must have looked annoyed, for he shrugged and said, "What? You're always scolding me for bad manners and now you scorn me for acting like a gentleman? No wonder no one wants to court you."

Marga ignored Hansel's insult. She addressed the duck respectfully and slowly, as if speaking to a potentially dangerous foreigner. "Hello there, good duck. We're grateful for your aid."

The duck beckoned her closer with a motion of its head. She waded into the cool, shallow water and turned to sit sidesaddle fashion on the duck's back. Her body sank a little into the thick feathers—an oddly comforting sensation. Still, she shuddered with nervousness as Hansel waved and said, "Bon voyage."

The duck pushed off with its feet and paddled away from the shore, floating along as if Marga weighed nothing. She grabbed onto a fistful of feathers to avoid falling off, gently, so as to avoid hurting the bird that had saved them twice. She tried to hold her legs up at an angle to keep all parts of her body out of the ominous-looking water, but it was no use. Her muscles were too worn out from their long hike through the woods. She let her feet and ankles dangle in the lake—and said a prayer that they'd not be nibbled off by something skulking under the surface.

As they drifted along, Marga wished she could have enjoyed the beauty that surrounded her instead of dreading the cottage ahead and the enemies behind them. The water was sapphire blue, and the lily pads were as green as the emeralds they'd taken from the witch's hoard. Turtles and frogs eyed her as she passed by, their little, dark eyes shining. The water sang in splashes and gurgles, and nearby birds trilled. Silver-finned fishes skimmed past.

There was something else, too. Something in the atmosphere that felt different. It was like the air hummed against her skin, or just beneath it. She'd felt it a few times before when walking close to the edge of the Igelwald in the late evening. It wasn't altogether unpleasant—but if it was magic, she did not want to experience it for any longer than necessary.

The sooner she was home again, enclosed by familiar walls, the better.

After a journey of a half-mile or more, the duck bore her into a patch of cattails. The brown and green stalks bent to make way for them to slip through to the muddy shore. More magic? Good magic, perhaps? Was there such a thing? It seemed possible, if the duck was any indication. It had shown them mercy and charity—in spite of Hansel's insolence.

The duck waddled onto the bank and sat so that Marga could dismount. It accepted her thanks with a nod before returning to the water to retrieve Hansel. *Himmel* help the poor creature, having to carry that weighty, bad-tempered load so far.

As she stood on the strip of pebbled beach and waited for her brother, her thoughts meandered into the bog of her dreadful childhood memories. That mean old witch, those weeks of endless torture and terror. She paced the shoreline and tried to force herself to consider pleasant things instead: the sour-sweet taste of a sun-warmed plum picked from their garden, her father's deep, rolling laugh, the soft lullaby her mother had sung before sickness and starvation had stolen her sanity, Eschlinsdorf's church bells pealing cheerily on Christmas morning...Still, her heart pounded uncomfortably in her chest and her stomach churned with anxiety. Why had the duck and Hansel not yet returned?

Shouting and gunshots echoed across the lake. Silence followed, as even the birds and frogs dared not to move.

Five

Marga held her breath as she sent up a wordless prayer for Hansel's safety. Her wide-open eyes scanned the water for a glimpse of him.

After a long moment, Hansel's voice shattered the quiet. "Faster, duck! For the love of mercy!"

They came into view, her oaf of a brother astride the frantically paddling duck. Hansel's legs were obscured to the knees by the dark water. He looked ridiculous, like a man riding a child's toy. A patch of red marred one of the duck's wings, but with Hansel's shackled, dripping wrist just above it, Marga could not tell for certain whose blood it was.

The duck drifted to the lake's edge. Hansel scrambled off its back.

"I could have swum faster myself," he grumbled as he trudged onto the shore. "Nearly got my head shot off, as well."

The big duck followed Hansel onto dry land. Marga

knelt down to examine its bloody wing with gentle fingers. The duck made a sharp, whistling sound, almost like a human gasp of pain.

"Its wing is peppered with lead shot," she said. "Poor thing."

"We'll be peppered, too, if we don't keep moving." Hansel shook himself like a dog and spattered her with droplets.

"Now that we've crossed the lake, I think we're safe from your friends—at least for a little while," Marga said as she petted the duck's head comfortingly. "They'd need to go all the way back to town to get a boat to cross the lake. Or, if they chose to continue on foot, the journey around the lake could take hours—if they dared to try it. You know how superstitious they are."

"They just *dared* to come as far as the lake. They might dare to keep coming after us," Hansel said, casting his gaze up the bank as if looking for a path. "We shouldn't linger. Leave the duck. It will live, I'd wager. Maybe even heal itself with its magic."

Marga stood and wiped her hands on her skirt. "I think if it was going to heal itself, it would have already done so."

"It will be fine. Let's go." Hansel held up his wrist to remind her of his need to hurry.

"No. This duck saved us. We must return the favor."

"Fine. Invite it along. You can nurse it at the witch's place. Use her herbs and such. But it's going to have to walk if it's coming with us. I've only got one good arm, you know."

With a pitiful quack, the duck started to shrink. In a matter of seconds, it was once again the size of a normal duck.

"Convenient," Hansel said. With his unshackled arm, he scooped up the duck and held it against his side. "Now, follow me."

A few clusters of beech gave way to the black-barked trees she'd never forgotten. Row upon row of them, lined up like ominous soldiers. Trunks smooth as window glass, branchless until twenty feet or more above her head. A few jagged-edged leaves lay curled at the trees' roots, as dark and menacing as the branches they'd fallen from. Hansel cursed the trees aloud—as if they were not already cursed—and led Marga into their shadows.

Chill breezes chased one another through the grove like invisible butterflies at play, yet not one leaf stirred. Marga's cheeks stung with the sudden cold. She tucked her hands into her skirt pockets as she followed Hansel across the flat, bare dirt. A mile. Two. Hansel seemed to be leading her in a straight line through the endless trees, but perhaps they'd been walking in circles. Her legs ached from trying to keep up with Brother Long-legs.

"Are we lost?" Marga asked.

"What do you think?" he replied churlishly.

The duck squawked and wriggled out of Hansel's grasp and onto the ground. It gestured with its head as if summoning them to follow and then waddled off the path. Hansel shrugged and walked after the duck. Marga fell in behind them and glanced downward. On the ground, barely visible, someone or something had laid a line of tiny black stones.

A trail of shining pebbles like Hansel had once used when their parents first tried to leave them in the forest.

"No," Marga said to the memories clawing at her mind. She whispered a prayer for courage. She had overcome so much of her past. She could endure this.

Soon, the duck stopped. Its bloodied wing drooped, brushing the ground. With beady, pleading eyes, it begged to be carried again. Hansel picked up the wounded creature and tucked it under his arm, forgetting to complain. Perhaps he had grown too tired to grumble.

The black trees thinned, yielding space to ordinary varieties of trees and bushes. Moving onward, they passed through the copse of pines depicted on Hansel's map. When they reached a burbling brook four or five feet wide, they stopped.

"Thank *Himmel*," Hansel said, stooping and setting the duck onto the ground. "I am about to perish of thirst." He cupped his unaffected hand and scooped up water.

"Don't," Marga said sharply. "You shouldn't drink that."

"It's fine," Hansel insisted. "We drank of it before and lived."

She had forgotten that. Still, it seemed reckless to drink of any stream in a forest tainted by magic. What was safe years ago might be deadly now.

"Don't forget that you grew into a giant, and I stayed the size of a child," Marga said. "This brook might have been the reason. We cannot know..."

He slurped up the water and then dipped his cupped

hand again. After three handfuls, he wiped his mouth on his sleeve. "Sweet as honey. What care I if I grow taller still? Perhaps the townsfolk would respect me more if I were ten feet tall, eh?"

"They might respect you if you'd act respectably," Marga said, too tired to rein in her temper. "Have you ever considered that?"

"And molder away in boredom like you? No, thank you, *Schwester*."

She pointed at his wrist. "You don't regret even that?" Blood trickled from all around the metal band and dripped to the ground. His fingers had turned a sickly shade of grayish-white.

Hansel lowered his forearm into the brook and let the water flow over the shackle. He looked up at her and said, "I would never trade my past adventures for your life of solitary misery. Besides, this will soon be gone, and I will be rich enough to have twice as much fun as before. And you can go back to wallowing in your spinsterly woe, as it pleases you."

Marga shook her head in disgust and set off across the brook, hopping from rock to rock to avoid the water's touch. The duck ambled after her, staying at her heels even after they reached the other side. She glanced down at the injured wing and hoped it didn't pain the creature much.

A hedge wall stood ahead of them, dense with deep-green, serrated leaves. Purple clusters of berries dripped juices onto the ground and scented the air with a cloying sweetness.

"Well, that's new," Hansel said as he stopped beside her.

"I don't remember it either. Much has changed in thirteen years."

Hansel grunted, and Marga knew he had in mind something meant to insult her. He'd been her brother long enough to be able to jab at her without words—and she'd been his sister long enough to have become immune to his jibes.

The duck waddled along the edge of the wall for a few yards, then paused. It quacked and pointed with its bill.

"Now what is it?" Hansel murmured. "We're supposed to waste time looking at some bug or fungus a duck finds fascinating?"

Marga ignored him and caught up with the duck. Now, among the leaves and vines, she saw what it had been trying to show them. "It's a door, Hansel. Well hidden, but there. Doorknob, hinges, and all."

"A door to what?"

"The other side of the hedge, I would assume." Marga turned the handle and the door creaked open to reveal more forest. As she stepped over the threshold, a single cuckoo sounded—not the live bird sort, but the kind found attached to wooden clocks.

She scanned the trees ahead and drew a sharp breath. From the lowest branches of every tree hung a single wooden clock with a brass pendulum and cylindrical weights. Every clock was painted differently, but each one had a small arched doorway above its face. A thousand faint tick-tocks filled the air.

Hansel swore in wonder.

All at once, every door sprang open and every cuckoo popped out. With hooting cries, the wooden birds proclaimed the time shown on their clock's faces. Hansel clutched his ears to block the deafening sound. Marga stood still as stone, mouth agape with astonishment.

One by one, the cuckoos retreated and their doors closed.

"What could that have meant?" Marga said, mostly to herself.

"I reckon it's probably just a bit of witchery meant to scare us away from the cottage full of treasure," Hansel said.

"But the witch is dead," Marga said.

"So we hope." Hansel wore the smirk he usually wore whenever taunting her. How could he joke about such a thing? The hag had almost eaten him when he was a boy.

Somewhere a few trees away, one last mechanical bird cuckooed. Hansel winced and clutched his banded wrist to his chest. "Well, whatever the time, we must be close to the cottage by now. Let's keep moving."

Marga lifted the duck, careful not to jostle its injured wing. It weighed less than she'd thought it would, and holding it close was almost like cradling a cherished doll, something reassuring and familiar.

They left the cuckoo forest behind and scaled a hill covered in evergreen trees. Little fir cones crunched underfoot. Slanted sunbeams fell in stripes across the path between her and Hansel. The duck lifted its bill and sniffed. Marga inhaled deeply then, smelling tree sap, damp earth, and, faintly, cinnamon and cloves.

"Hansel," she called out across the space that separated them.

He halted and turned. "*Ja*," he said. A greedy grin spread across his face. "The smell. Just as I remember it." He took off running like the starving little boy he'd been the first time they'd found the cottage made of cake. Only now, his hunger was for jewels, not sweets.

Marga tried to swallow the lump of dread in her throat. And then she forced her feet to carry her toward the place she most detested in the world.

Six

An army of spiders surrounded the cottage, all but coating the earth with their dark bodies. They stood motionless, their countless beady black eyes fixed upon the human visitors. Most were smaller than a coin, but some, furry and brown, were as large as Marga's palm.

These she remembered. The old witch had used spiders as border guards after she'd captured them. Once, to punish Marga for wandering too far from the cottage, the witch had commanded them to swarm over the little girl. Their myriad legs had poked into her nostrils, ears, and even her mouth when she couldn't stop herself from screaming. It had taken Marga years to overcome her fear of spiders. Now, she eyed them coldly. They were fragile creatures, abhorrent but not deadly. They would not deter her.

Hansel grunted in disgust. The duck wriggled in Marga's arms until she set it on the ground. Squawking and flapping its good wing, the bird rushed at the spiders, a feathered soldier plunging into battle. The spiders scattered in all directions, up trees and into the brush.

"Little cowards," Hansel said. He puffed out his chest as if he'd been the hero who'd saved the day.

"Thank you, duck," Marga said, hoping to make up for Hansel's lack of courtesy. He'd been such a polite and pious child. How dear little Hansel had transformed into a living example of the proverb "bad company corrupts good character" was a mystery she never expected to solve.

With the spiders gone, Marga turned her attention to the gingerbread cottage. Or what was left of it. A fir tree with sparse, brown needles lay across the building. Its fall had smashed part of the roof. In contrast, the ornate frosting swirls decorating the gables were as white and crisp as they'd been thirteen years ago, and the brightly colored candy windowpanes remained shiny and intact. There were very few nibbled spots on the walls, as if most of the forest creatures knew better than to seek nourishment from a place contaminated by magic and murder.

"Door still looks sound," Hansel said as he strode closer to the house. "If we sleep in the north end, we should stay dry and snug enough."

Nothing in his demeanor hinted that, in this place, he had endured unspeakable torments. Indeed, he had never seemed scarred by their experiences with the cannibalistic witch. Marga wondered, as she often had, why she alone had borne the aftereffects of their suffering.

A chorus of wolves heralded the moonrise. Hansel hissed with pain; Marga cringed in sympathy. It would be a miracle if he had two hands come sunrise. Yet they could not go back now, not without a lantern or weapons, through the tracts of enchanted trees and across the uneven ground. And if they made it to the lake alive, the injured duck wasn't fit to carry them across the water.

Hansel shoved the door open. A parade of mice scampered out, scurried over his boots, and continued into the woods. A wave of scent rushed into Marga's nostrils. The broken, abandoned house should have reeked of must and mildew. Instead, the air smelled of cinnamon and butter, apples and cloves—same as it had thirteen years ago.

Although the witch had perished in the oven, at least a portion of her magic had survived. There was no other explanation for the intoxicating scent and the fact that the cake and candy structure had endured the elements for so many years.

Marga let her brother enter the dark house without her. Her heart beat too fast just looking at the place, and she could not seem to catch her breath. From where she stood, her eyes caught a flash of light from inside. Seconds later, Hansel poked his head out the door. A yellow beeswax candle illuminated his face. The sculpted candlestick in Hansel's grasp was all too familiar. In their long month of captivity, she'd polished the horrid depiction of an imp's twisted face every day, while trying her best not to look directly at it.

"Come in, *Schwester*," Hansel said. "Not a soul is here but us, unless beetles and moths have souls, that is."

An unsettling feeling prickled up and down her body. She wouldn't call it fear. The sensation was more like an awareness, perhaps an impression of whatever magic the witch had left behind. It was stronger than the feeling she'd had at the lake, but similar. She tried to shake it off and failed. "Do you feel that, Hansel? It's like the air before a thunderstorm."

"All I feel is tired of walking. And that my hand is about to fall off. Please, come in so I can shut the door. There are wolves nearby, and *Gott* alone knows what else."

The duck prodded her leg gently with its head, quacking as if to reassure her.

Hansel blew out a slow breath. "So. I know it's hard for you to be here. If it will help, I'll go back in and light every candle I can find." The kindly tone was one she'd not heard from him since the day their father died. Perhaps being in the cottage again reminded him of their childhood bond and how she'd saved him from certain death.

"Thank you," she said. With a nod, Hansel ducked back inside, bending to avoid bumping his head on the top of the door frame.

After a few minutes, Hansel returned and said, "Come."

Marga drew in a deep breath, gathered her courage, and stepped across the threshold. The duck trailed behind her.

True to his word, Hansel had set candles and lamps in a dozen places about the room. Everything was as she remembered—only coated with gray dust and sprinkled with mouse droppings. The scarred wooden table with its three sturdy chairs, the blue-painted cupboard with its neatly stacked plates and cups, the shelves of bottled herbs, the tin water pails she'd left by the stone hearth. The witch's woolen cloak and linen apron sagged from hooks on the wall, embellished with layers of lacy cobwebs. Her favorite spoon, painted with gold and swirling red flowers, still rested on the mantelpiece.

The fallen tree sliced through the center of the room, blocking the view of the bedchamber. What a luxury that room had seemed on their first night there, when the witch had tucked her and Hansel into twin, feather-stuffed beds made up with snow-white linen—a room built just for sleeping, with its own little wood stove sputtering away in the corner. It was heaven on earth compared to the stark woodcutter's hut they'd come from.

Heaven had not lasted. After that one night, young Hansel had slept in a cage. Little Gretel had been allowed to continue to sleep in the bedchamber, but she had rarely slumbered, for the witch had occupied the other bed. The hag's snores had been like the growls of a demon, the very opposite of a lullaby. Inspiration to tremble and pray rather than slumber.

"You look spent, *Schwester*. Do you want to go lie down in the bedchamber?" Hansel said. "You can take a lantern. Two, if you wish. Although I'll be dashed if I know how you'll get there without crawling under that tree trunk."

"No," Marga answered firmly. "I could not sleep a wink here, not in this house. I'll take care of the duck's wing while you collect the treasure."

"Please yourself." He grabbed the tin pails and headed to a wooden chest disguised as a bench under a window, the last place they'd plundered before running home to their father. Back then, they'd left the chest half full because their pockets and sacks could not hold another gem.

Marga sought and found a small knife, a towel, and a

bottle containing a tincture of witch hazel. She set them on the table, leaving room in the center for her patient. The duck was resting on the floor near the fireplace, and she went to crouch beside it. She looked into its beady black eyes and said, "Will you allow me to remove the lead shot from your wing? I will be as gentle as I can. If the shot remains in your wounds, it could cause festering and fever. And if that happens, you'll probably die, I'm afraid."

The duck nodded, reminding her that it was not an ordinary duck, but one that possessed at least a little more intelligence than normal waterfowl—and enough magic to grow and shrink at will. Still, she wasn't afraid of the creature. It had saved her and Hansel twice, and had received only gratitude and injury in return. She owed the duck every kindness she could offer.

She lifted the waterfowl onto the wooden tabletop, then moved a pair of clay lamps and a brass candlestick closer to its body. After whispering a prayer, she set to work. The duck lay still and quiet, its breast rising and falling evenly as it endured her ministrations.

Across the room, Hansel opened the chest. He started to toss handfuls of gems into pails, filling the air with clinking and clanging. The duck seemed unbothered by the noise, thank *Himmel*. Marga gritted her teeth and tried to concentrate on picking out the bits of lead. She wouldn't waste her breath asking Hansel to be considerate.

Night fell hard outside the cottage, darkening the candy windowpanes. Owls hooted mournfully. Insects hummed and buzzed. A moth found its way in through the broken roof and flitted around Marga's head as she worked. Finally, after Hansel had fallen asleep in a chair by the sooty hearth, she extracted the last piece of shot from the duck. She tore a strip of cloth from one of the witch's aprons, and she bandaged the wing. With the rest of the apron, she made a nest in a basket.

"There now. Rest, and we'll hope for the best," she said as she set her patient in the makeshift bed. Sighing, the duck closed its eyes and tucked its bill under its good wing. Marga smiled wearily. She'd never known ducks could sigh so... humanly. It was rather endearing.

"Rest?" Hansel said groggily. Three pails and two baskets sat at his feet, full to their brims, and his pockets bulged with riches. "No, *Schwester*. We should head back now, while I still have two hands."

Marga wiped the dust from the short stool opposite her brother. She sat, and tried to forget sitting there as a girl, forced to darn the witch's woolen stockings after a day of chopping wood and scrubbing the floor. "As much as I hate to spend the night here, it's too dark to travel through the forest now, Hansel. There are bears and boars. Wolves." How quickly he'd forgotten forcing her into the cottage earlier to avoid such perils.

"Not to worry. We'll take lanterns and knives and make a lot of noise." He stood and stretched, keeping his injured arm snug against his belly.

She didn't believe for a second that wild things would be repelled by Hansel's scheme, but that was not the only problem she foresaw. "How do you plan to cross the lake? This duck cannot carry us in its condition, and we could never swim across with all that heavy treasure to bear."

"I thought of that. We'll make a raft. Take the big wooden door from the shed. Use branches as paddles. We're a clever pair. We will make a way, because we must. I refuse to forfeit my hand."

As if to support his argument, a fat drop of blood fell from his wrist to the floor. Hansel was right to want to hurry. His plan was risky, but if fortune favored them, it might work. "Fine," she said. "But we must take the duck back to the pond so it can heal in its own nest."

"Of course. Now, rest there while I take down that door. In a few hours, we'll be on the other side of the lake. We'll leave the Igelwald behind, I'll pay Frau Grüber and the men what I owe them, and you, dear *Schwester*, will return home to sip tea by the fire. Thank *Himmel* the shed is wooden and not made of cake, eh? A cake raft wouldn't carry us half a yard without sinking to the bottom, I reckon." A thimble-sized ruby tumbled out of his pocket and he bent to retrieve it.

Something howled outside the cottage. Marga glanced at the darkened candy windowpanes and had second thoughts. "Could we not wait an hour or two? Daybreak cannot be so far off."

Hansel gave a dismissive wave with his good hand. "Don't worry, *Schwester*. What's a little darkness when we have such nice lanterns? Besides, I got us here safely, did I not?"

Marga glared, but he failed to notice. Of course he would take all the credit for getting them to the cottage. She stood, moved the duck's basket to the hearthstones, and then started to tidy the table. As silly as it was to clean up after oneself in the abandoned cottage, she needed something to occupy her hands and thoughts. To help keep the bad memories from overflowing the dam she'd built in her mind to contain them, and to keep her from giving Hansel a swift kick in the shin for being a conceited numskull.

Lantern in hand, Hansel left for the shed. After a few more minutes of senseless cleaning, Marga sat at the table and lay her head down on her arm. No matter how heavily weariness weighed upon her, sleeping in the witch's kitchen was not something she was going to do. The odd, tingling feeling had not left her, the feeling that there was magic all around her, sizzling like butter in a hot pan yet not making a sound.

She closed her eyes to rest them for a moment, and imagined being far away from the accursed gingerbread cottage, safely home again, curled up in bed with a fat book.

And then she was dreaming.

She dreamed that Lukas Beckmann had baked a loaf big enough to house a family. Inside, she sat close to him at a table made of pastry, pouring him a cup of pink, rosehip tea. His warm, teasing smile made her blush. He reached for her hand and—

With a start, she awoke. Sunbeams poked through the hole in the roof. An empty feeling lurked in her gut—not only hunger, but an uncanny knowledge that Hansel was gone.

Seven

Marga found Hansel's note on the mantel, flanked by two guttering candles.

In a few lines of clumsy script, he claimed he'd been unable to wait a moment longer to go back to Eschlinsdorf, for the metal band had tightened again and he could see bone beneath its edge. Without her short stride to hinder his progress, he believed he could reach the brothel before noon. He swore to return as soon as he could.

She paced, hands in fists, wishing she could pummel her brother. Wishing he would treat her as an equal instead of a burden for once. Why did he never remember that she was the one who'd been brave enough to conquer the witch and save his life—at the age of eight, no less?

The heavy cinnamon and clove scent lingered in the kitchen like invisible fog, nauseating Marga while simultaneously provoking her appetite. In desperate need of fresh air, she went to the window above the metal washing trough, lifted the latch, and swung open the checkered pane of clear and pink sugar. A cool, morning breeze rushed in, bringing hints of pine, fern, and wildflowers. A black and white speckled bird came to perch on the windowsill. It eyed her for a moment and then flew away. Without the witch in residence, the cottage felt almost tolerable—until her thoughts strayed into memories of the past.

The aftereffects of the witch's cruelty could not be swept away as easily as ashes. One minute, the witch had been as sweet as the cake walls around them, the next, she'd chained their ankles together, bespelled them to dance, or cursed them to itch as if set upon by a thousand fleas. Everything the witch had done had seemed to amuse her. Her cackling laughter was more chilling than winter's harshest wind—a sound Marga wished to forget but could not.

When Marga had fled the hag's cottage with Hansel, she'd carried more than gems; she'd brought a collection of fears. Conquering them one by one had been a sort of game for her in the years thereafter. With no playmates and a brother who shunned her company, she'd used the game to pass the time as well as to fortify herself against future peril. For if there was one witch in the world, there were surely more.

She declared her creed to the rose bushes outside the candy windowpane. "I am not afraid of spiders. I do not fear the darkness of night, flocks of small birds, chicken bones, old women in headscarves, or the taste of candy. Someday I will not cringe at crumbs. I am strong and clever, loved by Gott, and I will live a good, long, and happy life."

Behind her, the duck quacked sadly in its basket nest. It was probably hungry and in need of a poultice. She had hours to wait before Hansel's return: tending to the duck would help fill the time. She rewrapped her shawl and went outside to find food and water for her patient.

The morning was bright and blue-skied. Behind the gingerbread cottage, butterflies flitted from flower to flower, honeybees tiptoed over chamomile blossoms and sipped from purple echinacea. Robins sang in the surrounding treetops. The witch had always kept a beautiful garden, and here it was, carrying on without her, lush and devoid of weeds.

In order to reach the spring, Marga circled around the now doorless shed. The weather-battered building leaned hard to one side. She wondered if Hansel had ventured within to see the cage in which he'd been imprisoned while the witch had attempted to fatten him. If she were Hansel, she would have set fire to the brittle boards. She had half a mind to burn it down herself before she returned home.

The sight of the shed made her uncomfortable, but what lay behind it was worse: the witch's huge clay oven. The place where Marga had committed murder to save herself and her brother.

She stared at the beehive-shaped, reddish-brown structure, the setting for years' worth of vivid nightmares. Too many times to count, her father had sat at her bedside in the wee hours, speaking in a soothing tone, trying hard to convince her to release the guilt she'd felt for shoving the witch into the oven. What else could she have done, after all? It was burn or be burned. Save herself and Hansel or surrender to painful deaths.

The witch's screams echoed in her memory now, shrill as the calls of some demon bird. The acrid smell of burning clothes and charred flesh seemed real in her nostrils. She begged *Himmel* for forgiveness and relief as she swayed on her feet.

What else could I have done? she asked herself again. She'd had to end the witch's reign of terror. In doing so, she'd likely saved other children from being tortured and eaten.

Still dizzy, she moved the pitcher from one hip to the other and strode in the direction of the spring. Hansel would be back soon. Even if he took a full day to return, she would find the fortitude to bear it. Preparing treatments for the duck would occupy her hands and mind. There were berries in the hedges surrounding the cottage, and herbs grew in wild abundance where the witch had once cultivated them—enough food to stave off hunger for both her and her patient. The stay would not be a holiday full of delights, but she could endure it without complaint.

The tinkling song of water drew her to the spring under the willow tree at the far edge of the garden. Marga filled the pitcher, then collected a handful of earthworms for the duck, depositing them into her pocket. The dress was already filthy from travel. A little dirt in the pocket was nothing to fret over. She made her way back to the cottage, averting her eyes from the oven, and stopping now and then to pick up sticks and dead grass for kindling.

It was late in the morning when she built the fire in the kitchen hearth—and learned too late that the chimney was clogged. The cottage would have filled completely with smoke were it not for the hole in the roof. It was a small mercy she did not take for granted. She needed every small mercy she could lay claim to, especially as the hours passed and Hansel failed to reappear at the door.

Hansel or no Hansel, the duck needed medicine. She moved its basket to the least smoky corner of the room, and then she set a kettle of water over the fire to boil. Her eyes stung and her throat burned, but she kept at her task. Quickly, she added herbs from the witch's shelf: valerian, lavender, calendula, slippery elm, and faerie nettle. Once the mixture steeped, she would soak a rag in it. After that, she'd wrap the rag around the duck's injured wing. Her childhood fascination with an old book of herbal remedies was proving useful—another small mercy to add to her collection.

The day wore on. She took up the witch's broom to sweep out mouse droppings, dust, and leaves. She nibbled one of the apples she'd brought from home; she ate a few red currants from the garden. When night fell, she lit candles, changed the duck's bandage, and gave up the silly hope she'd nursed of Hansel returning before dark.

Tiny embers glowed in the fireplace as she sat in the hearthside chair. The duck slept in its basket. From across the forest came the faint sound of countless cuckoo clocks proclaiming twelve different hours, followed by the howl of a solitary wolf. Inside the cottage, she didn't fear wolves. The old witch had bragged of setting a boundary against them, putting magic into the ground. Likely as not, the spell still held.

Neither did she fear being alone. For over a decade, she'd contented herself with reading, sketching, meandering down seldom-used alleys, and on occasion, venturing to the edges of the forest to forage for mushrooms or plants. There were worse things than being alone. She'd already survived some of them.

Time crawled by, slogging through thick silence. Her body begged for sleep. Not the upright dozing she'd done the previous night at the table, but proper sleep in a bed, with her limbs sprawled out and her head sunk deep into a pillow.

Her stomach turned at the thought of spending the night in the bedchamber she'd shared with the witch, but she needed good rest to prepare herself to journey home. Besides, the very fact that she was afraid to revisit the bedroom meant she *had* to. Fear would not be her master, not even within these walls. She blew out all the candles but one, then checked on the slumbering duck. The bird looked peaceful in its makeshift nest, so she took a short candlestick in hand and moved toward the tree trunk.

The bole rested at an angle, one end embedded in a chest of drawers and the other resting on a crumbled edge at the top of a wall. Along the trunk, branches jutted out, jagged and menacing, positioned as if meant to deter her passage. This journey, though short in distance, would not be easy.

She knelt and pushed the candlestick under a low branch, scraping it across the stone floor as far her arm's reach allowed. The flame flickered but kept burning, and thank *Himmel*, it didn't ignite anything. On her belly, she crawled under the trunk, keeping her head low. Twigs snagged her hair and scratched her forehead. The floor beneath her chilled her palms to near-numbness. Her apron caught on something and tore. All this to sleep in a bed? She ought to have slept on the bench in the kitchen. But it would be stupid to turn back now. She had only to crawl a little farther, maneuver over a low branch, and break through a section of clustered sticks before she could claim victory over her tree enemy.

The apron tore again, loudly, as she wriggled forward and over the branch. A sharp twig poked through her stocking and stabbed her shin. Hansel's favorite curse words danced in her head. She reached out and started to snap the sticks that blocked her way. They broke easily but there were more. Many more. She worked on and on, and her fingers ached and bled from the task, but she did not give up. When finally she'd made a good-sized hole, she pushed the candle through and then wriggled through herself.

With a small cry of victory, she rolled onto her back. She stared up at the cobweb-festooned ceiling while she caught her breath. After sunrise, she vowed, she was going to search for an axe, even if it meant going into the shed where Hansel had been caged. She'd chop the insufferable tree trunk into matchsticks.

The candle flickered beside her like a miracle—but one with only an inch of wax left to burn. She staggered to her feet. The bedchamber door yawned open before her, and she passed through it without permitting herself to hesitate. Dim candlelight glazed the room. It was just as she remembered it. She'd expected to tremble at the sight of the place, but either her self-training or exhaustion kept her calm. She eyed the room with detachment. The walls were merely walls. The furniture was merely furniture.

A painted wardrobe rested against one wall, and a small, tiled, wood burning stove sat in a stone alcove. There were two quilt-covered, narrow beds. Between them, a small wooden table held a dusty oil lamp and the dog-eared book of medieval love poetry the witch had read aloud from nightly, much to little Gretel's bewilderment. Above the table, an age-scarred looking glass hung on the wall—another odd thing for a hideous crone to possess.

Except for a layer of fine dust on the quilts, the beds had remained neatly made, just as she had left them. She threw back the covers of the closest bed and checked for unwelcome insects. Finding none, she set the candle on the table. With both hands, she yanked the quilt off the bed and shook the worst of the dust from it. Finally, she slipped off her tattered, sap-stained dress and petticoats. Her chemise was fine wool and sleeveless, not the best choice for a nightdress in a drafty cottage, but it would have to do. Her mother had instilled in her a conviction that wearing dirty clothes to bed was never acceptable. It was a silly rule, but one she had diligently kept since childhood. With a shiver, Marga flopped onto the mattress, and cocooned herself in the quilt. Before she could finish praying for Hansel's hasty return, sleep overcame her.

Eight

As if being a duck was not torture enough, now he was a duck with a mangled, painful wing. The girl, whom he remembered as Gretel, had done a passable job of treating the wounds. If he'd possessed human speech, he would have requested gefress root soaked in dandelion milk to help him sleep, but alas, all he could do was quack like a slow-witted waterfowl. At least she'd not poisoned him with her concoctions. He supposed he ought to be grateful for that gift from the gods.

He had not been surprised in the least to see the big brother tiptoe out of the house like a treasure-laden thief while his sister slept. The man obviously cared about nothing but getting free of the bloody, enchanted shackle that clenched his wrist. The duck could only imagine what mischief the fellow had done to earn such a painful punishment.

No matter, thought the duck. He did not need the

uncouth lummox to break the spell that held him in thrall. The girl was the one for whom he'd been waiting.

He tucked his head under his good wing and closed his eyes. Before he slept, he remembered the one thing he'd been straining to recall since leaving the lake: his human name.

Ansgar.

He repeated it in his mind, again and again, the good, strong name his mother had bestowed upon him: Spear of the Gods.

He was Ansgar. He'd been an elegant, intelligent person with powers worthy of respect before he'd become a simple-minded waterfowl. He would be that man again.

Nevermore afterward would anyone dare to call him "duck."

* * *

Beams of sunlight streamed through the candy windowpanes above the bed where Marga had slept, yet the air in the cottage was cold and damp. She sat up, yawning. Goose bumps spread across the exposed skin on her arms as she shrugged off the quilt. Vague memories of a dream lingered like wisps of fog in her mind. She'd been dreaming of Lukas the baker again. They'd been laughing, sitting close together on a velvet sofa. His smile had warmed her through like a winter tonic, and he'd spoken to her of bread making, but in such a way that his words sang like poetry. He'd kissed her knuckles tenderly, lingeringly.

Such a ridiculous dream. Her nocturnal mind was silly indeed if it could imagine that a respectable man like Lukas would court a witch. The townsfolk would go without bread before buying it from such a man.

She set her feet on the cold floor and turned her thoughts to Hansel's return. *If we set out as soon as he arrives and hurry along the path through the woods, tonight we will sleep in our own house.* First, though, she needed to dress.

In the light of day, her clothes looked far shabbier than they had the night before. She was fairly certain that, as she'd slept, mice had chewed additional holes into her garments. Big holes. Her dress and petticoats were nothing but rags now. Unwearable.

But she knew where to find other clothes.

A black wardrobe painted with bright flowers and flourishes of gold stood against one wall. The witch had forbidden her to touch it, but little Gretel had managed to glimpse the clothes inside a few times as the witch retrieved a dress or cloak. Now, Marga opened the door cautiously, hoping not to startle any bats or rodents that resided there.

She peered inside and found only clothes.

For a moment, she hesitated. She closed her eyes to think. Would it be wise to don the witch's clothes? Like an actor in a play, would she take on the witch's attributes upon slipping into her garments? Already she'd been dwelling in the witch's house, drinking from her cups, using her herbs, and sleeping in her bed. The suspicious townsfolk would have taken these things as ample proof that she was indeed a wicked enchantress, the successor to the old witch of the wood. But Marga knew her own character. She had no inclination to work dark spells or command armies of spiders.

Clothes are just clothes, she told herself. *Be practical.* She took a deep breath and opened her eyes.

Three dresses hung on hooks, and two were not the plain, sturdy, dark gray linen that the witch had worn day in and day out. One was a gown of sky-blue silk, fit for a countess attending a ball. The other was a dress blacker than any Marga had ever seen, with the sheen of a crow's wings and hundreds of tiny tucks sewn all over the bodice. A dress fit for a mourning empress. On the floor of the wardrobe, folded neatly, lay more clothes. She pulled them out, her fingers digging into the thick mass of fabric.

Marga unfolded the garments and spread them flat on the mattress—a full set of expertly tailored men's clothes: a cream-colored shirt, tan breeches, a pale gray silk cravat, and a sapphire blue, brocade waistcoat—all softened by age but immaculate.

The choice between wearing the witch's clothes or the clothes of an unknown gentleman took not a second to make. She stepped into the breeches. They hung to her ankles instead of her knees, thanks to her shortness. She slipped the shirt over her head, atop her chemise, and stuffed the long hems of both into the top of the breeches before buttoning them. On a whim rather than out of necessity, she tied the dove-gray cravat at her throat in a loose knot. She might look ridiculous, but it was a relief not to have to wear the child-eating witch's clothes.

The garments were surprisingly comfortable, and there was something refreshing about wearing clean clothes after a hard journey—or two, if one counted crawling under a tree. In spite of their long storage, they still smelled faintly of the witch's homemade lavender soap. Marga finished tidying herself by combing her hair with her fingers and twisting it into a knot on the back of her head. The oval looking glass glinted above the little table between the beds, tempting her to check her appearance, but she shoved aside the vain inclination. No one but a duck and, she hoped, her brutish brother would gaze upon her today.

Her stomach growled as she slid her feet into her own shoes. Only then did she remember that she'd have to climb through and under the fallen tree again to reach the kitchen. Her fresh clothes would be ruined, and she'd garner more scratches and bruises. Unless...

Marga eyed the sugar-paned window high in the wall above the bed she'd slept in. The thin candy glass should shatter easily, but it would be a miracle if she could fit through the narrow opening of the window frame. Had the wall been made of stone or brick, there would have been scarce a chance of enlarging the hole, but the walls were built from cake. Sturdy cake several inches thick, yes, but probably nothing that could stand up long against the blows of an axe or hammer. She had neither tool, but she recalled that the witch had kept a brass bed warming pan with a long wooden handle underneath her bed. In a matter of seconds, she retrieved it. The brass pan was weighty, and promised to be effective as a bludgeon.

Marga climbed atop the mattress and steadied herself with a wide stance. She gripped the handle and punched through the candy pane with the pan. The glass fell in shards, mostly to the outside of the cottage. Now she jabbed hard at the cake along the edges of the window frame. After much bashing, grunting, and sweating, the cake started to fracture into fist-sized chunks and smaller crumbs she tried not to look at. With a shout, she shoved the pan into the wall one last time, and an enormous piece toppled to the outside. Enormous as in the size of the kitchen door.

"*Dummkopf*," she scolded herself.

She dropped the pan onto the bed and wiped her brow with her hand. She'd gotten carried away. She might have to spend another night in the bedroom if Hansel were delayed. The weather and whatever animals dared to approach the cottage would share easy access to the room thanks to her "renovations."

From the kitchen came the duck's forlorn quack. Marga attempted to climb out through the hole gracefully, but her exit became a brisk tumble over the broken cake wall and into some rose bushes. For a moment, she lay still. The work of demolition had sapped her strength, and the shock of ending up in unfriendly shrubbery had left her limp-limbed and short of breath.

The duck quacked again in appeal. The sad sound roused her from her stupor. She extracted herself from the bushes and brushed horrid brown crumbs off her clothing—while trying not to throw up. Her face and hands were scratched and sore, but her clothes appeared to be undamaged—so she'd achieved one of her goals. Yet she could not help but regret the entire business of the morning. Next time, she'd consider the possible consequences of her actions before knocking down a wall.

She glanced upward as she walked away from the bushes. The bright sunshine made her squint. Judging by where the sun sat in the sky, noon was nigh. She'd both slept and worked much longer than she'd intended. The poor duck was probably ravenous.

Truth be told, she too was growing hungrier by the minute. She started across the garden, eyes fixed on a patch of berry bushes near its edge. A bird swooped low, so close to her head that its passage stirred her hair. The wood pigeon perched on a low branch in a gnarled pear tree. It ruffled its feathers and cooed insistently. Attached to its leg was a tightly rolled scroll of paper tied with a scarlet string.

A message.

Slowly, warily, Marga stepped toward the pigeon. The bird stared at her with glassy black eyes as she unfastened the tiny scroll. As soon as she held the paper, the pigeon launched itself skyward with a whoosh. "In a hurry, are you?" Marga said as the bird disappeared over the mountaintop.

She sat, pressed her back against the bumpy tree trunk, and unrolled the note. The handwriting was tiny but neat, the ink unsmudged in spite of the missive's unusual delivery.

Greetings, Fraulein Holzfäller,

My name is Ada. We met once in the market when we were little girls, I think.

Your brother Hansel wishes me to inform you that he has paid all his debts in full. He is certain his wrist will heal in due time. With regret, he cannot return to you without risking your life. A fever spreads through Eschlinsdorf like fire set upon straw, and the townsfolk blame the "Holzfäller witch" who so recently fled—and that means you, of course. Were he to go to you, he would be followed. You would surely die at the hands of the townsfolk whose children have perished this week. Hansel cautions you that several grieving fathers have been seen going in and out of the woods, and that they have publicly sworn an oath to capture and kill you.

Your brother and I leave for France today, having purchased my freedom from Frau Grüber. We shall soon be married, and plan to live near Lourmarin, where my mother was born. Send the enchanted wood pigeon back to Frau Grüber right away, for she loves it quite well. You do not wish to incur her wrath.

Your soon-to-be sister,
Ada Haas

Post script: Frau Grüber says to tell you that should you ever desire to train to become a true witch or one of her ladies, she would gladly offer you her protection, guidance, and profitable employment. (Not so profitable for anyone but her, in truth, but leastwise you'll never go hungry or be forced to sleep out of doors.)

Post script to the post script: Warning. Do not dare to tell anyone she's a real witch. You will not be believed, and she will take swift revenge upon you.

Another post script: Please come find us in France someday. Hansel says there are still enough jewels in the shed to pay for your journey. I have always wanted a sister. I know I could prettify you and find you a husband in no time at all. Nothing would please me more.

~A

A breeze ruffled the paper, and Marga looked up. The recently clear sky now roiled with dark clouds. A moment later, rain poured as if dumped from a hundred overturned buckets. It drenched her to the skin before she managed to stand up. Lightning flashed, and she dashed toward the cottage.

She all but dove through the kitchen door. Thunder boomed and rattled the windowpanes. The duck quacked miserably as she shook the rain off her sleeves and pushed soggy strands of hair away from her face. Thanks to the letter, her stomach had quit begging for food and instead churned with anxiety and anger. How dare Hansel abandon her and run off to France with a girl of ill repute? Surely he could have found a way back to the gingerbread cottage without being followed, if he'd wanted to badly enough. Instead, he'd left her stranded deep in the magic-infested forest, forced to hide in a damaged house with an injured duck.

And how much time had passed outside the Igelwald, in Hansel's world? Every day she grew more convinced that time within the forest was a slippery, changeable thing. Even the amount of time it took to cross from one end of the garden to the other seemed to vary greatly between mornings, although the breadth of the land did not visibly change.

In any case, she'd been gone from town long enough for a fever to take hold and spread—and to be blamed for it.

A puddle formed under her feet. She undressed again, until all she wore was her damp chemise. She draped the man's clothes over the wooden chairs and table. Hansel would have laughed at her, dressing and undressing in the space of an hour, standing there as angry as a wet hen. She took her shawl from the hook where she'd left it the night before and wrapped it tight around her chilled shoulders.

Marga took out a mortar and pestle and pounded and smashed ingredients for a salve. She insulted her absent brother in every way she could think of. He'd treated her so kindly when they first arrived at the cottage, with all the candles and reassurances. Why could he not have remained that man? Why did he have to be so selfish and so...Hansel?

The violence and foul words failed to lift her spirits. She applied the potent-smelling paste to the duck's wing, careful not to take out her frustration on the poor bird.

Her stomach roared. She searched the cupboards and cabinets for something still edible after thirteen years, but found only a half-full jar of honey among the dried herbs and bottled oils. Until her clothes dried, honey and herbal tea would have to serve as a meal.

There could be no tea without a fire. Her shoulders slumped. She dreaded using the fireplace with the clogged chimney again. The room still smelled of smoke after yesterday's fire. Perhaps she could use her old friend the bed warmer to poke some of the debris loose from inside the masonry. But when she turned toward the hearth, she noticed a large pile of soot and dark clumps spilling onto the floor in front of the fireplace. Her first fire, or perhaps the storm, must have loosened the clog during the night. This was a blessing she would not count as small.

She made use of her anger toward Hansel, took up the witch's broom, and whisked the pile of sweepings out the door within the space of a few minutes.

The duck stared hard at her as she restarted the fire and heated a kettle of water. It had nothing else to do, she supposed, although she wasn't fond of being watched so intently by anyone, least of all a magic bird. She poured hot water into a china cup, then added a good measure of honey and a pinch of dried lavender from the witch's shelf. This was not the sort of breakfast she was used to as the daughter of one of Eschlinsdorf's wealthiest families, but it would take the edge off her hunger until the storm abated and she could forage for something more filling. Certainly she had survived on little as a child during the famine, in the months before her parents had abandoned her and Hansel in the forest.

She took a seat at the table and sipped the sweet, flowery drink. Its warmth soothed her nerves a little. The rain ceased and a few birds began to trill. As her anger at Hansel started to fade, she considered what to do next. If she and the duck had to stay longer than another day (and there was no question they would), they would require food, heartier fare than a few berries and boiled nettles. They'd need firewood—although the tree already inside the house could be counted on for some of that. And then there were the holes in the cottage. The roof and wall would have to be made weatherproof—and she had no experience in matters of construction.

By *Himmel*, she hoped the duck would heal quickly so they could leave soon. She glanced over and found it asleep in its basket near the fireplace, looking peaceful as a slumbering child. The duck could go home to the lake, but what home could she go to?

Marga spoke softly to herself as she stared into the fire. “Once the duck is well enough to return to the lake, I must set out on my own. Perhaps I might become a ladies’ maid in some city to the north or west, where no one would call me a witch. Until then, I must pray that none of the townsfolk find me here, and that winter doesn’t come early.”

She sipped the dregs from her cup. Her stomach growled as she imagined Hansel tucking into a plate filled edge to edge with warm rolls, thick slices of ham and cheese, and boiled eggs cut in half to reveal creamy, pale orange yolks. Would he think of her as he breakfasted with his rosy-cheeked bride? Would he fret while wondering if she had enough food to keep from starving? No, not Hansel.

If she had been the powerful witch the folk of Eschlinsdorf thought she was, she would have seriously considered turning her brother into the pig he so frequently resembled.

Nine

Ansgar plucked a loose feather from his side with his bill and spat it toward the fire. It could be deduced from the girl's cross demeanor, mumbled curses, and conversations with herself that she'd discovered that her oafish brother Hansel did not plan to return.

If a duck could have smiled, Ansgar would have. He'd been thinking and planning since he'd carried the siblings across the lake—shallowly at first, constrained by the slowly shifting limits of his duck mind. Now, although he retained the outward shape of a drake, he'd regained most of his human intellect. Perhaps because he was close to fulfilling the favors required by the spell, the magic had loosened its grip upon his consciousness. Perhaps it was the influence of the enchanted gingerbread cottage. He would not waste time puzzling over such matters when he had better things with which to occupy his thoughts.

His latest plans were both ingenious and exciting.

With his keen little eyes, he stared at Gretel as she

mopped up a puddle the storm had left on the kitchen floor around the tree trunk. She was clever, possessed a fair hand with remedies, and would soon be desperate for help. If he squinted his eyes and concentrated, he could perceive the tiny sparks of magic encircling her—enough innate ability to work with, enough to shape and coax into more.

Someday soon, should it please the gods, she might become powerful enough to rise to the station for which she'd been chosen. He'd have a hand in the perpetuation of the old witch-queen's legacy. He had no choice if he wanted his old life back—but that did not mean he would not take pride in grooming the girl to reign properly and powerfully over the Igelwald.

Ansgar tried to stretch his injured wing and was rewarded with a surge of pain. In his mind, he let loose a string of curses that would have shocked even uncouth Hansel. As much as he wanted to carry Gretel across the lake again, it was simply not yet possible.

The problem with being a duck was that he was limited to doing duckish things and a bit of amateurish weather manipulation above the cottage. Forcing Gretel indoors with a rainstorm was effective if he wanted attention, but it didn't help him achieve his grander goals. He certainly couldn't heal himself with weather.

The situation called for patience—a quality Ansgar lacked whether clad in feathers or manly flesh. How often had his beloved wife said as much in their many years together?

How long had passed since he'd thought of her?

Pain and regret filled his small, thumping heart. Human

emotions were not something he'd missed while a duck. He shoved them down now, covering them over with spite and anger. Were it not for his wife, he wouldn't be in such a state.

Yes, anger felt better, more powerful.

He relished it.

* * *

Marga spent a day and a half hacking away enough of the fallen trunk to allow easy passage into the bedchamber. Her hands bore blisters from gripping the axe handle, but she forced herself to stack the branches and logs on either side of the wide kitchen fireplace. The wood was enough for a fortnight or two, depending on the weather and her frugality. *Please Gott,* she prayed, *may I not remain here as long as that.*

On her foray into the shed to look for the axe, she'd found a piece of oilcloth large enough to cover the hole the tree had gouged into the kitchen roof and the top edge of one wall. Now, she used a piece of rope to secure the folded oilcloth to her back. After uttering a quick prayer for safety, she climbed the rose-covered trellis attached to the side of the cottage. A hundred savage thorns punished her for trespassing, scratching her hands and face. Her knees trembled as she inched her way across the cinnamon-biscuit-shingled roof to the hole. The biscuits looked brittle and the roof sloped precariously. If she were to fall, no one would hear her cries for aid—except wild beasts. She dismissed the thought of being dinner for scavengers and kept crawling. Finally, she reached the hole. She tucked the edge of the cloth under the shingles, securing it as best she could. With luck, it would keep out the rain and snow for a while.

The next day, although her arms and back ached, she turned her attention to repairing the bedchamber wall. She'd been spending nights on the settle in the kitchen, far away from the wretched hole she'd made, on alert for the scritch-scratching of unwanted visitors in the bedchamber. She'd never sleep well anywhere in the house as long as the opening invited visits from bats, rats, and other unseemly guests.

Clothed again in her dirty, torn dress (for she was loathe to ruin the man's finery), she made good progress the first morning. She used an axe and hoe to level the hole, and then she shoveled the resulting gingerbread rubble into the weeds at the edge of the garden, her stomach churning at the presence of so many crumbs. She pilfered stones from an old wall behind the house and filled a wooden garden cart with them. She made thick mud in a basin to use as mortar. Her work did not have to be pretty, just sturdy enough to keep out animals until the duck recovered.

But as soon as she placed a stone and turned her back to grab another, the stone fell to the ground as if shoved by an invisible hand. Not one to give up easily, she tried again and again, using different sizes and shapes of stones and thicker mud. Every stone fell out. The witch's gingerbread wall seemed to be rejecting her attempts to repair it.

As dusk shadowed the forest, she went inside. She sat beside the fire, coated head-to-toe in gingerbread dust and mud but too tired to care. Other matters were more important. How could she fix an enchanted wall? Before a single idea came to mind, she fell asleep. All night, she dreamt of wildlife invading the cottage to ravage and eat her and the duck.

At dawn, Marga drank some honey-water and filled the duck's bowl with the same. The duck honked as if dismayed with the offering—but since its health seemed to be improving, it could wait a little while for its breakfast. Her nightmares had inspired her to try harder to fix the wall. She went outside, mixed new mud, and tried using small logs to patch the hole.

Every time she turned her back, the logs fell out. Clearly, the cottage hated her.

Marga sank to the ground and wiped her brow with her muddy wrist. She smelled like a gingerbread-spiced bog and probably looked like a grimy swamp beaver. *Of course* magical gingerbread walls wanted only magical gingerbread patches. She laughed at the absurdity of the situation.

If I were a witch, she thought, *none of this would be a problem for me*. A shudder passed through her as she realized that she'd almost wished to be a witch. What a dreadful thing to desire! How, for a single moment, could she have forgotten the absolute wickedness of the child-hungry crone who'd cast little spells to frighten her into submission, making flame-eyed rats nibble her stockings, or turning her porridge into a bowl of writhing vipers?

Never, never would she become a witch. She'd rather be buried beside Papa before she drew another breath.

She blamed the dark turn of thoughts on her poor diet. After almost four days with little to eat but wild onions, some mushrooms and greens, and a little honey, constant hunger gnawed at her insides. She was starting to feel she could eat almost anything, even pieces of the cottage or the grubs she dug up for the duck.

She might even eat the duck.

"*Himmel* help me," she prayed. Of course she'd eaten duck before, but to eat a magical duck, the very duck that had kindly helped her cross the lake twice, would be a terrible thing. An atrocity worthy of a witch.

Marga stood and shook dried mud off her skirt. Her stomach roared. It was time to cease her striving to repair the wall and find food. During the last famine, when the Holzfäller family lived in the woodcutter's cottage, her mother had boiled acorns and ground them into flour for pancakes. She could do the same. She made her way toward a stand of oaks she'd noticed while gathering mushrooms. If the squirrels had not been too greedy, she might harvest enough for a few meals.

A blast of bitterly cold wind swept in from the west, whipping her skirt around her legs and stinging her cheeks. As the wind began to keen, it pelted her with sharp crystals of ice. Too weary from her fight with the wall to battle the weather for a few acorns, she retreated into the warm kitchen.

The duck lifted its head and gestured with its bill toward its empty water bowl.

"Poor soul," Marga said as she refilled the bowl from a pitcher. "I've neglected you while trying to fix the house. Well, you'll be happy to hear I'm done trying. Unless you're capable of baking magical gingerbread?"

The duck blinked in reply.

"In that case, the bedchamber door will have to remain

shut. We can't have wild beasts wandering in, especially with you unable to fly to safety. And I'll be sleeping on the settle for as long as we're here."

She looked up at the oilcloth that covered part of the rafters. In spite of the wind, it had remained where she'd put it. Perhaps, in spite of her lack of experience, she wasn't altogether hopeless at taking care of a house, even if she couldn't fix the wall. One thing was certain: she would never again take for granted the comforts of a sound dwelling and a full larder.

The duck pecked at the empty dish beside its water bowl and gazed at her beseechingly. Marga listened for wind and hail, but hearing neither, grabbed a cloak from a peg near the door.

"I'll find something for your supper," she promised. "If the weather doesn't turn foul again, that is."

As she left the cottage, she could have sworn she heard the duck chuckle.

Ten

Ansgar enjoyed vexing the girl with hail and rainstorms, but enchanting the weather cost him dearly in strength. Ducks, even the most special of them, simply did not have the constitution for wielding much magic.

Exhaustion would not help his wing heal, and the meals Gretel offered (hardly enough to sustain a puny duckling) left him lethargic. If only he'd had the ability to speak, he could have manipulated her with words instead of weather. Cunningly and gently, of course, in the manner of a kindly old uncle whom no one ever suspected of pocketing the silverware. Shouting was for peasants, after all.

Not that the temptation to shout—or quack loudly, as it were—never arose within him. The girl's clumsy attempts to clear the fallen tree had driven him half mad. If she'd used the smallest spell, the most basic of enchantments, the job would have been done in minutes rather than hours. But Gretel had no inkling of her potential.

He dunked his bill into the dish of tepid water and

tipped his head back to swallow it. He could no longer endure lazing about in a basket like some tiny-brained pet. Pain notwithstanding, it was time for him to rise from his sickbed, exercise his wing, fetch a decent meal, and nibble some trefoilluna plant from the witch's herb garden to speed his recovery. Autumn was upon them, and winter would follow fast on its heels. Although he could control a cloud or two, he could not hold back the entire, brutal season. Unless he took action, they'd freeze or starve to death inside the broken cottage before Yuletide.

Ansgar preened his feathers as he plotted his next move and the ones to follow. By the gods, he hated the taste of feathers. He wouldn't miss them or his inelegant webbed feet. Once he threw off the witch's spell, he swore by every star in the universe that he'd never again set foot in a lake.

If all went according to plan, he'd be restored to human form within a fortnight. He'd fulfill all his obligations and fly —no, *walk* away from the gingerbread house forever. Away from the memories, good and bad, that hung in the air like smoke that refused to slip up the chimney.

Pacified by hope, he'd allow himself a fortifying nap, and then he would convince the girl to take him outdoors so he could nibble healing herbs. He was becoming quite the expert at making his wants known by gesturing with his head and using variations of his quacking voice. And she was so biddable, so easily coerced to fawn over him. If he'd miss anything about his time as a duck in the gingerbread cottage, it would be having Gretel as his servant. The irony was most delicious. She all but groveled and bowed as she offered him little bowls of berries and earthworms every day, oblivious of her destiny.

Soon, she would know. And then they would both take their rightful places in the world. Until then, he would continue to play the poor, helpless duck—and milk the situation for all it was worth.

* * *

One morning, perhaps a week later, Marga awoke in the bedchamber. She yawned and stretched still-weary limbs. She'd spent another uneasy night in the drafty room, sleeping only lightly and in brief stints, her senses continually tuned to catch any hint of creatures attempting to enter through the broken wall.

The slant of the dull sunbeams streaming through the remaining window spoke of winter's nearness. It might already be winter for all she knew. She'd lost count of the days and weeks she'd spent at the cottage—and yet the duck seemed no stronger. It would live, certainly, but not for long if she were to release it into the wild. Some fox would have it for supper within a day.

The duck was not the only one in trouble. Marga had grown too thin. Without proper nourishment, her thoughts were frequently hazy. She slept too much, and she was cold no matter how close she stood to the fireplace.

The time had come to do something—before she became too weak to do anything but die.

Marga pulled on two pairs of woolen stockings and then the

breeches she'd become accustomed to wearing. She buttoned the brocade waistcoat over the layered chemise and man's shirt, then added a fitted jacket she'd found in a drawer, a pretty thing made of heavy green silk that would have been fashionable on a well-to-do gentleman decades ago. She buckled a leather belt low across her hips to hold the small hatchet she'd found in the shed. Finally, she pulled a knit cap over her braided and pinned-up hair.

Sunlight glinted off the looking glass that hung over the table between the beds, inviting her to peek at her appearance. She was afraid to look, knowing the toll hunger and exhaustion had taken on the parts of her body she'd seen when washing.

She was afraid, so she forced herself to look.

She moved a wooden stool and climbed atop it. Heart racing, she peered into the glass.

Her mother's face stared back at her: gaunt, sharp-edged, and pale, as Mutti had appeared when Marga had last seen her—the day before she had met the witch. The reflection was false, Marga told herself, a trick played by hunger and the shifting light. She closed her eyes. She pictured *Mutti* as she'd been before the famine, a woman of simple yet striking beauty, resourceful and spontaneous, the type of person little Gretel had wished to become one day.

When Marga opened her eyes, the mirror's image had altered to include features she recognized as her own: the nose she'd inherited from her father, the scar on her chin from a childhood stick fight with Hansel. Still, the face was too much like the haggard face her mother had worn at her life's end.

Too much like the face of a woman who, driven mad by

starvation, had convinced her husband to leave their two children in the woods to die.

"You're stronger than Ilske Holzfäller," a woman's voice said from the mirror. "Stronger than she ever was."

"Who's there?" Marga said, leaning closer and placing her hands on the wall on either side of the oval frame. Her knees shook. Her chest felt hollow with fear. She wanted to run, but she'd trained herself for so long to confront and conquer things that made her afraid. She steadied her stance on the stool.

"Only Margarethe," the voice, now exactly like hers, replied. Marga watched the reflected mouth as it formed words she was not speaking. "Margarethe Holzfäller, daughter of a woodcutter and his poor, sickly wife. Gretel that was, Gretel that shall ever be."

"I'm not Gretel," Marga replied. "Not anymore."

"True enough, yet not wholly true. Are we not who we were as well as who we are and who we shall become?" the looking glass Margarethe said.

"My mind is playing tricks because I'm hungry." Marga blinked hard, hoping the vision before her would become nothing but a true reflection of her face. It didn't work.

"Hungry, yes. Hungry and broken like your mother, Ilske, was in the end," the mirror said.

"Never like she was then. Never." Marga had endured enough. She tried to look away and step off the stool but found her limbs frozen in place. She fought hard to move her foot, her hands, even a single finger—to no avail. Her body grew cold, and colder.

"True in a way, yet not wholly true," her mirror voice

said. "Ilske became nothing but hunger. Violent need wearing a woman's skin. But you..."

"Let me go."

The reflection continued, "You, child, could become more than your mother ever was. More than pathetic, weak Margarethe is. Magic still bides here in this cottage. It has been waiting for you, longing for you. Feel it in your marrow now. You could wield it. You could save yourself. You could punish your brother and the townsfolk as they deserve. You could have everything you desire, if only you'd take up the magic."

"No!" With every ounce of strength she could gather, Marga shoved hard against the wall. She toppled off the stool and fell hard onto her backside, gasping for breath.

She had to get out of the cottage. Now.

She rose from the floor, muscles aching from having been held in thrall by the mirror's magic. She never should have given into the vain temptation to look into the glass.

As she scrambled out of the bedchamber, she tried to convince herself she'd been hallucinating from lack of food. Better that than conversing with some spirit left behind by the old witch.

Marga crossed the threshold between the two rooms and an odd jolt of energy rattled through her body. Her thoughts went blank. What had she been doing in the bedroom? Dressing and...? She'd seen or heard something strange, perhaps? Well, it mattered not. What mattered was getting to town and back quickly. What mattered was getting food and help. She felt more unwell by the minute.

"I'm going out, duck," she said, although the duck appeared to be asleep. "I'll be back as soon as I can."

Her hands shook as she poured water into the duck's dish. She dumped a few shriveled berries and leaves into its food bowl, the last of the food she'd gathered. She filled a small water skin and tied it to her belt. From a hook by the door, she took a heavy, black cloak—one large enough that it too might have belonged to the man who'd owned the clothes she now wore. She wrapped herself in it, secured the button at her throat, and left the cottage.

The cold morning air stung her face and ears, but also invigorated her. A good thing, since she'd felt as weak as a kitten after dressing. As she hurried down the garden path, she covered her head with the hood of the heavy woolen cloak, concealing the knit cap that hid her tightly braided crown of hair. She wasn't altogether convinced she could pass as a young man, but she hoped not to meet anyone who'd wonder as she traveled toward Eschlinsdorf.

Her boots crunched through an inch of crusty snow as she walked. She passed the vined wall, the cuckoo clocks, and the black trees. The farther she strayed from the cottage, the nicer the weather became. Not a speck of snow could be seen. The air smelled of dried autumn leaves. Squirrels and birds chattered in the trees and on the forest floor. Marga dove for a patch of mushrooms and stuffed them into her mouth without regard for manners or the soil clinging to their stems. Never had fungus tasted so wonderful.

She trudged onward, ever careful to retrace the path she'd trod with Hansel. He'd taken the map when he'd abandoned her, of course, but she was prepared. A few summers ago,

Marga had trained herself to navigate using landmarks, the stars, and the sun. She would never repeat Hansel's mistake of relying on pebbles and bread crumbs for guidance.

She pushed the hood of the cloak back, warmed by the brisk walking and sunshine. Her plan to cross the frozen lake on foot might not come to fruition, given the temperature. Well, she'd find another way over the water. She had to procure food, better medicine for the duck, and advice about fixing the wall before winter truly set in.

She needed help. And help she would have, even if she had to swim across the lake and crawl into town on her knees.

Even if she had to beg Lukas Beckmann, the baker.

That was her plan, after all. She swatted at a branch that blocked her path, wishing she could banish her memories of the silly romantic dreams she'd been having of that man. She needed to focus on practical matters, not girlish fancies.

She needed his mercy, not his kisses.

Her face went hot. How was it possible that she could embarrass herself with mere thoughts of Lukas Beckmann? Honestly, sometimes she was every bit as silly as Hansel always said she was.

In an attempt to outpace the unwanted feelings, she doubled the speed of her feet.

Eleven

Marga leapt over a puddle of something black and foul-smelling without slowing her progress toward Eschlinsdorf. A squirrel darted across the path, scattering the last leaves of late autumn—for surely it was November by now. And then she was thinking of Lukas again, how his hair seemed threaded through with the same gold as the leaves at her feet.

When, she wondered, had she come to think of the man not as near-stranger Herr Beckmann and instead, far too familiarly, as Lukas?

She could only hope Lukas—*Herr Beckmann*—didn't blame her for the fever Hansel's fiancée had mentioned in the letter, the one that had killed many townsfolk. If he did, perhaps she'd spend a night locked in the cellar that served as Eschlinsdorf's jail before her execution. There, her jailers might provide a hunk of stale bread and some watery soup for her last meal. Stale bread sounded like a wonderful treat to the girl who'd not had a crust in ages, even if it shed nasty crumbs everywhere. The following morning, they would burn her alive or hang her.

If she died, the duck would starve alone inside the witch's gingerbread walls. It deserved better after all it had done to help her and Hansel.

No. Lukas would be kind and helpful. He had never treated her with disdain or suspicion. The last time they'd met, he'd fretted over her lack of a cloak and offered to lend her his own. He'd even offered to walk her home—as if he didn't care that some sleepless busybody might have seen them alone together in the moonlight.

She had to trust that Lukas would keep her hidden, and that he'd trade the gems she'd brought for the things she needed. She had to hope he'd give her a recipe for sturdy gingerbread so she might try again to fix the cottage walls and roof before winter.

A light breeze played with the hem of Marga's cloak and coaxed the scent of pine from the trees. The weather here was most pleasant. Why was it so different around the cottage? Was the witch's residual magic that strong? With all her heart, she wanted not to return. But the duck was there, and she owed it her life. She wasn't one to run away from obligations, unlike Hansel.

Onward she trudged. The ground was far from flat, and all too often branches blocked her progress and she had to climb over, under, or through them. Thank *Himmel* she'd worn breeches and not a cumbersome skirt puffed out with petticoats.

Nightfall was imminent when she reached the lake. The day had lasted a week, or so it seemed. She'd heard once, perhaps from the old witch, that enchanted places did not abide by mortal man's ideas of time. Maybe that was why the cuckoo clocks in the grove disagreed with one another. Well, no matter the hour, she was tired. Ready for the journey to end—although still miles from town.

The water sloshed against the banks of the vast lake—unfrozen, as Marga had feared. Right away, she took the small hatchet from her belt and set to building a raft from branches and vines.

The sun disappeared and a bright moon took its place, shedding just enough light to allow her to keep chopping lengths of wood and tying them together. Hours passed. Her arms ached and her fingers stung, full of tiny splinters. Her body begged for sleep, but she forced herself to continue.

Not long after the earliest birds began to sing the sun into rising, she tied one last knot and declared the raft done. She still needed to fashion an oar or two, but first, as inconvenient as it was, she needed to rest. She lay down on a patch of cushiony moss and surrendered to sleep.

* * *

With a start, Marga awoke. She sat up straight, and her hand pressed onto something hard and round. Someone had left a pile of walnuts and small red apples beside her while she slept.

High-pitched giggling drew her attention to the base of a thorn bush. Two tiny figures, dressed in layered leaves and wearing acorn cap hats, waved to her before turning and rushing into the undergrowth. *Faeries.*

She'd heard many tales of the little folk, but she'd never before seen a faerie. She opened her mouth to thank them but stopped as she remembered what she'd read of their customs. Woodland faeries disliked being thanked and would repay words of gratitude with pranks or mischief. Better to leave an offering of sweets for them when she passed this way again.

The little meal strengthened her. She got up to examine the raft. The light of day revealed many gaps and weak spots. It would not hold her, even as thin as she'd become. She hurried to gather more vines, and then spent several hours knotting more branches together until her fingers ached and her hands were stained green.

This time when she looked over her work, she was satisfied. But she still needed some sort of paddle. She searched among the trees for something to use. It took only a short time for her to find a four-foot-long, bare pine branch ending in a V-shaped flourish of green needles. It would do. The raft's construction had already taken up much of the day; the last thing she wanted was to spend another night sleeping on the floor of the enchanted forest. The faeries had been kind to her when last she slumbered, but she'd been lucky. If she slept again, some toothy resident of the Igelwald would likely have her for dinner.

She lugged the raft and the makeshift oar through the cattails and into the water. She waded in up to her knees, frightening tiny minnows so they darted into the deep. The duck would have made a meal of them, no doubt. As she pushed the raft away from the shore and clambered aboard, she wondered how the duck was faring. This water and these shores were its home. If only she could have brought it back here, but that would have slowed her journey. Besides, the duck wasn't yet well enough to survive in the wild. She offered up a prayer for its well-being. Worrying would help neither of them, but hurrying might. She took up her oar.

On her knees, Marga rowed, dipping the branch-paddle and stroking along one side of the raft and then the other. The raft wobbled without ceasing but showed no inclination to sink, thank *Himmel*. She tried to ignore the ominous bubbling around the raft. If fortune favored, only fish and frogs surrounded her, and not ravenous, long-tentacled lake monsters.

A cluster of lily pads parted as the raft drifted into the center of the lake. Marga was thankful at first, for the plants grew so densely there that she'd been sure to become caught up in them. But then she noticed several of the flower-topped leaves gliding smoothly, forming a circle. Trapping her.

One of the lily pads lifted from the water. Two more did the same. Marga whisked the branch-oar out of the water and brandished it like a weapon. The dripping masses of pine needles looked more pitiful than threatening, but the only other weapon she'd brought was the small hatchet and it was too well-secured to her belt to be quickly accessed. She could hardly imagine striking any sort of living creature with a hatchet, anyway.

The lily-leaf-crowned heads and bare shoulders of three young women arose, one in front of her, one to her left, and one to her right. They were not identical, but almost. Long tendrils of coppery hair framed their fair faces. They gazed intently at her with doe-like, dark eyes as they took hold of the raft's edge with slender fingers. The skin on their necks was striped with delicate, silvery gills.

They were not women but water sprites. Nixes. Creatures she'd read about in her father's fat book of mythology. Known for being as deadly as they were beautiful.

"Please let me pass," Marga commanded. She kept her voice steady, but her heart beat so fast she feared it might burst.

"You cannot leave the wood," the nix in front of her said in a high, clear voice. Her companions' lips moved as if silently repeating the words. In their mouths, Marga spied sets of needle-sharp teeth.

"I must fetch medicine for the white duck. Surely you know the one. It has lived here for many years, and can ferry passengers over the lake. The duck will surely die if I'm delayed."

The nixes looked at one another questioningly but without uttering a word. They returned their gazes to Marga.

"Are you the human Gretel who ate of the witch queen Truda's cottage? Do not lie or we shall drown you," the nix on the left said, narrowing her eyes.

"I am," Marga said. She was a terrible liar and a worse swimmer. It was not worth the risk.

"The white duck told us not to let you leave the wood," the middle nix said.

"This he commanded many years ago, when first he came to us, but we forget nothing," the nix on the left said.

"You cannot leave the wood," said the nix on the right. Her silvery neck gills fluttered as she spoke. "The one he spoke of must stay. The white duck must be obeyed since we have no queen."

Marga lifted her chin and conjured her most authoritative tone. "If you are beholden to the duck, you will let me go. The duck is very ill and needs my care."

"One must stay," the nix on the left insisted. The center nix hissed and gathered her sisters into her arms. They whispered like reeds in the wind, in a tongue unknown to Marga, their pale shoulders bobbing amid small waves.

Finally, they separated. The center nix said, "You must swear by the moon and stars to return within three days."

The sister on the left let go of the raft and raised dripping hands heavenward as she spoke. "You must swear, and if your oath proves false, your firstborn daughter will have gills and be bound to this lake from the day she is born. For the one must stay in the wood. Too long have we been overseen by bones and a bird."

"One must stay," all three said. "Give us your hand and your oath."

With a shiver of trepidation, Marga promised to return. She offered her hand to the center nix, expecting her to clasp it in a handshake. Instead, quick as a striking snake, the nix bit her finger and whisked a drop of blood into a tiny vial made from a snail's shell.

"The oath is sealed. Should you break the vow you have taken, your firstborn shall be ours," the right nix said.

"You have three days and only three," the nixes sang together as they joined hands and sank under the surface.

The lake stilled for a moment, and then the lily pads separated again, this time to form a channel wide enough to allow the raft to pass through. Muffled echoes of mischievous laughter drifted up from the depths. Nixes were fickle things. Marga could not afford to hesitate, lest they decided to drown or eat her after all.

She plunged her oar into the water and paddled fast. The nixes were terrifying, but something equally dangerous—or many somethings—might lie in wait between her and the shore, waiting to vex or to eat her. The sooner she reached dry ground, the better.

Twelve

Ansgar bellowed with rage.

If he had been a man, he would have cursed in seven languages and hurled things against the walls. Confined by his injured, avian form, he let loose a trumpeting quack and shook his good wing at the gods in fury—for the girl was gone.

Just like her cowardly brother, Gretel had slunk off without a word. And there was a strong possibility she would not return. She was a little thing, and the forest was rife with ravenous creatures too stupid to know better than to tear their future queen to shreds.

Pain darted through his bad wing as if he'd been shot all over again. He hissed and sank into his basket. The brief outburst had left him hot and light-headed. His belly seized with pain. He needed more medicine or magical intervention. In Gretel's absence, deprived of her poultices, the wounds had started to fester and poison his body. Without her care or a miracle, he would perish within a day or two.

For a period of time, things had gone according to his plan. On days when the weather was fair, Gretel had set his basket outdoors so he could take in the good sunlight. She'd left him there while she foraged or fetched water, and he'd seized the opportunity to help himself to healing herbs from the witch's garden. He'd nipped the plants to the ground—and they had much improved his health. So much so that he'd had to feign illness to keep the girl at his beck and call.

But the herbs would not grow back until spring, and he was more ill now than ever before. Even if the heavy door were not in his way, he wouldn't have had the strength to walk deep into the maze of the garden.

Another round of cursing quacks spewed forth from his bill.

He ought to have been more careful. He should have used his weather manipulation to better effect, or perhaps enlisted the aid of faeries or magic-blooded animals. He'd been too confident, too arrogant, too patient.

If he died without fulfilling the enchantment's demands, he'd fail not only himself, but the entire realm of the Igelwald. The repercussions would be immeasurable. He'd tried to keep that weighty truth in the back of his mind until now. After all, there was only so much one could do to set the world right as a heap of quacking feathers.

The truth was this: the last witch's ashes had made for a poor queen. After thirteen years without firm governance, the magical creatures of the wood took more liberties and more risks with every passing solstice. Too often they interfered with humankind and risked being discovered and destroyed. The forest folk needed a new queen, and she who had vanquished the witch-queen Truda owned that role. It was the natural order of things, as well as the supreme will of the Igelwald.

One spring day, perhaps twenty years before his fall into avian form, the speaking pool in the Igelwald's greenest glen had whispered a secret to the wizard Ansgar: the little daughter of a woodcutter would wander to the cottage, one who would grow up to take Truda's throne. Of course he'd kept this prophecy to himself. He did not fancy having a kettle thrown at his head by his irate wife.

He'd long been a duck by the time Gretel arrived at the gingerbread cottage. Truda, who occasionally saw visions of the future, must have recognized her for who she was. He imagined that rather than preparing the girl to reign, power-mad Truda had sought to thwart fate by killing her.

Little good that had done the old hag.

The tale had been carried through the forest, passed from mouse to bird, from bird to sprite, from sprite to frog—and then to his duck ears. When Truda had been about to shove the girl into the oven, the girl had outwitted her, and fed Truda to the flames.

He flinched, regretting that he'd referred to his wife as a hag. Great gods above, Truda had been a beauty once. How she'd made him burn with passion then! They'd scratched and tumbled like wildcats, smashing meadow grasses flat while howling with pleasure. The early years of their marriage had been the best time of his life.

Alas, every spell she'd cast had eaten away at her loveliness. A hundred years of casting spells had rendered her wrinkled, bent, gray, and almost toothless. Still, he loved her for her daring heart, her fortitude, her cleverness, and the purity of her abhorrence for unmagical humans.

For all her offenses against hapless humans, Truda had been the perfect monarch for the forest folk. One could scarcely blame her for eating a few peasant children after she'd discovered that doing so would restore her beauty for a time. He'd heard this from a pair of chatty sprites he'd once carried across the lake long before young Hansel and Gretel. This information had not shocked him. If one could have counted vanity as a virtue, Truda would have qualified for sainthood.

Ansgar's body shivered as his fever rose. Bah, why did he waste time worrying about the Igelwald's future? Why should he mourn the loss of dryads, moss folk, elves, and the like? His feathered throat constricted as his attempt not to care proved futile. He was loath to admit it, but the notion of so much wild beauty, feral joy, and primal mischief coming to an end pained him more than his wing ever could.

If only fate had chosen him to be the next sovereign instead of Gretel...

Such speculation was useless, unprofitable. Better to rest and to hope that fate yet had its unseen hand firmly on the girl the forest had chosen to become its next sovereign, coaxing her magical potential from ember to conflagration in a way a duck never could.

* * *

The sun had set, vanishing in a blaze of color as it yielded dominion to the silvery-gray moon. Marga sat on the roots of an enormous tree and huddled inside her cloak, trying to stay warm as she waited just inside the forest's borders. The best chance she had to avoid the townsfolk and to find Lukas Beckmann alone would be in the hours just before dawn.

The journey to Eschlinsdorf had taken much longer than she'd intended. For the hundredth time, she hoped the duck was not suffering in her absence.

The nixes' comments about the duck had been curious. They'd spoken about the creature as if it possessed great authority and wisdom, but for as long as it had been in Marga's care, it had behaved much like an ordinary duck. It hadn't done anything magical since changing size at the lakeside. Perhaps its injuries had taken an unseen toll on the creature.

While Marga daydreamed, time passed at a snail's pace. Finally, when the moon had sunk partway down the sky, she decided she'd waited long enough. She rose and stretched. Her heart pounded with apprehension as she re-knotted her cravat and attempted to brush dried mud off her breeches. Thank *Himmel* the big, black cloak would cover her from head to ankles, and mask any untidiness.

An odd sensation gripped her as she neared the last of the trees, the feeling of someone cupping their hands around her hipbones from behind. Like something tried to hold her back. Perhaps it was the power of the oath she'd sworn to return, but leaving the bounds of the forest did not sit well with her.

She remembered leaving the woods with Papa and her brother soon after she and Hansel had escaped the witch. How ill she'd been the instant she'd stepped out of the Igelwald and onto the slope leading to town. Her bones had ached so badly that Papa had been obliged to carry her. But surely that was a coincidence. She'd made no promises to nixes when she was eight. Anyway, after a few days, she'd felt fine.

Stubbly grasses crunched and snapped underfoot as she strode over them in the milky moonlight. Someone had harvested hay for their livestock there, someone not afraid to venture close to the Igelwald. Not many in Eschlinsdorf possessed such boldness. In the street and in the pub, they were forever warning one another of the dangers of wolves and wild boar, of poison trees and tricky fairy folk. And the old witch, who may or may not have been dead.

The same witch whose stockings she was wearing, and whose cottage had given her shelter for weeks.

Marga hurried across the wooden footbridge over the millstream, with her head bowed and her hood well forward. She didn't expect to meet anyone on this side of town so early, but she couldn't afford to be incautious. Within minutes, she found the narrow alley that passed behind the candlemaker's and cheesemonger's shops before ending abruptly at the big stacks of firewood owned by the Beckmann family.

She stopped and pressed her back against the alleyway's stone wall. Would it be better to forget involving Lukas Beckmann in her business? If she could sneak back to her own house to gather food, medicine, and clothes, she could return to the cottage without bothering the baker...if the townsfolk had not already ransacked the place. And if they did not catch her coming or going.

If she made it back across the nixes' lake alive, then regained a little strength from food and rest back at the cottage, she could chop enough firewood to keep the main room warm until the duck healed. If they ate sparingly, whatever she brought from home might last for a while.

If the tarp on the cottage roof held, rain and snow would not seep into the kitchen.

If...

There were too many ifs. She could not change the plan she'd made before she'd left the witch's cottage. She had to find the baker.

Her legs ached with weariness as she took slow steps out of the alley and then lingered among the bakery's wood piles to watch for Lukas.

Several tin lanterns hung on poles in the yard behind the bakery, giving the place an almost festive appearance. But the bakers were hard at work, not indulging in a party. They did most of their baking before dawn so the townsfolk might have fresh bread and rolls for breakfast. Two huge, hive-shaped, outdoor ovens roared, their bellies full of wood and flames, their mouths open wide to accept unbaked loaves.

The heady aroma of fresh bread almost caused Marga's knees to buckle. Dear *Himmel*, she could endure the detestable sight of crumbs for the sake of one bite of a crusty brown loaf. Although she stood yards away from the big ovens, their intense heat warmed her skin and made her suddenly drowsy. In the shadows, she stretched her arms and legs, trying to throw off the mantle of sleepiness and the urge to snatch a loaf.

She found a place to crouch and hide among the piled

wood. Now, all she could do was pray that Lukas, and not one of his surly, superstitious brothers, would soon come to fetch fuel for the fires. Hansel had always said that the Beckmann brothers were meaner than old billy goats and wore so many little brass charms against evil that they jingled when they walked. Men who would not take kindly to a so-called witch's clandestine, pre-dawn visit.

A baritone voice rang out nearby. Marga recognized the traditional song. The townsfolk sang it every autumn as they aided neighboring farmers with the harvests. When Marga's family had first settled in the area, the townsfolk had invited them to help, but before a year passed, the rumors about the Holzfällers had sprouted up and spread like weeds. They'd never again been asked to assist in the harvest or to join in the feast that followed—but that hadn't stopped Marga from spying upon the festivities.

When the song ceased, a steady *shush-shush-shush* followed as the bakers slid long wooden paddles in and out of the ovens to remove finished loaves. The bread aroma increased tenfold. Marga tried not to inhale, fearing she might be overcome by the desire for food and rush into the brothers' presence when it was unsafe to do so.

"Lukas!" one of the bakers bellowed. "Stop stargazing and attend to your work. Gott gave fleas more sense than you. At least they keep to their business and don't waste time writing poetry to imaginary sweethearts." The man cleared his throat loudly and spat.

"Coming, Jacob," Lukas replied from across the yard.

Marga peered between the wood stacks and watched Lukas plod to a pile not far from her hiding place. The grumpy brother, Jacob, hefted a basket full of loaves onto one shoulder and trudged toward the bakery's back door.

She hesitated. What if Lukas betrayed her? What if he, too, believed that she'd caused the deadly fever? In trusting him, she might lose her life. Was the life of a duck—even a magical duck—worth such a sacrifice?

On the other hand, could she live with herself if she betrayed the duck's trust, when its kind service to her and Hansel had resulted in grave injury?

"Lukas," she whispered. She stood and took a step closer. Her knees trembled inside her breeches. She wanted to hide again, but that would help nothing and no one. Louder, she said, "Lukas Beckmann."

He turned his head. His blond hair was mostly covered by a loose, gray linen cap. He wore an apron smudged with ash and flour. She'd forgotten how tall he was, probably the tallest man in town save for freakish Hansel. The sight of him sent her heartbeat racing. If she blamed uncertainty and fear alone for the state of her pulse, she'd be a liar. There was a word for it: infatuation. It was exasperating, truly, that her heart reacted to his presence in such an irrational way.

Lukas set the wood back on the pile. His gaze swept over the yard. "Who's there?" he asked in a low voice. "Show yourself."

Marga moved into his line of sight and shoved the hood back from her face. "It's me. Margarethe. Fraulein Holzfäller."

Thirteen

Marga tried not to cringe as Lukas assessed her appearance with a wide-eyed gaze. What must she look like after trudging, half-starved, through the Igelwald in a set of old-fashioned, men's garments?

His face was a mixture of concern and dismay. "Fraulein, what has happened to you? You're skin and bones. And those clothes! Your hair!" Instead of waiting for a reply, he nudged her back into the gap between the stacks of firewood where she'd been hiding. "You must not be seen. The townsfolk want you dead. They think you cursed them with fever."

"I know. But I'm in desperate need. I could think of nowhere else to go." Her vision blurred and she grabbed onto the wood pile to keep from collapsing in a faint. Of all the times for her body to betray her, it had to choose now, in front of a man she still wasn't sure she could trust.

"You're not well. Sit, before you fall," Lukas said softly but firmly. "Stay here. I'll bring you something to eat."

Marga sat on a piece of log and peered up at the baker. "You won't alert the town councilmen?"

He shook his head and offered a smile so kind that it brought tears to her eyes. She was unaccustomed to people treating her without suspicion or malice. And she was tired, so tired.

"Stay here," he said again before striding away.

Marga leaned back and rested her head against the woodpile. She felt safe in Lukas's care, which was sure proof of her exhaustion. She was in as much danger now as she had been within the enchanted woods—yet she could not keep her eyes from shutting.

A few minutes later, a hand brushed against her forearm. "Fraulein Holzfäller?"

Marga opened her eyes. Lukas crouched in front of her. His big hands presented her with a mug of milk and a round roll draped with a thick slice of ham. "I would have brought something more, but I heard my mother's footsteps on the stairs."

"Thank you." She drank the milk in a few gulps. She bit into the ham-covered roll like a wild animal consuming its prey, without regard for the crumbs sprinkling onto her borrowed clothes. She shamed herself by eating without any regard for manners, but nothing she'd ever eaten had tasted better, not even the walls of the gingerbread cottage she'd nibbled as a starving child.

"Lukas! Where the devil are you now?" Jacob shouted from beside the ovens. "Hurry and help me get this batch out before it burns." He grumbled a few curse words.

"There's a shed just over there." Lukas pointed to a place beyond the tallest wood pile. "Hide inside, and I'll come to you soon as I'm able." He stood and rushed toward his nagging brother without awaiting her reply. "Coming, Jacob!"

She watched him go and tried not to miss him. There was something about him that seemed so good and so reliable. And he was as handsome in person as he was in her recurring dreams. Handsomer. Which was something she really ought not to dwell on now. Or ever.

She tipped her head back. The sky above Eschlinsdorf sparkled with stars. Soon, the first light of day would erase them. The bitter smell of burnt bread drifted on a current of crisp air. Marga set down the mug and got onto her haunches. After a minute or two, she crept like a thief toward the shed as Jacob berated Lukas for the ruined loaves. When she reached the unpainted wooden building, she pried open the door wide enough to squeeze through—and thanked Gott it didn't squeak or fall off its hinges. She felt her way through the darkness, shimmying past boxes and barrels, bumping into shovels and old furniture. Sticky cobwebs clung to her face and fingertips. When her hand met the back wall, she turned and sank to the floor. She covered herself with the cloak so she might be mistaken for an old sack if anyone came to fetch a tool.

It was a good place to hide, *if* Lukas did not betray her.

Protect Lukas, dear Gott, she prayed. *And whether he chooses to help me or turns me over to those who wish to kill me, please let the wait be short.*

* * *

Ansgar stepped out of his basket. Fever raged within him. He kept forgetting whether he was a duck or a man. He was hot, and hungry, and thirsty enough to drain the Danube River. He quacked for the girl's help, but she did not come. He quacked again, insulting her in the most vulgar of terms, and then remembered she'd left. He would have to see to his own needs, blast it all.

His webbed feet slapped the cold stone floor as he waddled unsteadily across the room. Everything spun and swayed as if the cottage itself danced to the music of an invisible orchestra. Possessed by fierce and utter desperation, he eyed the door.

And then he remembered he had no way to open it, for he was a duck.

He had no hands.

In his feeble state, he had not even a spark of magic with which to summon a beetle to come ease his hunger pangs.

Never once had he wept in all his years as a duck. He had not thought it possible. Now, ill, alone, and dizzy with the need for sustenance, twin tears leaked from his eyes and rolled down his feathered cheeks.

Was this pitiful scene to be his last? He'd expected to end in triumph, to perish in some grand and colorful explosion of magic. At the very least, he'd hoped to expire in his true love's arms with poetic words upon his lips.

No, he exclaimed, although the protestation came out as a weak quack. He refused to die as a cursed waterfowl. He simply would not accept such a humiliating and ignoble fate.

Lifting his chin with proud determination, he waddled forward, taking a slow tour of the room. He found a few dead moths and a live, very stupid housefly. He choked them down and slurped the last of the water from his bowl. It wasn't much of a meal, but it was enough for now.

Death would not own him this day.

Fourteen

Shards of sunlight poked through the wall of the shed where the old boards had cracked or decayed. Marga guessed that the hour might be as late as noon. In the narrow space she'd occupied since before dawn, she stood and yawned.

She hadn't meant to doze, but resting had renewed her strength—as had the little meal Lukas provided. He'd been so kind, so anxious to care for her. She wanted to trust him, but why had he not yet returned after so many hours? *Because he is busy baking, or sleeping, or waiting until it is safe. Have patience.*

Cobwebs and twigs clung to her cloak. She removed it and looked for a place to hang the garment so she could brush it clean with her hands. Nearby, atop a dresser, she spied what looked like a rectangular, gold-framed looking glass, the size of a large book. The mirror sparked her curiosity. What did she look like after trudging through the woods, building a raft, and climbing through a dusty shed? Earlier,

Lukas had seemed quite surprised by her appearance—shocked, really. Could she look so terrible?

Curiosity coaxed her into squeezing through a gap between boxes, stepping over a crate, and then wedging herself between the dresser and an empty bookcase. She wiped dust off the glass with her palm. She'd never been vain, but she had always striven to be tidy. *There's no sin in tidiness*, she told herself. Of course her concern with her appearance had *nothing* to do with the fact that she found Lukas handsome.

As she shrugged off the cloak and hung it from the corner of the dresser, something within her cautioned against peering into the glass. She paused, searching her mind for a rational reason to refrain from looking. Something to do with the witch of the gingerbread cottage, perhaps? Had the crone used mirrors to cast dark spells in her presence long ago?

She waited a minute or two, allowing time for the remembrance of such an episode to arise from the depths of her brain, but no memory came. So she leaned closer to the mirror.

In the age-speckled, cloudy glass, Marga discerned her image. She gasped. She'd expected to look pale, bedraggled, and hunger-stricken, but she had not expected *this*.

Two, inch-wide streaks of silver striped her hair, starting at her temples and winding around the sides of her head. At the corners of her eyes, deep creases like the footprints of birds fanned outward. When last she'd studied her reflection, she'd looked far younger than her twenty-one years. Now, she could be mistaken for a woman twice her age. Maybe thrice.

The shed door creaked as it opened. Marga grabbed the cloak and crouched low, draping the garment over her body, hiding. She held her breath.

"Fraulein Holzfäller?" Lukas whispered from far across the shed—or someone who sounded like Lukas. He had so many brothers that Marga could never remember all their names.

"Fraulein?" the man repeated.

"I'm here." She stood, still trembling from the shock of seeing her altered appearance. The cloak fell to the floor as the door thudded shut. She rose onto her tiptoes to catch sight of Lukas fumbling to fasten a hook and eye latch at the top of the door.

Once again, she questioned his intentions. Did he mean to keep others out or to trap her inside? Even if he had left the door unlatched, she could not have escaped him. Too much furniture and too many boxes, and Lukas himself, filled the space between her and the exit. He could catch her with barely an effort, for he was well fed and long-limbed, while she was malnourished and cursed with a short stride.

"Wait there. I'll come to you," Lukas said. His journey through the room was punctuated by thuds, bumps, and mumbled exclamations of pain. After a particularly loud crash, he said, "I fear I am too large to navigate this maze, Fraulein. Are you well enough to make your way to me?"

The noise caused by Lukas's clumsy movements had agitated Marga's already jangled nerves, but his sheepish tone soothed her and drew her to him as if she were a rat and he the piper from the old tale of Hamelin. She threaded her way through the furniture and boxes to meet him in a vacant corner. Marga's face grew hot with embarrassment, knowing the baker could see what she'd seen in the looking glass—and then hotter still as she scolded herself for caring. A woman of character would be concerned about the risk Lukas was taking on her behalf rather than whether or not he found her pretty.

"Here." Lukas offered her a cloth sack. The warm skin of his big hand brushed against her fingers as she accepted it. "Something more to eat and a bottle of cider."

"Thank you."

He turned to the desk beside him, lifted an upside-down wooden chair off the top, and set it in front of her. "Please. Sit. I am used to standing all day, and it is bad for the stomach to eat while standing. Or so my mother says."

She sat and tried to take ladylike bites of the apple, cheese, and sweet roll he'd brought.

Lukas stared alternately at his feet and the piles of furniture, his fair cheeks tinted rose-pink. For such a big man, he sometimes seemed as timid as a kitten. When half her meal was gone, he said, "Would you tell me what happened, Fraulein? They say you were driven out of town, you and Hansel, because you bewitched Herr Zetter's flock and made them act unnaturally."

His words made the food in her mouth taste bitter. Swallowing it felt like swallowing gravel. Hansel's gambling acquaintances must have concocted the preposterous tale in order to conceal their own wicked deeds. The story might have made her laugh if it had not imperiled her life. What unnatural things would bewitched sheep do? Dance and sing? Walk on their hind legs and recite Shakespeare?

She set aside her questions about the sheep. She met Lukas's gaze, hoping he'd believe her words. The ever-present kindness in his blue eyes inspired her trust. "The truth is that Hansel owed money to half the men in town, and *Himmel* knows how many women. Too much to repay. And you know what they have always said about me, I'm sure. The rumors. We were chased out of our home in the middle of the night like rats. Like vermin."

"You hid in the forest?"

"Yes. We hoped no one would dare to follow us into the Igelwald." She didn't want to tell him yet that they'd sheltered in the witch's gingerbread cottage. And as much as she wanted to trust him, it seemed imprudent to admit she'd been nursing a magical duck back to health.

Nor did she want to remind him of the gossip he must have heard about her, the gingerbread cottage, and the witch. Because, after all, everyone in town knew something about the Holzfäller children's month of living with the witch, thanks to her brother.

Hansel had taken up hard drinking when he was thirteen, and whenever his belly was full of spirits, he'd regaled one and all with his version of the shocking tale of young Hansel and Gretel, lost in the Igelwald. How the townsfolk must have loved the boy's stories of torture, magic, and murder.

Over the years, someone had always brought drunken Hansel home, leaving him weeping or passed out on the doorstep. His friends never knocked upon the door, for that might have summoned his sister, the odd girl with the unseemly habits. The girl who'd spent weeks being mothered by the forest's famous, child-eating witch. Little Gretel could not have helped but learn the witch's wicked ways before she'd killed the crone.

Marga had heard things about Lukas as well, years ago when she'd still dared to browse the open-air market on occasion. Lukas's sister Berta fancied herself a matchmaker. Without shame, she loudly extolled her brother's virtues to every suitable girl she met in the town square: Lukas was quiet, obeyed his Mutti, had muscles like Goliath, read books in three languages, said his prayers both morning and night, and made pastry light as butterflies' wings.

But never in a thousand years would Berta have matched her brother with an alleged witch.

"Where is Hansel now?" Lukas asked, bringing her thoughts back to the present.

She'd finished the cider but still held onto the bottle with both hands as if it might lend her some kind of fortitude. "He ran away. To France."

"There is more that you're not saying, I think. You can trust me." Gently, Lukas took the empty bottle and set it on the desk. "Please. Allow me to help you."

His goodness made her want to throw herself into his arms or to fall at his feet in supplication. She could do neither. She'd fought for years to prove herself capable to her father and brother, and she was not about to allow this man to undo her. She had no time to indulge in girlish nonsense, no energy to spare on fluttering eyelashes and coy speeches.

"I can take care of myself," Marga blurted. Loudly. She flinched, and so did he. Such rudeness was inexcusable. She looked up into his surprised face. "I'm sorry. I should thank you. I *do* thank you. I came here to ask for your help, after all. You've been very kind."

"Don't be sorry. I have no doubt that you can take care of yourself, and have done so many times. But to ask for help is an act of courage, and to accept help is braver still."

"You do not believe the rumors about me?" Hope sprang up inside her like a seedling seeking sunlight.

"The Good Book says *Gott* will judge all people. I would not presume to take his place."

Tears burned Marga's eyes but she blinked them away. A lump formed in her throat and kept her silent.

Lukas offered a gentle smile. "Now, Fraulein Holzfäller, tell me how I can assist you, before my brothers come looking for me."

The story spilled from her lips like water bursting free from a broken dam. She told him everything, from Hansel's revelation of the wrist-crushing shackle to her encounter with the lake nixes. She told him of the sickly duck and her obligation to stay in the witch's cottage with the bird until it was well—a cottage damaged by the elements and her foolishness. How winter was coming and that she'd probably have to reside there until spring. How she needed a baker's help to repair the cake walls so she and the duck wouldn't perish from the cold. That she had brought gems to trade for food and whatever was needed to fix the walls, and that he could take all the riches he could carry home with him when the job was done.

Lukas nodded from time to time but said nothing. His face retained the same pensive look whether she mentioned magical ducks or boiling pine needles for tea.

Hearing her tale aloud, Marga realized how mad it sounded. How mad *she* must seem to this sensible, hard-working man. Perhaps she *was* mad and had imagined it all. She gripped the seat of the chair with both hands and waited for Lukas to respond. Minutes as wide as hours passed.

Lukas nodded once more. “I believe you,” he said softly.

“You do?” Her tears returned and overflowed. She covered her mouth with both hands but could not hold back a sob.

He crouched down beside her and looked straight into her face. “My great, great grandfather built the witch’s house. And I am going to help you fix it.”

Fifteen

Spiders.

Ansgar hated the way arachnids crunched in his bill, how their spindly legs twitched within his throat.

A wee measure of his magic had returned after his meal of moths. To stave off starvation, the small magic allowed him to summon spiders a few at a time. Spiders, but nothing else. Greatly he longed for the tasty little trout that roamed the lake, or even a fat frog.

The possession of such paltry power rankled him far more than being reduced to eating spiders. He'd wielded such magic once! Somehow, someday, he vowed with a dismal quack, he would be formidable again. He'd move more than spiders and storm clouds. Someday, he'd feast on the finest foods. He'd wear fine silk and soft leather, jeweled rings and gold pocket watches. His servants would bow and grovel and treat him like royalty. In his future mansion, feathers would be forbidden.

Would he be happy without Truda beside him? He

dismissed the sentimental question and hardened his duck-sized heart. He could find another wife—or do without the trouble. Bachelorhood might suit him. Why not try it, when he was a man again?

A new man with a new life.

With all his being, he willed the girl Gretel to come back to break the spell that bound him. The concentrated effort made his head hurt—and likely affected nothing else in the universe.

Wearied, cross, and famished, Ansgar settled onto the cold hearthstones to wait.

And wait.

* * *

Marga glanced up at the starry, cloudless heavens as Lukas locked the door of the storage shed they'd just raided for flour. The night was frigid, but at least the clear sky would not dump snow upon them during their journey.

She turned her attention to Felix, the shortest, thinnest, and youngest Beckmann brother. The metal charms Felix wore on his wrists clinked together faintly as he raked his straight, fair hair off his forehead. Yawning, he eyed her suspiciously as Lukas laid a huge sack of flour across his back. The town's church bells tolled midnight. A rooster crowed in the distance, confused by the brightness of the moon.

"Will you be able to bear that for a few miles?" Lukas asked his brother.

"I'm fifteen, not five. And why did you wake me if you

thought I couldn't?" Felix asked, grimacing under the weight.

"Who else could I have asked? Old Astrid the housemaid?" Lukas hefted two sacks onto his own broad back.

"Astrid's too pious. She never would have agreed to help a..." Felix reddened and did not finish his comment.

"I'm not a witch." Marga picked up two big wicker baskets filled with the spices and jarred honey Lukas had brought from inside the bakery. "If I were, I would not need your help." She wondered what Lukas had told him about their plans.

"Perhaps you would, if you were bad with spells," Felix said.

"Enough, Felix." Lukas grabbed the handle of a wooden cage containing a pair of cross-looking hens. "The moon is bright now, but the way the wind is picking up, the skies might cloud over soon. We'd best be on our way. Quietly."

"You'd better make this worth the trouble," Felix grumbled. "My bad shoulder aches already."

Lukas gave his brother a reproachful look. "Stop whining like a baby and let's go."

"You left a note for *Mutti*? She's not going to be happy when she wakes to find us gone."

"I did," Lukas said. "She won't expect us home for a day or two. I wrote that we'd gone to help old cousin Horst repair his barn."

Felix's eyes bulged with surprise. "You lied? To *Mutti*?"

Embarrassment reddened Lukas's face. "Stop stalling, Felix. Ready, Fraulein?"

"This way." Marga set off at a brisk pace. She'd been

shocked when Lukas showed up at the shed with Felix, but of course they needed help to transport the ingredients from the town to the cottage deep in the forest.

With the large flour sacks, the baskets of supplies, and the two men to ferry over, her little raft would have to make multiple trips across the lake. *Himmel* help them if the nixes acted up. Should those lusty females take a liking to the bakers, the men might find their enticement irresistible. Perhaps it would be better if Felix didn't try to cross. He was so young, so steeped in golden-haired beauty. Taking him onto the lake would be like baiting hungry lionesses with fresh meat.

She'd speak to Lukas about it before they drew near to the water.

The hens warbled softly in their cage as the trio reached the tree line. Marga cast a glance behind them, over the moon-washed field of short, frost-glazed grass. Not a soul followed. She thanked Gott under her breath and led the bakers into the forest.

Her body tingled, as if the forest magic embraced her with invisible arms. She shook herself, trying to throw off the feeling, and hoped Lukas hadn't noticed her odd wriggling. He might think she had fleas.

The strange sensation settled down, seeping into her bones. She couldn't deny that it felt right to be once more surrounded by the old trees of the Igelwald. Every step she took away from the hateful Eschlinsdorfers was a good one, surely, even though the forest offered its own challenges and perils.

"How much...farther?" Felix asked, panting under the weight of his burden.

"A good many miles, I'd wager," said Lukas. "We can rest once we're a better distance from town."

Felix stumbled. His flour sack fell to the ground with a thud. He dropped to his knees and swore.

Lukas scowled at his brother. "Every time you speak a foul word, I'll deduct a coin from your pay."

"You're paying him?" Marga said.

"I had no choice," Lukas said. "We needed another strong back, and I trust no one more than my brother. Even if he is lazy, prone to complain, and too fond of money."

Felix got to his feet and shoved Lukas with both hands. The boy wasn't big enough to actually move his older brother an inch. In truth, Marga was surprised that scrawny Felix had managed to carry his burden this far without stopping.

Lukas laughed and set his flour sacks against a tree trunk. A puff of dust rose into the air. "All right, then. I suppose we could rest here for a minute or two. This part of the woods seems harmless enough."

A breeze stirred the treetops and rattled the dry leaves that still clung there. Marga watched a ghostly white owl swoop from one tree to another. "I don't believe that any part of the Igelwald is harmless. We should trust nothing here easily."

With a loud huff, Felix took a seat on a tree stump and mopped his brow with a handkerchief. "Well, this is charming. Have I mentioned to you, brother, that I've always dreamed of meeting my doom in a nice patch of pines?"

"Hush," Lukas said. "You'll be fine. Home soon without a scratch. Probably."

"We shouldn't linger," Marga said, gripped by a sudden, certain awareness of creatures watching from every angle. She adjusted her hold on the baskets and tried to remain calm. Felix seemed too close to bolting without her mentioning the things that hid in the bushes and boughs.

"Right." Felix stood and rubbed his shoulder. "Might as well get this over with, then. A little help, brother?" He gestured toward the sack he'd dropped. He inclined his body and Lukas hefted the load onto his back.

"All right?" Lukas asked.

"Oh, never better," Felix said wryly.

Lukas lifted his own flour sacks and settled them onto his back as if they weighed no more than a single loaf.

"With such impressive skills, one would think our Lukas would have found a wife by now," Felix said. "You wouldn't consider wedding a strong but somber man who's always coated in flour, Fraulein? I think he must fancy you a little, since he's going to all this trouble for you." He chuckled as a hot blush spread over Marga's face and throat.

"I thought Berta was the matchmaker in your family," Marga said. She started walking briskly, wishing to leave the irksome conversation behind. Even if Lukas dared to love her, his family would never accept her. They could not risk losing their business. Few Eschlinsdorfers, if any, would buy bread made by the hands of a witch's husband.

If Fate deemed her a spinster, a spinster she would be. No matter that her heart fluttered like the wings of a tiny sparrow every time he looked at her with those earnest blue eyes of his.

The brothers followed her, their boots crunching twigs as they trod the shadowed path.

Lukas cleared his throat and changed the subject. "I only hope we've brought enough flour."

"*I* only hope my spine doesn't snap like a sapling before we get to wherever we're going," Felix said. "And good *Himmel*! If she can eat all this before spring, she'll be fatter than Jorgen's prize heifer."

Marga looked back over her shoulder at Lukas. "Are all your brothers so ill-tempered and vulgar?"

Lukas smiled. "Every last one. They take after our dear *Mutti*."

"It's true, Fraulein," Felix said. "Six of us, and only Lukas inherited Papa's tender heart. Even our two sisters turn mean as wet cats if you rile them."

"Enough talk, brother," Lukas said. "Save your energy for hiking."

Felix grunted but obeyed. Forest sounds replaced the conversation: the cries of night birds, the buzzing of insects, the rustling of leaves. With the aid of the moonlight, Marga recognized a bent tree here and a boulder there as she continued to lead the brothers along the path she and Hansel had taken to the lake when they'd fled from Hansel's enemies.

That journey seemed a year ago.

After a while, as Felix mumbled something about his legs falling off, Marga caught sight of her wooden raft among the weeds. She'd forgotten how small the raft was. How many crossings would it take to carry all the supplies over?

One might be too many for the brothers, should they encounter the nixes. Marga berated herself under her breath. In her eagerness to keep moving, she'd neglected to speak to Lukas about the malevolent faeries before they arrived at the lake.

Sloshing water whispered an invitation to hurry, but Marga stopped and turned to face the young men. "You must be cautious now," she said softly.

"I thought we *were* being cautious," Felix said, too loudly. Lukas frowned and shushed him.

Marga took a step closer to the brothers and whispered, "There are nixes in the lake. Dangerous water faeries shaped like comely maidens. They'll try to take you. To seduce and drown you."

"Doesn't sound so bad." Felix grinned as if she'd been teasing. "If one has to drown, why not drown happily, in the arms of a feisty woman?"

"It is not a laughing matter," Lukas said to his brother. "They are real, and they will kill you for sport, given the chance."

Felix dropped his flour with a thud. A little white dust trickled out of a tiny tear in the coarse fabric. He scowled at Lukas. "How would you know, brother? Are you suddenly an expert on faeries? *Himmel*, if I'd known you were going to be so cross and dreary, I would have let you carry all your own stupid flour, money or no money."

"Hush," Marga said. "You're here now, Felix, so let's make the best of it. The raft is small, so we'll have to take turns crossing with the supplies. I'll go first, and try to talk the nixes into sparing you from mischief."

"Must we cross the lake at all? Is there no path around it?" Lukas asked.

Marga shook her head. "From what I've observed, thick brush and steep stone walls surround much of the lake. With the flour and everything, it might take days to get to the other side by land, if it's even possible."

Felix narrowed his eyes accusingly. "But you've crossed the lake safely before. More than once, from what Karl and his friends have been saying in the tavern. And you expect me to believe that these saucy water wenches never tried to steal your dashing brother away?"

Felix's words failed to provoke Marga. She had years of experience in being prodded by an annoying brother. She answered in a calm, rational manner. "Hansel and I crossed twice together with the aid of a magical duck. I cannot tell you why the nixes left us alone then. Perhaps they fear the duck."

Felix took a big step backward. "Ho, there. First nixes and now a magic duck? I'll be going home now, Fraulein. I agreed to help carry flour to your cottage so you could survive the winter. Lukas said nothing about all this magic nonsense. I did think you made up the nix thing to frighten me, but now...Let's have the truth, Fraulein. Admit you're a witch."

Lukas rested a hand on Felix's shoulder and gazed down into his eyes. "I've taken good care of you since before you were old enough to speak, and I continue to now. You must trust me, Felix."

"So she *is* a witch?" Felix said.

Lukas shook his head. "Fraulein Holzfäller is only a young woman betrayed by her brother and slandered by her neighbors. There is magic in these woods, yes, but it has been here for centuries—as well you know from the tales told by every grandmother in Eschlinsdorf."

"That's just what you'd say if she'd bespelled you."

An eerie song drifted on the air. Lilting voices invited the wanderers to come and rest in their arms. Felix turned his head toward the sound.

"The nixes. Cover your ears. Quickly." Marga lunged toward Felix, pulled the scarf from his neck, and wound it around his head like a bandage. Lukas clamped his hands over his own ears.

Glassy-eyed, Felix clawed at the scarf. "Get back, witch," he said, raising a fist in readiness to fight her off. "I want to hear the song. Never have I heard such beautiful voices."

"No," Lukas said. "Felix, don't!"

But the boy tossed the scarf into the grass. Grinning, he rushed toward the water. "I'm coming," he called. "Wait for me!"

Sixteen

Lukas sprang like a wildcat and knocked Felix to the ground. Lying atop his squirming, swearing brother, the big man covered his own ears again.

"I'll ask them to stop," Marga shouted. She sprinted to the water's edge.

The three nixes bobbed in the shallows, long coppery tresses floating and swirling around their bare shoulders. Atop their heads, they still wore lily flower crowns. Their open mouths spewed words in an unfamiliar tongue. They sang in harmonies no human could replicate. Although their song enticed Felix, it aroused only panic in Marga.

She splashed into the water. The muddy bottom sucked at her shoes with every step. "Stop!" she yelled as the water swept over her knees. "I beg you, stop singing!"

The nixes gazed at one another and broke into laughter.

"Attend, my sisters. She has kept her oath to return, but she does not care for our song," said the closest nix. She smiled with sharp teeth and dragged languid fingertips over the surface of the water.

"She wants to keep both men for herself," said the one on the right, pouting.

"Selfish girl," said the third nix. "Here is a bargain. Give us one and you may keep the other."

"You may have neither," said Marga forcefully. "They are not for you."

"Selfish, selfish," the three nixes sang.

"What will you give us in his stead?" asked the closest nix. "We are lonely here. So lonely."

"We hunger," said the nix on the right. "Who shall satisfy our longings?"

The nix on the left scowled, pointed teeth edging over her scarlet lower lip. "We do not deal in kindnesses. If you will not give us a man, you owe us payment for their passage."

"What will you give us in payment?" they chorused. Their arms skimmed over the surface of the water in a unified motion, back and forth, back and forth. Marga felt a cold stream of water encircle her ankles like a loose rope. Had the nixes called up a magical current from below? Would they drown her and take the brothers no matter what she said?

No, she would not allow these creatures to take Felix or Lukas. They'd spoken of the white duck with trepidation before. She would use that to her advantage now. She straightened her spine and declared, "You will let me pass, as the white duck would wish. In return, if you let these men cross unharmed, I will bring you cake and wine at Yuletide. I kept my oath to return to the lake, and I will keep this oath I make now."

The closest nix splashed hard with both hands, spattering Marga's head and clothes. "Cake? What care we for the food of humans?"

"These men are great bakers. One of them possesses an age-old recipe for a cake special enough to please even you." This was conjecture, perhaps even a lie, but she was desperate to subdue them. If they drowned either baker, she'd never forgive herself for leading them here.

"We must let her pass," whispered the closest nix to her sisters. "For one must stay, and she is to be that one. So said the duck, and so I feel, in the marrow of my bones."

"If that be so, we must yield to her, even as she is now, small and weak," said the nix on the left in a voice of sad resignation. "If these men are hers, they are hers."

"But I hunger," whined the nix on the right. "I want and I need."

The closest nix scowled. "Quiet, sister, else you stir the one to awaken her powers. Do you not know she could quench your hunger forever—and you with it?"

Marga tried to maintain an authoritative stare in spite of her confusion. These nixes were either fickle or mad, the way they threatened her and then cowered as if she could destroy them.

"You will not share?" the nix on the left asked sweetly, batting her long lashes. "We would gift him with a most pleasant end."

"No, I will not share," Marga said.

The nixes exchanged a look. "So be it," they said in unison.

"We grant you and the menfolk safe passage this day, as much as it is ours to give," said the nearest nix.

The other two nixes pouted as they plunged into the murky waters.

"Hurry across," the remaining nix said. "When darkness comes, our wilder natures shall rule us, vow or no vow." She started to sink but then rose again. She waved a beckoning hand and a dark-green lily pad twice the size of Marga's raft drifted toward them. Its edges curved to form a pretty boat. "Borrow this vessel, and use no other upon these waters. And when you reign, I beseech you to remember that the Three Sisters of the Lake treated you with mercy."

"I will remember your kindness always," Marga replied. The more they said, the more their words perplexed her, but she would not waste time questioning capricious faeries.

The nix submersed herself so that only her water lily crown remained above the water. The lily drifted away, and two others followed in its wake.

Behind Marga, Felix swore and Lukas exhaled a loud breath. She turned and waded back toward the men on the shore, towing the lily pad boat by a vine connected to its prow.

"We must hurry," Marga said. "They've loaned us this boat and promised safe passage, but I don't trust them not to change their minds."

The men were standing now. Lukas looked relieved but Felix's expression was one of anger and mistrust.

"What the devil was all that?" Felix asked, unwinding the

scarf from his head to free his ears. He threw the scarf to the ground as if it had offended him. "See, brother? This woman is a witch, just as they say. She consorts with water spirits and accepts their gifts. You *saw* it."

"Shut your mouth, Felix. This is no time for such talk. The longer we stand about, the more likely it is we'll attract something worse than nixes. Help me ferry the goods across and carry them to the cottage. After that, you can complain and accuse all you like, and give the Fraulein a chance to rebuke you. Or run home to cower under our mother's skirts, if you prefer."

Felix stared Marga up and down, as if searching for physical evidence of witchery, perhaps some scar or mole that would help his case against her. Undaunted, Marga returned his stare. Felix's sharp-edged countenance bore little resemblance to Lukas's rounded, benevolent face. Only the shape of their eyes and the blondness of their hair hinted at a common lineage. Felix was slender and of average height, whereas Lukas was built broadly and could look down upon most men—other than freakishly tall Hansel, of course.

"Very well," Felix said coldly. "But I won't stay at the witch's house. Not for one hour. I'm not a coward, but neither am I a *Dummkopf*."

"You'll be free to go as you please," Lukas said. "Now, let us waste no more time here. Help me load some of the flour onto the boat, and then one of us can row across, empty it, and return for the others."

"By 'one of us,' you mean *you*," Felix said. "My shoulder hurts too much for all this lugging, loading, and rowing back and forth. I cannot imagine you have enough coin to pay me for so much work."

Marga bit her tongue, wishing she could tell Felix that limited imagination was a sure sign of limited intellect. Such banter wouldn't speed their journey to the cottage and the poor, sickly duck.

Lukas lifted a sack of flour and walked over to deposit it onto the beached lily pad boat. Still grumbling, Felix followed suit. Marga placed the caged hens on board, leaving only enough room in the boat for one man.

"It looks seaworthy," Lukas said, perhaps to reassure himself as much as anyone else. "Help me drag it out into the water, Felix."

The hens warbled questioningly as the brothers shoved the boat away from the shallows. When the water lapped at Lukas's waist, he clambered over the side of the boat and took up the leaf-shaped oars the nix had provided.

"Be safe," Marga said to Lukas's back as he paddled away. Felix stood beside her—but not too close, as if she might contaminate him. Together, they watched the vessel skim across the water as if it was ice.

"More witchery," Felix murmured, his gaze fixed on his brother as he fingered the charms tied to his wrist.

Marga ignored the comment. "Your brother is kind-hearted and full of courage," she said as the boat disappeared into a patch of mist.

"He's too trusting. It will be his undoing."

"Perhaps. But it is better to act bravely than to be ruled by fear."

Felix stepped between her and the lake. He glowered

down at her. "Do you call me a coward, Fraulein Holzfäller? You are more brazen than I thought."

Felix's attempt to use his height to intimidate her failed. Hands on hips, she looked up into his face. "I see in you what I once was, a child set on edge by a hundred little terrors. If you ever manage to overcome them, you might aspire to become a man as strong as Lukas."

"Good *Himmel*. You're in love with him." Loathing dripped from his words.

Marga's face flushed. "That's a petty accusation. And quite unoriginal."

The young man moved a fraction of an inch closer. Still, she held her ground.

"If I were a gambler like your rotten brother, Hansel, I would wager everything that I am right," Felix said. "Alas, *my* mother brought me up to scorn the sin of gambling."

A faint whooshing caught Felix's attention and he turned toward the lake. Marga stepped to the side and watched the mist part to reveal the lily pad boat. The vessel sailed with such speed that Lukas's blond hair blew back from his brow. A boyish smile dimpled his cheeks. Marga smiled back and offered up a silent prayer of thanks. He had not been accosted by nixes or monsters, and his return had come sooner than she'd expected.

"This lake is enormous," Lukas said as he leapt from the boat to the shore. "A mile across at least. But the boat is swift. I hardly had to paddle."

"Witchery," Felix said again, but neither Lukas nor Marga paid him any mind.

Lukas set to reloading the boat with Marga's baskets of

supplies and the rest of the flour. As he worked, Felix muttered under his breath, spewing complaints and curse words. The charms he wore on his wrist clinked together like thin coins. Marga doubted any faerie creature would be deterred by them. If anything, their shininess might attract the fae.

Lukas turned to Marga. "You and I will go together this time, Fraulein. You can sit upon the bag of flour. The vessel can carry two passengers, but I would not risk three. I'll come back for Felix after we unload."

"Wait a minute, brother," Felix said. "You would leave me here by myself? With those...those female water demons lying in wait for me? I think not. They nearly tempted me to my death an hour ago, if you recall."

Laughter came from a nearby cluster of bulrushes.

"They did promise to leave you alone, Felix," Marga said. "But if you are afraid, go with Lukas now. I will wait."

"Fraulein, no," Lukas objected. "Felix can wait. I insist on it."

Marga lifted her chin. "I have traveled through the wild Igelwald without a man's aid. I think I can look after myself until you return. Or I could follow you on my little raft."

Lukas shook his head. "The raft lying back in the weeds? Did you not see that something had gnawed through the vines that bound it together? It could bear nothing larger than a squirrel."

"I didn't notice," Marga confessed. "Well, then. I'll just wait for you to return for me. I'll be fine. I promise."

"You heard the girl. Let's be on our way." Felix waded into the water and tugged at the edge of the laden lily pad to inch it out of the shallows. "Sooner begun, sooner done, as Mutti likes to say."

Lukas rested one of his big hands on Marga's shoulder. "You're sure you want to wait? You could go with Felix instead."

Grateful for his kindness, Marga smiled up at him. Goodness, he was tall. A good five or six inches taller than Felix and far more pleasant to look at. His thatch of blond hair. The endearing wrinkle of worry between his eyebrows. She attempted to replace her smile with a look of unwavering confidence. "Go. I will be fine."

His hand squeezed her shoulder gently. There were promises in his eyes, unspoken things that made her stomach flutter. Half-remembered dreams of him lurked in the corners of her mind. "I will be back as quickly as I can manage," he said, his round cheeks pink as autumn's first apples.

"Go," Marga repeated, and he obeyed, climbing into the leaf boat and taking up the oar as his sour-faced brother sat on a flour sack throne.

Just before disappearing into the mist, Lukas glanced back at her. He looked more heroic than a baker from Eschlinsdorf had a right to. She hadn't lied to Felix; she did not love Lukas. No, that would be silly. They had met only a handful of times—outside of her dreams. Besides, what good could come of it if she did love him? She was an outcast, and he was needed by his family, the bakery, and the community.

She told her heart to slow its foolish galloping, and she set her mind on the things she needed to accomplish. She had a gingerbread cottage to fix, a duck to heal, and winter to survive. She was a grown woman tasked with living in an enchanted wood, not a silly, parlor-bound *Mädchen* with time to scribble love notes and daydream of handsome gentlemen.

The little waves that constantly lapped the shore grew larger. A nearby clutch of bulrushes rustled. The hidden nixes whispered as one, speaking in their faerie tongue. As hard as Marga listened, she couldn't understand a word. Something in the atmosphere felt wrong. Gooseflesh rose on her arms.

A scream tore the air and echoed across the lake. A man's cry of pain.

Marga held her breath and prayed—for Lukas first, and then for Felix.

Seventeen

Through half-closed eyes, Ansgar watched weak, wintry sunlight dapple the floor. Another long night had reached its end. He had barely slept. He cursed the happy chirrups of the birds outside the candy windows. No one had a right to be so cheerful at such an hour.

Ansgar used his bill to pick at the feathers of his good wing. Every time he plucked one from his skin, he felt a sharp jolt of pain. The pain was good. It kept him alert, ready for Gretel's return.

If she did return.

But she had to. Fate was a powerful matron—not one to be defied by a diminutive, ignorant snip of a girl.

He tore out another feather. How he despised his duck-shaped body. His wife, Truda, had known well his disdain for waterfowl and had chosen to ensnare him within this ridiculous form for that very reason. She'd known all his secrets, that woman. He'd kept nothing from her...

Until the larch tree incident.

The larch tree faerie had caught him by surprise. Before that summer day when he chanced upon her, he'd never once had dealings with a tree faerie. He'd heard tales and ballads of the creatures, narratives he would have considered warnings if he'd spent any time considering them at all. But one balmy evening, as he strolled through the forest—trudged, actually, simmering with anger after a particularly nasty fight with Truda—the larch tree faerie stepped out of her wooden abode and opened her leafy arms to him.

In the early days of Ansgar and Truda's marriage, a good fight had always ended in laughter and fervent kisses. After a decade or two, none of their fights were good fights. They fought with unsheathed cruelty, stabbing each other with sharp words and hateful looks. Sometimes, they flung little spells back and forth, ending their arguments with singed hair or unreachable itches. Yet no matter how many dishes or insults were hurled, they'd kept their vows of fidelity and steadfast love.

Of course Ansgar's dalliance with the larch tree faerie had nothing to do with love. He did not set out to break his marital vows on purpose. He'd simply been as stupid and thoughtless as a young sailor lured overboard by a siren's call.

Nothing about Truda had ever been sweet, but the larch tree faerie had offered him all the sweetness of fruit ripened to perfection. Nothing about Truda had been light, but the larch tree faerie's countenance had sparkled with stolen specks of starshine. Although he'd hated himself for succumbing to the larch's skillful caresses, he'd returned to her again and again, desperate for more.

The affair lasted only a week. In retrospect, Ansgar was

surprised Truda had not noticed sooner. He'd reeked of fresh leaves. Sap had marked his flesh like sticky bruises. When Truda had finally called him to task, he'd been relieved to be free of the cloying, clinging faerie and the burden of his shame. On his knees, weeping, he'd begged Truda for forgiveness. Instead, the witch had meted out harsh punishment.

With a wave of her hand and a few ancient words, she'd made him a duck. A clumsy, grub eating, ineloquent duck.

Years had passed since then, but he'd been unable to count them.

Ansgar stood and waddled toward the closed door, his stomach twisting with hunger. A draft tickled his scaly ankles as he turned back toward the hearth.

A *draft*.

Of course. He'd overheard silly Gretel complaining about the hole she'd made in the bedchamber wall and failed to fix. The previous night's strong wind must have pushed the bedchamber door open a little.

Wide enough for an emaciated waterfowl to squeeze through.

He was no longer trapped, thank the gods. If he'd been one to pray, he would have begged the heavens to grant him success in his forthcoming search for sustenance. With the season such as it was, and far from any lake or pond, his appetite would probably not be entirely sated.

But something was preferable to nothing, when one was a nearly starved duck. With renewed vigor, he waddled toward the broken wall and the promise of a meal.

* * *

The man's screams echoed in Marga's mind.

Each minute felt like an eternity as Marga waited for one of the Beckmann brothers to sail into view aboard the lily pad boat. She paced and prayed. She imagined Lukas bleeding, drowned, carried off by a giant, fang-toothed, frog monster. And then she imagined the same scenes with Felix as the victim. Finally, gripped by desperation and anxiety, she called out for the nixes.

The three faeries swam close to the shoreline. One after the other, they lifted their pretty, flower-crowned heads out of the water. Their wet hair gleamed like polished metal.

"Mistress?" said one of the nixes. Her two sisters lurked behind her, blinking at Marga with wide-eyed expressions of innocence.

Marga refused to fritter time away with polite conversation when Lukas or Felix might be dying. She asked boldly, "What has happened to my friends? Have you broken your vow to leave them alone?"

The lead nix frowned. "It is not our custom to make oaths in vain. Not a finger have we laid upon your menfolk."

Balling her fists at her sides, Marga stepped into the mud at the edge of the lake. "Surely you heard the screaming. Tell me what has happened. Now."

"The cullberfish, I should think," the second-in-line nix said as she braided her dripping hair. "I did tell him to behave, but he is keen to fatten himself against the scarcities of winter."

"Winter's wrath is nigh," said the third nix. "A wild creature cannot be blamed for making preparations."

"Cullberfish?" Marga asked.

"More of a water dragon than a true fish," the first nix said. "The size of one of your men, but born with the strength of ten of such. The cullberfish's teeth are long, his bite full of venom."

"Powerful poison," said the second sister.

"Such as can fell a buck in the space between two heartbeats. I have seen it done," said the third nix. "Many times."

Marga shivered as fear slid coldly through her veins. "Please. You must hurry. Go and see if the men need help."

The nixes turned to face one another. They held hands just above the surface of the water. "We should do as she asks. We should please this one," the first nix said, and her sisters bobbed their heads in agreement.

"But here is a better idea, my lady," the first nix said as she left the circle to swim closer to Marga. "Come, take our hands. We shall escort you through the waters in safety and with swiftness."

"We offer what help we can, as the white duck would counsel," said the second nix.

Marga did not hesitate. She rushed into the lake waters, hands outstretched. The nixes grabbed hold of her with their thin, cool fingers. Would they drown her and leave her as food for fishes? She had to hope they would not. If there was any chance that she might help Lukas or Felix, she had to take it.

But as the water surrounded her, it was Lukas's face alone that stuck in her mind, her heart.

Eighteen

The nixes tugged Marga through the frigid lake, almost crushing her fingers with their grip. The tops of their lily-crowned heads skimmed above the surface, but everything below their eyes, they kept underwater. Marga lifted her chin and tried not to breathe in water as they sped along. Nevertheless, the dank scents of algae and fish seeped into her nostrils to worsen the sickness in her stomach.

Lukas had to be safe. Felix had to be safe as well, or Lukas would never forgive her. She disliked herself for that selfish thought. She should want Felix to be safe because he was a person, loved by his family, and still so young. His life was worth as much as his brother's, no matter how churlishly the boy behaved.

Faster and faster the nixes swam, much to Marga's surprise. Their delicate features and slim arms had given no indication of the strength they possessed. They pulled her past the leaf boat that now drifted and bobbed, empty, carried away from shore by some unseen current. Soon, the toes of her shoes brushed against underwater plants and sandy mud. She found her footing and gulped in big breaths.

"Fraulein!" Lukas shouted from the shore. He waved both arms above his head. "Over here!"

"Thank Gott!" Marga wriggled free of the nixes' hold and scrambled up a sloped, pebbled beach. "What happened?"

Face pale as milk, Lukas reached for Marga's dripping hand. He pulled her along almost as quickly as the nixes had.

"We must make haste. A monster rose up from the water and seized Felix's arm with its jaws," Lukas said as they reached the place where the pebbles gave way to rough grasses. "I fought the beast off with a few blows, but Felix is gravely injured. Talking nonsense. Bleeding badly."

"Brew nettle leaf and foxglove root, oak apple and heart-of-turtle," one of the nixes shouted from the water. Marga did not turn to see which one had spoken.

"Add twig of myrtle and powder of trout scales," another nix said.

"Still, he may die," said the third nix, with an air of indifference. "The cullberfish's bite fells larger prey than bony boys."

Lukas stopped pulling Marga forward. At their feet, Felix lay prostrate on a patch of brown grass. Eyes shut, he moaned and rolled his head back and forth. Blood oozed from a wound on his right arm, just below his elbow. His entire sleeve was missing, torn off as he struggled to escape the beast, no doubt.

Marga knelt beside him and peered more closely at the damage done by the cullberfish's teeth. The grisly sight made her gag. It was a wonder Felix still had a forearm. Thank *Himmel* Lukas had known to tie a handkerchief above the bite to slow the bleeding.

Lukas fell to his knees beside her. "Can anything be done for him?"

"I don't know. The nixes say the monster's venom is powerful. If we can get him to the cottage, we could try the remedy they described. The old witch's shelves are still well stocked with herbs and powders."

"We must make haste, then." Lukas stood. "We'll leave the flour for now. I'll come back for it when Felix is better." He offered his hand to help Marga to her feet. Weary, she took it. Once standing, she felt as unsteady as a sapling in a windstorm. Lake water dripped from her hair and clothes. She tried not to shiver but she couldn't remember ever being so cold, even in midwinter.

She gazed up into Lukas's earnest, trusting face. She wanted to promise she'd cure Felix, but that might turn out to be a lie. A man like him deserved the truth. "I cannot swear I will make him well. I am neither witch nor doctor, Herr Beckmann."

"I believe in you. I believe we can save him, together, if we try hard enough and pray hard enough," Lukas said. His words were brave but his eyes glistened with unshed tears. He scowled at her wet clothes. "But this will not do. We cannot have you falling ill as well." Without asking her leave, he undid the button at her throat and removed the sodden cloak. He dropped the wet garment onto the grass, and then removed his mostly dry cloak and wrapped it around her shoulders—just as he had done in the graveyard.

The cloak settled on her like a blessing, heavy but comforting. It was too long by several inches, so she rolled the neckline and then secured it with its tie. She wanted to thank Lukas, but could not speak with the lump of emotion clogging her throat. Lukas was so virtuous. His family was blessed beyond measure to have him. To know him well, to see his kindly face every day in the bakery or across the table at mealtimes.

Lukas lifted Felix and draped his body over his shoulder while Marga picked up one of the food hampers piled beside the flour sacks. With her other hand, Marga grabbed the rope handle of the hens' crate. Inside, the hens cooed and clucked. It would be cruel to abandon the chickens, and besides, the baker would need eggs to make the gingerbread to patch the wall. Many, many eggs.

"Ready?" Lukas asked. The full weight of his worries rested on that single word. Nothing Marga could say would comfort him, she knew. All she could do for now was to help him get Felix to the cottage quickly.

"Come," she said. And something within her whispered affirmation, sweetly, gently. She might have let the odd stirring rankle her, but instead, she accepted it as encouragement that she was doing the right thing. That Felix would be fine.

They trudged deep into the shadowy forest. The path was becoming all too familiar. Marga moved among the trees and over the rocks with confidence, even in places where thick layers of overhead branches blocked most of the daylight.

Walking as fast as they could, they crossed a small meadow, startling a pair of deer. Behind her, Lukas started to sing softly to his moaning brother, an old folk song. His voice was deep and rich. Marga glanced up at the scattered stars. While Lukas's singing soothed Felix, it stirred up a thousand little butterflies of longing inside her.

The butterflies were most unwise. She willed them to lie still, but they continued to flit and flutter as Lukas repeated the verses.

What business had she, who the townsfolk called "the witch's adopted daughter," falling in love with the good baker? His reputation could not elevate hers, and her reputation would likely ruin him and his family. A temporary friendship was all they could share. This hard truth sent a sharp pang of grief through her heart.

The final note of Lukas's song faded. Marga took note of where they were. She cleared her throat and said, "I should warn you. We'll soon find ourselves in a grove of cuckoo clocks."

"Clocks?"

"Hundreds of them, dangling from trees, no two alike."

"Fascinating. It is magic, this display of clocks?" Lukas sounded more curious than frightened.

"Yes. It must be."

"And are the clocks dangerous?"

"No, I don't believe so. Hansel and I passed through the grove on our way to the cottage, and I walked through alone on my journey back to town. It was strange—and exceedingly loud when the clocks struck the hour—but it did us no harm. Indeed, the clocks were a beautiful sight. Such bright colors illuminating this dark forest."

Lukas grunted as he rearranged the unconscious brother

on his shoulder. "I should have liked to have visited such a marvelous place with you under better circumstances."

The baker's subtle flirtation brought heat to Marga's cheeks. His boyish wonderment was weakening her resolve. She eyed the sleeping hens and took a deep breath to calm herself. And then another.

She increased her pace, adding several inches between her body and Lukas's, as if that would help. "Well, we have no time to admire the scenery. For Felix's sake, we must continue to make haste."

"Yes, of course..." He paused, but she sensed he wanted to say more. He caught up to her easily, matching his stride to hers.

"We should be quiet, and not draw attention to ourselves," Marga said without glancing over at him. "There are creatures, wild and magical, hiding in the brush and branches here." She felt their presence with as much certainty as she felt the baker's.

"Yes, of course," Lukas said again, and he stopped to let her proceed before him through a gap between two trees. His manners made Hansel seem like an untamed beast—although Hansel hadn't been brought up to behave badly. If Hansel had been half the gentleman Lukas was, she'd still be living quietly in town. She wouldn't be responsible for curing a sick duck, or risking her life traveling through the Igelwald.

And she most certainly would not be wondering what it would feel like to be enfolded in Lukas Beckmann's strong arms. To rest her cheek against his bread-scented chest. To feel his broad hands on her back.

Again he hummed the lullaby to his brother, and her inner butterflies spun and danced.

Onward they walked, over morning-dappled hills and through thick stands of pine and oak. And Marga was not afraid of anything but herself.

Nineteen

Ansgar hopped over the crumbled gingerbread wall and waddled back into the dusky bedchamber, his belly taut. He'd gorged on grain he'd found hidden in the back of the shed, and thereafter indulged in a dessert of mushy, windfall apples. His memory of the details of his duck life was arbitrary, but he presumed that never before in his waterfowl existence had he consumed so much food.

He gazed at the prettily made-up beds and belched. If not for his injured wing, he would have flown up onto one of the fat mattresses and settled among the plump pillows for the night. Instead, he chose a spot on a little woolen rug that had somehow ended up crumpled in the corner.

By the gods, when he regained human form, he'd move to Paris or Rome and commission the crafting of the most sumptuous bed imaginable. He'd lie in it for a month, wearing a silk robe that settled on his skin like a thousand tender kisses. Pretty, vapid wenches would wait upon him at all hours, bringing him rich dishes and the best wine.

Propped up by dozens of velvet cushions, he'd read poetry and pen plays when he chose to be awake.

Life would be grand—when the girl returned and helped to free him from Truda's spell. He imagined how it would feel to stretch arms and legs, to run his hands through his hair, to wear fine clothes, to ride a fast horse again. To live rather than to simply exist.

Cheered by the feast, Ansgar dared to believe that Gretel would return soon. It would not be long before she'd willingly assume the role for which she'd been chosen.

And if she were unwilling, it would be his pleasure to coerce the silly girl with his boundless cleverness and charm.

Presently, his excursion and feasting rendered him drowsy. Sleeping seemed like a grand way to pass the time he had left as a clumsy lump of feathers. He started to tuck his bill under his wing, but something caught his eye. Underneath one of the beds, almost obscured by darkness, he spied the black box in which Truda had kept her most treasured book.

He stared, watching tendrils of magic hover like black smoke over the box. The thing was useless to him, but he found its presence comforting. He almost felt as if his wife were in the room with him as he drifted to sleep.

* * *

Damp, decayed leaves clung to Marga's boots as she guided Lukas through a maze of oak saplings. Her feet had gone numb, but she did not slow her pace. They'd been obliged to stop several times so Lukas could rest or switch his feverish, mumbling brother from one shoulder to the other, but otherwise, emboldened by her past journeys, she'd led with confident efficiency.

She glanced through the treetops to glimpse fat clouds meandering across the sky. Today, the distance from the lake to the witch's cottage seemed both longer and shorter. It might have been either, or even both, given the magic she now sensed at work all around her. They passed into the grove of emerald-green firs Marga remembered. A moment later, she caught sight of a tan biscuit chimney sticking up beyond the hedge. The scent of spiced walls beckoned her forward. Lukas must have smelled it, too, for he inhaled sharply.

"There," Marga said, pointing to a gap between the trees. "The cottage." Relief washed over her. Felix was still alive, and here she could treat his wounds with the remedy the nixes recommended. The boy might soon return to the bakery and forget this trial.

"Praise Gott," Lukas said. Not as blasphemy, she knew, but in heartfelt thanksgiving for their arrival. In spite of the coldness of the air, a sheen of sweat covered Lukas's brow. He'd frequently stumbled during the last few miles of their journey, and his eyes were swollen with tiredness.

Marga led him through the open gate and toward the front door. She tried to see the house with his eyes, to perceive it as she had the first time she'd come upon it. To little Gretel, the scene had been miraculous, a starving child's sweetest dream made real. But the wonder and bliss the cake and candy cottage had once inspired was now replaced by a hint of dread and a trace of hunger.

"What a marvel," Lukas said as he followed her inside. An expression of boyish delight lit his face as he scanned the room from floor to rafters. "Hard to believe it's made of flour and sugar."

"And magic," Marga said—and immediately wished she had not. But then she realized it didn't matter that she'd said it aloud. There was no question that he knew there was magic within the sugary mortar and bright candy windowpanes. Any house built of plain cake would have decayed and collapsed long ago.

Lukas paused to shift his brother's weight on his shoulder. "Where should I put him?"

"This way. There's a bedchamber. The wall is broken, but it will have to do for now." Marga stepped over a pile of duck droppings. Where was that duck? The basket by the hearth was empty, save for a few feathers. She hoped it hadn't wandered off to die in her absence.

Now that she was inside the cottage again, the nixes' words about the duck and its authority seemed farfetched. The duck had magic, certainly—enough to grow and shrink in size—and it seemed intelligent, but she'd never have described the bird as commanding.

Lukas lowered Felix onto the bed nearest the door. Felix sighed as his head sank into the soft pillow. With a groan, Lukas straightened his back and then massaged his left shoulder. He turned to face Marga. "For such a skinny lad, he weighs a lot. Am I imagining it or is that a duck asleep in the corner?"

"Ah, there it is," Marga said, relieved to see the duck's body moving as it breathed. "You remember the wounded duck I spoke of? The one the townsfolk shot as it carried Hansel across the lake?"

"That was too strange a tale to be forgotten."

"I suppose it grew tired of its basket by the fireplace and chose to nap here."

The duck opened its eyes and quacked weakly. The sound struck Marga as contrived, now that the nixes had set her wondering about the bird. She was about to go to it, to assess the state of its health, when Lukas took a step closer to her. Worry creased his forehead. "Will you make the medicine now?"

"Yes. As tired as I am, as we both are, we cannot afford to wait." She'd see to the duck's needs later. Felix's dire condition took precedence.

Lukas reached out and rested his hand on her shoulder. "Thank you, Fraulein."

Impossibly, the warmth of his hand seemed to pass through all her layers of clothing and into her skin. Her face heated, too, and she gazed at the duck instead of Lukas's face, praying he did not notice her blushes. "You may thank me if the cure works. I haven't managed to heal the duck, you know. Perhaps I'll do no better for Felix."

"Hope is what makes the bread rise," Lukas said, removing his hand but leaving behind the warmth. "It's an old family saying. It means that everything needs hope to flourish. Or faith, if you prefer to name it so. What we do, we must do believing we will succeed."

"I have never been much good at baking," Marga said. "Or at hoping for much beyond the ordinary."

"Perhaps I might help you with that."

"Baking?" She stared at the duck as her face grew hotter. The duck stared back disapprovingly—or so she imagined in her exhausted state.

"For a start."

Felix stirred upon the bed. Marga and Lukas flew to his side.

"Mutti! Help me!" Eyes open wide, the boy clawed at the wound on his arm. His head thrashed from side to side.

Lukas struggled to wrench his brother's hand away from the oozing bite. Finally, he pinned Felix's wrists to the mattress, but the boy continued to fight and writhe.

"Do you have something to calm him?" Lukas asked.

"I think so. I ...There should be something." Marga rushed into the other room, skidding to a stop in front of the wall of shelves. She squinted at the witch's spidery handwriting on the labels of the jars and bottles. "Burdock leaf, cough remedy, for insect bites, purgative, wart remover...yes! Sleeping powder." She held the brown bottle up to catch the light from the window. "Half a teaspoon in a cup of warm water," she read.

The clay pitcher on the table still held water. It wouldn't be warm, but Felix needed a dose without delay. To gather wood, make a fire, and heat the kettle could take an hour or longer. She dumped a generous spoonful of powder into a teacup, added water, and then stirred the mixture while running back to Felix's side. A little sloshed onto the floor, but most of it remained in the cup until she halted next to the bed.

In Marga's absence, Felix had stilled and quieted. Lukas

had removed his brother's stained, torn shirt. Now he covered him to the neck with the patchwork quilt.

Felix stared up into Lukas's face with glassy eyes. "Am I going to die, brother?" he asked in a wobbly voice. "You must...speak truthfully."

"No. No, of course not," Lukas said. "Look, here is Fraulein Holzfäller with medicine for you."

Lukas helped his brother to sit up, adjusting pillows behind his back. Felix's ashen face paled as the quilt slipped down to reveal his bare chest. "Get out, witch. You ordered that creature to attack me, and now you mean to kill me with your potion."

"Calm yourself. You're safe now." Lukas smoothed his brother's hair back from his forehead.

"Get out, in the name of *Gott*, witch," Felix demanded with such raw spite that Marga winced.

Lukas pushed his brother back against the pillows. Felix swore but did not resist.

"She's bewitched you too. You'll see," Felix said. His breathing became labored. He turned his head away from Marga as if she were too terrible to behold.

"You're safe, brother," Lukas repeated, covering Felix with the quilt again. "I swear it. No one will harm you here. Trust me. You're *Mutti's* favorite, are you not? Why would I risk her wrath by putting you in danger?"

The boy didn't reply. After a minute of tense silence, his breaths slowed and he closed his eyes.

"He's always been one to fall asleep quickly, ever since he was a babe," Lukas said. He wiped a tear from the corner of his eye. "But sleep is good. Sleep heals many ills, they say."

"Yes." Lukas's tenderness touched her heart, while Felix's cruel outburst had left her shaky. She was too tired to wrestle with her feelings, and besides, she had practical matters to attend to. She set the cup of medicine on a table by the bed. "I'll leave this. I'm taking the duck to the kitchen so I can tend to its wing."

She started to cross the room, but stopped when Lukas said, "Fraulein? I'm sorry my brother spoke to you in that way. Felix is..."

Marga forced a small smile. "He's unwell. He cannot help himself."

"You give him grace he does not deserve, I think. But yes, see to the duck. And if you have any ointment and linen to bandage Felix's arm...?"

Marga nodded. She lifted the duck and left the bedchamber. Felix suddenly hurled more insults in her direction, but she did her best to ignore his tirade. Had he been asleep at all? If he had, the nap had done nothing to improve his temper.

"Dirty witch! Daughter of the devil! Trollop's spawn! You'll burn. There will be no escaping it ..."

She'd not borne such a tirade of abuse in years—not since she'd learned to stay home and avoid the hateful townsfolk. She'd forgotten that words could sting like hornets, leaving swollen, aching wounds on one's spirit. Against her will, tears welled in her eyes.

"That's enough, Felix. Enough," Marga heard Lukas say as she deposited the duck into its basket by the hearth. "One more uncharitable word and I'll tan your hide—no matter how sickly you are."

He's defending me, Marga thought. It helped to lessen the pain Felix had inflicted.

The duck uttered a pleading quack. It rested its chin on the basket's edge and stared at her like a sad puppy.

"Let me look at that wing, and then I'll find you something to eat."

She crouched down and used her fingers to part the feathers where the shot had lodged. "It looks a little better."

The duck made a pitiful sound, something between a honk and a moan. Marga petted its head where a single dark feather mingled with the white. The nixes' strange words about the white duck echoed in her memory, puzzling her still. If the duck were as wise and powerful as they suggested, why did it not use magic to heal itself, or point out the herbs it needed?

Perhaps this was a different duck than the nixes had known. She stroked its feathers one last time. "Hush now. I'll take care of you until you're well. I promise."

The duck shut its eyes and sighed.

Sighed like a *person*.

Marga shuddered.

Twenty

Ansgar kept his eyes trained on the girl as she bustled about the kitchen. His stiff bill refused to curve, but inwardly, he grinned.

She promised to care for me until I am well. Foolish girl. She does not know that a promise made to a wizard within his home cannot be broken—except by the hand of Death.

By the gods, he wished he were capable of producing a fiendish chuckle.

He shook himself to right his feathers, imagining that he looked regal in the basket beside the newly laid fire. The girl mumbled to herself as she worked, consulting one of the handwritten books Truda had collected, stirring things into the witch's favorite kettle with a spoon he'd whittled one summer's evening long ago.

He watched the girl concocting, creating, as Truda had done in that same way, in this very space. Becoming, finally, more than a simple, silly child. Stepping firmly onto the path of destiny.

Could she feel the magic building around and within her as she sprinkled various herbs and whispered her wishes? Ansgar could see it, swirls of blue and yellow mist encircling her body. She breathed it in; she breathed it out.

This was good. Exceedingly good.

The potion sputtered. A spray of red sparks leapt out of the kettle. The girl gasped and jumped back.

"The book didn't say that would happen," she said as the tall man stepped out of the bedchamber and approached the hearth.

"A chemical reaction of some kind," the man said. He leaned to peer into the kettle. "I had a fondness for scientific books when I was a boy."

Ansgar laughed. It sounded nothing like his robust human laugh had, being more of a high-pitched wheeze. Science indeed! Such balderdash. He hoped the new queen wouldn't choose this asinine peasant to be her lifelong mate. The tall, muscular blond was attractive in a rustic sort of way, but as devoid of magic as a dead beetle.

Well, the future witch queen's *affaires de coeur* were nothing to fret over. Let her have her youthful flirtations. Her suitor would most likely spurn Gretel's company and run home to his mother the minute he discovered who and what she truly was.

The big oaf would never have the mettle to push her into an oven.

How amusing it would be if the new queen turned the fellow into a duck for breaking her heart. That was something he would very much like to witness.

"I think it has cooked long enough," Gretel said to the

man as she wrapped her hand in a towel and lifted the bubbling kettle from its hook.

The man peered at the liquid. "Will it counteract the venom?"

"The book says this reverses the damage of snake bites. I could find nothing specific to treating the bite of a lake monster. Some of the ingredients the nixes suggested weren't on the shelves, so..." Gretel set the kettle on the wooden table. A bit of greenish gray liquid splashed out and soaked into the boards with a faint hiss. "It needs to cool before we try it, anyway."

"It looks terrible and smells of rotten meat," the man said. "Felix will not want to take it."

"He would object to taking it no matter how it looked or smelled, since I made it."

The man took a step backward, coughing and waving a hand to ward off the potion's fetid fumes. Never would such a weakling be a suitable partner for Gretel. "Well, I shall convince him. Force him to swallow it if I must. And we will pray. Perhaps by morning, he will be healed."

Had Ansgar been able to speak, he might have suggested otherwise. Without powdered turtle's blood and a sprinkle of pink nettle, the potion would do the boy no more good than a cup of boiled goat urine.

Ah, well. It pained him to watch, but there was no real harm in allowing the lovesick humans to bask in their childish hopes for a little while. As an English poet once said, "Ignorance is bliss." They could have their meager taste of fleeting contentment; soon he would feast upon victory.

If he knew anything of Gretel's character, the medicine's

ineffectiveness would only drive her to try harder. And the harder she tried, the more she'd stir up her gifts. Every time she used the magic, it would grow stronger and become more ingrained, more inseparable from her—until she had no choice but to bow to her destiny. Indeed, she might soon desire to take up Truda's mantle with little prodding. He had a strong suspicion that the girl had never in her life wielded any sort of power. Truda's legacy would bestow upon her the ability to rule and reign, to crush her enemies, and to possess all the riches of the Igelwald. He envied Gretel not a little. The thrill of coming into one's magical potential was something one never forgot, like a first kiss but far more intoxicating.

The potion glowed with orange-gold light. It was ready. Pleased with Gretel's progress, Ansgar closed his eyes to dream sweet dreams.

Marga spied on the brothers from outside the bedchamber door, beyond Felix's range of vision. Silently, she prayed for Felix to give in to Lukas's pleas and take the medicine she'd made. Thus far, he had refused, saying he'd prefer to die than to drink a witch's brew.

The argument between the brothers went on for what felt like an hour. Would she have to help Lukas force the medicine down the boy's throat? It seemed cruel to do so, but kinder than letting him die of stubbornness and superstition.

Finally, after he'd made Lukas dip the metal charms from

his bracelet into the cup "to kill off any magic," Felix agreed to swallow the dose. The boy coughed and sputtered afterward, as if he'd been forced to drink manure-tainted ditchwater.

A cold draft snaked from the bedchamber into the kitchen in spite of Lukas's efforts to partially block the hole in the wall with furniture. Marga shivered. The little wood stove in the bedroom corner, though blazing away, did not prevent Felix from shivering as well.

"Are you trying to kill me, too, brother?" Felix asked, shoving the cup away. He wiped his mouth with the back of his hand, then pressed his head deep into the pillow. "Nothing so foul could possibly cure a person."

"Do not waste your breath speaking nonsense," Lukas said wearily. "Rest now, and let the medicine do its work."

"Well, if you insist. I did have plans to scale a mountain this evening, but..."

Lukas tousled his brother's hair. "At least you still have your humor."

"And my looks. Unlike you."

Lukas laughed and pulled the blankets and quilts up to Felix's chin. "Sleep, brother." He started to walk away, but Felix grabbed his sleeve.

"Lukas? She is a witch, you know. Be careful, else you end up transformed into a pet mouse for her pocket."

"I am always careful. And I would trust Fraulein Holzfäller with my life."

"You mustn't. You are bewitched. Bewitched and besotted." Felix cringed and paled as a gust of wind surged outside the cottage. He yanked Lukas by the sleeve, drawing him closer. "I hear ghosts howling. I feel their cold fingers on my face. They want to take me. The witch must have called them."

"It is only the wind. There is a hole in the wall, one you must help me to fix as soon as you are well."

"They'll find another way in. We cannot stop them."

Lukas freed his sleeve from Felix's fingers. He rested a hand on the boy's cheek in a fatherly way. "Hush now. There are no ghosts. You are ill from the lake creature's bite and imagining things. Now, you must rest."

"It is only the wind. You're sure?"

"Listen. It's slowing down." Lukas patted the bedclothes. "Sleep, brother."

Felix looked calmer, though still glassy-eyed with fever. "I will try."

"Good." Lukas strode out of the bedchamber quickly, as if trying to escape before his brother could object.

Marga backed away from the doorway to let him pass. "Hungry?" she asked.

"Always, but more so now that Felix has taken a dose of your medicine." He gave her the gift of a small smile as he brushed past her. It was worth more to her than a handful of gems.

She followed him into the kitchen and took out plates and knives, mugs and a teapot. She wished her mind could be occupied as easily as her hands. She wished her cheeks would stop burning and her heart would stop fluttering in the presence of the baker who stood by the hearth warming his big hands in the fire's glow. The patient, gentle way Lukas dealt with his brother had endeared him to her more.

He would be a fine husband for someone, but never for her. She must remember that, no matter how much she might want him. Still, she allowed herself to admire him from across the room, as one might admire a red-gold sunrise.

From its basket a few feet away from Lukas, the duck hissed. Or perhaps the sound had come from a piece of damp firewood. It was impossible to know for certain, but Marga cast a glance in the waterfowl's direction. The duck stared back with cold, black eyes, and she wondered what thoughts played inside its plumed head. It looked unsettled, perhaps dangerous. But that was probably her fault. Too long had passed since she'd fed or watered the poor bird. Most creatures became grumpy when hungry and ill.

No more admiring Lukas or trying to discern the thoughts of a duck. She had a mess to clean up and a meal to prepare for a duck and a disturbingly handsome baker.

Twenty-One

Marga and Lukas sat at the table, facing one another. The fire crackled as it blazed in the hearth, thanks to Lukas's expert attention. The room smelled like Christmastime as the gingerbread cake walls warmed and released their scent. A surprising feeling of contentment settled over Marga, and then a twinge of guilt. Felix and the duck were ill. She was living in the cottage of an evil witch. How dare she feel so comfortable?

"Are you well?" Lukas asked as he poured lavender and honey tea into his mug.

"Yes. Tired, I suppose. Here." Marga picked up a platter of cheese, ham, and apple slices and passed it to him. The dish looked paltry in the baker's wide hands. The usual appetite of a man his size could not be satisfied by so little, and this man had carried Felix for miles. Since then, he'd spent an hour or two taking boards from the shed and arranging them to block the hole in the bedchamber wall.

The cottage had not objected to Lukas's temporary patching of the wall—so far.

"I'm sorry there's not more," Marga said as he looked at the platter. "You must be very hungry. But there was not much food in the basket I brought, and the hens have yet to lay a single egg."

Smiling, Lukas used a knife to slide almost half the food from the platter to his plate. "Do not apologize. I'm grateful you had the presence of mind to bring the hamper of food when we left the lakeside. This is a fine supper. This cheese is my favorite, and my uncle grew these apples on his farm."

Marga bowed her head and said a quick prayer of thanks.

"Amen," said Lukas. He used his fork and knife to slice a morsel of ham. His table manners were perfect. His mother had trained him well, of course. According to gossip Hansel had once passed on, she'd come from a titled Zurich family. If Frau Beckmann could have seen her fine son supping alone with a so-called witch, she probably would have disowned him—or scratched Marga's eyes out. Thank *Himmel* Frau Beckmann was miles away.

They ate without conversing. The gentle clinking of silverware and the low roar of the fire were as good as music to Marga's ears. A quiet dinner with Lukas was far more pleasant than listening to Hansel brag about money-making schemes or his latest romance.

Lukas's plate was empty. He set his fork and knife down, rested his forearms on the tabletop, and leaned toward her. "I do not believe the gossip, you know. I have never believed you were a witch. People are too often cruel. They let fear and mistrust overtake good sense and courtesy."

Heat flooded her face and chest. She looked into his too-blue eyes and words poured from her mouth. "What if it is true, or becomes so? I felt something today when I was making the medicine, an odd, sparking sensation beneath my skin. A power, perhaps. And at the lake, I heard the nixes say strange things, that I was 'the one,' and that I would rule over them."

"Nonsense. The nixes are tricksters, and you are exhausted. Dreaming on your feet. Do not frighten yourself with such imaginings, Margarethe." Two red circles appeared on his cheeks as he corrected himself. "Fraulein Holzfäller, I mean. Forgive me."

"Of course." She longed to ask him to always use her given name, for its syllables spilled from his tongue like a song—but since they were currently without a chaperone, observing some formality seemed wise. She trusted the baker, but could she trust herself? Minute by minute, she felt more irresistibly drawn to him, like a magnet held near iron.

Lukas leaned back in his wooden chair and crossed his arms. "You look worried."

"I confess I am, and not only about the nixes' words. Your brother's illness, the state of this cottage with winter coming, the duck—"

"We have done our best for Felix. He is in the hands of *Gott* now. I promised to fix the walls, and I will. But if I'm to bake according to the old recipe, I must go back and fetch the things we left beside the lake."

"I wish we had a horse. There's a small wagon or cart in the shed, I think." A shiver passed through her, and she pulled her shawl tighter around her shoulders.

"I can serve as the horse. The supplies cannot weigh much more than Felix."

His smile, tinged with humor, warmed Marga through like swallowed sunlight. She stood and briskly gathered the empty dishes. She had to do something practical—because what she wanted to do was kiss him.

To kiss him! The outrageousness of such a notion, the impertinence!

The witch would have kissed him, she thought as she wiped the plates with a wet rag and set them on the cupboard to dry. She remembered the witch telling her, little Gretel, of the handsome man she'd wooed and won when she'd been young and beautiful. The witch had not hidden behind rules of etiquette when she'd spied the man she wanted. She'd acted boldly and she'd reaped the rewards. Such a strange thing to remember now. It was almost like the ghost of the witch lingered in the cottage and whispered into her ear, *Do as you please. Go on. Who would know?*

"No," Marga said aloud.

"I beg your pardon?" Lukas said behind her.

She glanced over her shoulder. He was kneeling close to the fireplace, rearranging the logs with a blackened metal poker.

"Oh. Nothing. I was just thinking." She wiped her hands on a towel. Supper sat in her belly like molten lead.

Lukas rose and faced her. "Are you finished there? Would you like to see my great-great-grandfather's journal now? The one with the recipe he used to build these walls?"

"Yes. Very much."

He gestured for her to be seated on the chair by the fire

and then retrieved the book from the pocket of the cloak he'd hung near the door.

"I've marked the page," Lukas said as he gave her the brown leather journal. It was smaller than his hand. A blue ribbon stuck out from its pages.

Marga opened the book as Lukas leaned against the stone wall of the hearth and observed. Lukas's forefather's handwriting covered the pages in neat, perfectly spaced rows. The ink had faded from black to yellowish brown over the years. The marked entry bore the heading, 20 April, 1703, and began with, "Dearest Bettina."

"Bettina?" Marga glanced up at Lukas. "Your great-great-grandmother?

"No. The woman he married was named Ermegard. Bettina was Great-great-grandfather's first love, the daughter of a wealthy mine owner. Her father forbade them to wed and sent her to a convent, where she took vows and later died of consumption."

"How sad," Marga said.

"He wrote to her almost every day in this book, telling her everything he could never tell her in letters. I'll be quiet now so you may read."

Marga angled the pages to catch the firelight. She read:

Dearest Bettina,

I have mentioned before the strange woman who runs what passes for an apothecary's shop here in Eschlinsdorf. She is beautiful, although not in a conventional way, and not as lovely as you, Liebling. *She is beautiful like a brightly colored serpent, or ripe, red, poison berries on a twisted vine. She overpowers men and women alike with her words or a gesture of her hand.*

It is magic, though few care to name it such. Even Pastor Althaus, leader of the local church, changes the subject of conversation if it is mentioned. He is more a sheep than a shepherd—and a skittish one at that. But that is another subject for another time.

The apothecary makes demands of me. More than once she has cornered me in a dark alleyway or blocked my path as I wandered the public garden. She wants a fine house built of sweets. She knows—and how she knows is a mystery—that I possess a recipe for magical gingerbread. I wish I did not own it, but it came to me as the eldest Beckmann son, as it has been passed down for hundreds of years.

Though some have tried to burn or tear the parchment upon which it is scribed, the recipe survives.

She has offered me treasure, land, and favors. I have refused them all. Again and again, I have refused. But she grows impatient. Angry. Her offers have become threats against my family, our bakery, and my health. Were I a bachelor, I would care little what became of me, but my wife is but twenty years of age, innocent as a dove, and recently delivered of our second son. I cannot let them come to harm.

Oh, Bettina. I will soon be forced to go into the Igelwald, to build a house of cake and candy for a witch, and I know that no good will come of it. Old Frau Keiser, who has the gift of foresight, has prophesied that a terrible famine will soon come upon this land, and I cannot help but think the witch will use the house to tempt the starving into doing whatever evil thing she commands. And then there are the tales of witches supping upon children to renew their youth. These thoughts haunt me. But what can I do?

Perhaps it was your good fortune not to wed me.

Marga turned the page and found a piece of pale yellow vellum. Age had rendered the writing upon it almost illegible. Common words were spelled in uncommon ways. Ingredients were called for in "handsfull," "half a thimble," and "goodly sized bukkets."

Lukas spoke as she stared at the list. "He disappeared the same day as the apothecary abandoned her shop, and he didn't return for months. Almost everyone thought she'd seduced him and convinced him to run away with her, but his wife knew the truth. Ermegard had helped him assemble the spices and pack the eggs in straw for the journey."

"His wife was of a stronger temperament than the journal suggested," Marga said.

Lukas nodded. "When my great-great-grandfather returned, he'd aged years instead of months. His hands trembled so that he could never decorate fancy cakes again. He even gave up writing in the journals. Ermegard and her brother had to take over the running of the bakery until the sons grew old enough."

Marga turned the journal page. Lukas's words were true. The handwriting was shaky and crooked, as if the writer could barely hold his pen. The last entry read:

I am old before my time, Bettina. My hands are stiff, my fingers bent and knobbed. I will write no more. But I shall speak to my memory of you in the orchard, under the apple tree where we met and dreamt of the beautiful future that eluded us.

"Perhaps you shouldn't use this recipe," Marga said as she closed the book and shifted in her chair. "By all appearances, it cost your great-great-grandfather his health, and stole years from his life."

"I believe the recipe was left to me for a reason," Lukas said, his back still pressed against the wall next to the fireplace. "To be used for a noble purpose this time. To help you."

"To help me?" If he had offered to give her the actual moon, she could not have been more stunned. "No. If the recipe is dangerous, and its use might cause you harm, then no. It would be unfair—"

"Pardon me, Fraulein. What is unfair is how you have been treated for the last thirteen years. Scorned, slandered, driven out of town—and for what reason? How have you ever harmed a single soul?"

His compassion had taken her by surprise. Again. Would she never grow used to it? If he sacrificed his life for her by using the recipe, she would never have a chance to grow used to it. The world would be a poorer place without Lukas Beckmann.

She met his gaze and shook her head. "You're not responsible for the actions of others. Their wrongs are not yours to right."

"I watched. I kept silent. I did nothing when I knew you needed a friend. Not doing the right thing is as much a sin as doing the wrong thing. I am as guilty as they are." Now his cheeks were as pink as Marga suspected her own were.

"You judge yourself too harshly," Marga said. "Always you have been kind and good. You gave me your cloak when I was cold. Years ago, you left bread at the door when I feared going out. You helped me when I came to you in desperation and hid beside your wood piles."

"Wait. You saw me when I brought the loaves?"

Marga nodded. "I'd forgotten it until just now. It was when I was ten, and Papa and Hansel had gone to the Christmas market in Bronnbach. Our housemaid's mother fell ill, and she abandoned me and left me to look after myself. I was afraid of everything then. I couldn't venture farther than our garden gate. I ran out of food."

The logs in the fireplace shifted and crackled. Lukas said, "My father was still alive then. He knew everyone's habits, and believed in the principle of loving one's neighbor. When your maid didn't come to collect the order for your household, Father knew something was wrong. He sent me with the bread. I was too shy to knock."

"You'd probably heard I was a witch. Even then, the rumors flew about the town like a plague of crows."

"Father had no tolerance for rumors. I was taught to seek

out the truth and form my own opinions. So no, I didn't fear you because of rumors. I feared you because you were pretty, and I was twelve. I knew that if you spoke to me, I'd become tongue-tied and you'd think me stupid." A little grin teased the corners of his mouth, and Marga could see him as the sweet, awkward lad he'd been.

"Well, thank you for the bread." She tried to ignore the fact that he'd called her pretty. His smile alone was enough to make her heart beat unevenly. She stood and handed the journal back to him. At the brush of his fingers, her breath caught.

"You'll permit me to make the gingerbread?" he asked.

"Let's wait until the morning to decide." Marga folded her arms around her middle. She wanted to say no again, but if she did, she suspected Lukas would argue his side until dawn. "It's late. Go and spend the night in the bedchamber with Felix. I'll sleep out here. The settle is long enough for me, short as I am."

"I'll feel like a swine, sleeping in a comfortable bed while you lie on a hard bench."

"There is no other option. He is...you are...men. Brothers."

"Ah, yes. I have so many sisters that I forget too easily the rules of propriety." He smiled again, his hand resting on the wall as if the cottage was his own. "But do not take that to mean that I see you as a sister."

A blast of wind surged down the chimney. Lukas took a step back as ashes and sparks flew toward him. The mighty draft snuffed out the candles on the table and shelves. The duck sneezed.

"How strange," Lukas said, brushing soot off his sleeve. "The night seemed so still." In the golden light cast by the flames in the fireplace, the tall blond man looked like the stained glass image of the angel Gabriel she'd admired in Eschlinsdorf's church.

Transfixed by the sight, Marga stared at the baker for a moment. And then she forced her eyes to gaze at the dirty floor. "I'll sweep up the mess and bank the fire," she said. "You should check on Felix. Try to sleep. Come and wake me if he takes a turn or needs anything."

"Good night then, Fraulein Holzfäller."

"Good night, Herr Beckmann."

As soon as Lukas disappeared into the bedchamber, Marga took a deep breath and released it in a slow sigh.

"Please *Gott*, help me," she whispered. "Tame my foolish heart."

She had to stop feeling the way she did about Lukas Beckmann. Immediately.

Even if the townsfolk miraculously decided to see her as a harmless woman rather than a witch, she despised crumbs the way some people hated snakes or rats. She could never be a baker's wife—no matter how generous and handsome he was.

Who knew there were such good men in the world? And why weren't the unmarried women of Eschlinsdorf lined up at his door, competing for the honor of becoming his bride?

After she banked the fire, Marga spread several woolen blankets over the seat of the settle and folded herself inside them. When she closed her eyes, Lukas appeared, as radiant and glorious as the stained glass Gabriel. She tried to mentally add crumbs to his finery, to ruin his allure, but her efforts were for naught.

She still wanted to kiss the man.

* * *

In front of the fireplace, Ansgar stood and turned a full circle before settling down again in his basket. He'd quite enjoyed sending the blast of wind down the chimney, in spite of the fact that it had besmirched his feathers with soot.

His joy was tempered with the frustration that had driven him to whip up the wind.

The attraction between the girl and this Herr Beckmann fellow was growing by the minute. Earlier in the day, Ansgar had thought it harmless to allow them to trifle with one another, but as night fell, he found he simply could not endure another second of their stolen glances and maidenly blushes. They acted as if they were a pair of twelve-year-old children, all shyness and hesitation, rather than passion-filled adults. And thank the gods for that mercy upon his eyes!

The more he saw of Herr Beckmann, the less he liked the big lout. The future witch-queen deserved a better husband than a giant-sized, mouse-brained baker.

Ansgar ought not to have cared whom Gretel chose to wed, yet he did. He believed with all of his heart that Gretel should marry a man gifted with magic. An ordinary man could never truly appreciate the complexities of her powers, nor could he help her hone her talent.

Nevertheless, he'd been pleased to hear that the baker intended to repair the cottage with his special recipe. The drafts from the bedchamber lowered the temperature within the kitchen by many degrees. Ansgar hated being cold, and his limited command over the weather would not enable him to hold back the inevitable onslaught of winter's fury.

If he had to spend another winter as a duck, he preferred to spend it someplace snug and warm. He'd allow Beckmann to stay long enough to fix what needed fixing, but then something would have to be done to rid the place of him. If necessary, he could surely use his bill to cautiously concoct a poison to stop the fellow's heart.

An owl hooted outside. It was late. He stood once more and shook out his feathers, as he was wont to do before sleeping. Bits of soot sprinkled onto the floor around his basket. Across the room on the settle, Gretel breathed softly. The sound soothed him into drowsiness, and he allowed his eyes to close.

After he'd dozed for a few hours or more, the faint sound of a whinny woke him.

Well, well, well. Little Gretel was blossoming more quickly than he'd expected.

It remained to be seen if she'd connect the granting of a spoken wish with her innate power, or if she'd attribute the horse's arrival to mere chance.

He could hardly wait to find out.

Twenty-Two

Something is trying to break down the door.

Marga sat up fast, shoving the blankets to the floor. Dawn barely illuminated the colored candy windowpanes, and the embers in the fireplace pulsed with the palest orange glow. Even before she'd awoken fully, panic had set her heart to racing and dried her mouth. She stood, but couldn't think of what to do next.

THUD. THUD. THUD.

If whatever was outside kept at it, the door would break.

"Did you hear that?" Lukas asked as he ran out from the bedchamber, fully dressed.

Marga pointed at the door. Another thump sounded against the thick boards of brown cake.

And then the mysterious visitor huffed and whinnied.

"I think it's a horse," Marga said with a little laugh of relief. "What in the name of *Himmel* is a horse doing wandering about the forest? And why is it pummeling the door?"

Lukas's expression shifted from perplexed to serious. He looked away from her like someone forced to keep an uncomfortable secret. Marga remembered then. She'd *wished*, out loud, in the witch's cottage, for a horse.

"No. It cannot be," she said. The blood drained from her head and the room swam about her. "I didn't mean to..."

"Sit before you fall, Fraulein." Lukas took her by the elbow and returned her to the settle. "Breathe, Margarethe."

"Go and see. Open the door." She trembled as if caught in an icy draft. Had she really done this...this magic? Had she brought a horse by simply uttering a wish? But that would make her a...She threw out the thought like dirty bathwater. Refused to entertain it.

Marga focused on Lukas, watching him open the door. Still seated, she leaned forward to glance outside. A few feet away from the doorstep stood a chestnut mare, regal and muscular. The animal greeted Lukas with a soft exhalation.

"Hello," Lukas said to the horse as it bowed its head. "You're a pretty one."

A sob swelled inside Marga's chest. She covered her mouth with both hands. Lukas would leave now.

He would leave her, because she was a witch. He wouldn't tell the townsfolk. He was not the gossiping sort. But he *would* unburden his heart to his mother or one of his sisters, and they would tell everyone, everyone, and then a crazed mob would come and burn her alive. She'd die just like the old witch she'd killed, in flames. Unloved.

Lukas would never love her.

She closed her streaming eyes. She'd ruined everything, without even trying. *Because she was a witch.* She'd somehow ended up the thing she hated most. It would cost her the small, tender, unwise hope she'd had of being loved by a good and honorable man. It would cost her everything.

Lukas's strong hands encircled her wrists. She kept her eyes shut. How could she look at him now?

"Margarethe. Marga, please. Don't weep."

She shook her head, mindful not to wish him gone. For if her unfamiliar, untamed powers erased him altogether, what a loss that would be for the world.

"You did nothing wrong," he said. He sounded close, as if he knelt before the settle where she sat, but she refused to open her eyes to find out. "How were you to know that a wish held such power? Were you ever taught such a thing? Did you beseech the devil for his aid in this? No."

"No," she said, still overcome with sorrow. She let her hands drop into her lap and Lukas freed her wrists from his grasp. The tears flowed no matter how tightly she clenched her eyelids closed.

"Will you look at me?" He spoke with infinite kindness —and only made her feel worse.

She shook her head. "Not now. I couldn't bear it."

"Am I so ugly?" His voice carried the hint of a smile.

"You must not tease me. Please, take Felix and the horse and go home. If you have any pity in your heart, go quickly."

"I will go, but only to fetch the flour to fix the walls. Felix is not well enough to travel. And besides..."

When he paused too long, Marga opened her eyes, ready to argue forcefully that they must leave. But before she could say anything, he smiled at her.

Smiled. At her. *A witch.*

He was on his knees, as she'd imagined. He looked penitent, like he was the one at fault. "If we are airing our secrets, Fraulein, I will confess mine to you now. I do not wish to leave you, not ever. I—"

"Stop. I beg you," Marga said. "You see what I have done. What I have become. How do you know you are not ensorcelled by me? How would we ever know if anything between us was true and real, if we were together? You must not throw away your life on what might be an illusion, Lukas. You must not."

"My life is my own, as is my heart. If you have ensorcelled me, then it is a good thing. Since that morning I found you behind the bakery, I have been happier than ever before in my life—may poor Felix forgive me. It is you I want, magic or no magic."

"Herr Beckmann—"

"Call me Lukas, as you did before," he said. "I never cared for my name until I heard you say it." He stood and pulled her to her feet.

Marga looked up into the baker's earnest, round face. "Lukas," she said. She was still crying, but she managed to add, "I'm unsuitable for you in so many ways. I'm far too short. Too strange. Everyone in Eschlinsdorf hates me, and besides, I hate crumbs. The sight of them makes me ill."

"I don't care for crumbs either," he said, pulling her closer. "And the townsfolk are fools. And as for being short, well, I think *Gott* made you perfectly."

Still smiling, he bent down to press his mouth to hers. She rose up on tiptoe to welcome the miracle. The kiss was salty and sweet, and, within the strong circle of his arms,

Marga forgot all her sorrows and objections. Warmth spread through her body. All she wanted was Lukas, and more of him.

The horse stomped and snorted. Tiny hailstones clinked and clattered against the windowpanes and roof. In the next room, Felix coughed. Lukas broke the kiss. Marga took a step back and tugged at her apron to straighten it.

"Are you...well?" Lukas said. His cheeks were rosy and his eyes had a dreamy look.

"Quite well," Marga said. "And you?"

"Very well indeed." Lukas gestured with his head toward the still-open door. "But it's hailing."

"Oh. Oh, I see. I didn't wish for that, if that is what you're asking."

"Good. You are happy then? I did not offend you by—?"

Marga reached out and took his hand. "If I ruled the weather, the sun would be shining."

Lukas grinned like a small boy. "Good," he said again.

Awkward silence fell between them. Hail continued to beat against the cottage. Some pea-sized pellets rolled over the threshold.

"We ought to shut the door," Marga said, releasing Lukas's hand.

"The horse needs shelter," Lukas said. "I will take it to the shed."

"And I should make more medicine. And tea. I'll make tea." Marga glanced at the horse, the wall, her stocking-clad feet. Two minutes ago, everything had felt right and natural. Now she felt discomposed and unsure.

Had she wished for the hail without realizing it? Had she wished Lukas into kissing her?

Lukas brushed her cheekbone with his fingertips. She met his gaze and saw nothing there but joy. Still...

"Tea would be welcome," Lukas said. "I'll see to the horse. And then I'll be back."

Marga shut the door behind Lukas. She felt as if a swarm of aggravated bees had been let loose inside her head and her heart. She wanted to relive the kiss in her memory, to bask in the bliss she'd known in Lukas's embrace, but all she could think about was the horse arriving because of her wish.

She was tempted to try to wish away her wishing power, but something told her it would be futile.

As she measured and mixed Felix's medicine, she scrutinized her memory, trying desperately to recall if she'd wished aloud to be kissed by Lukas Beckmann. Perhaps her wishes didn't have to be spoken to be taken seriously by whatever magic indwelled the gingerbread cottage.

Or perhaps he had kissed her because he wanted to.

How she hoped that was true. She felt that she might be able to bear anything if Lukas loved her, even being forced by Fate to wield magic.

She caught sight of her reflection in the water she'd poured into the big kettle. The image made her stomach lurch like she'd seen a hundred crumbs. Her hair was far more silver-streaked than the last time she'd seen her image. Deeper creases fanned out from her eyes. Her back pained her as she bent over the pot.

Was there no end to the dead witch's cruelty? For suddenly, Marga had no doubt that the magic growing within her and the unusual aging were cruel gifts from the old woman who'd enticed her and Hansel into the gingerbread cottage thirteen long years ago.

She was nothing more than a moth trapped in a spider's web. She could wriggle, but could she ever break free?

* * *

Ansgar hissed when he awoke to see the girl and the big oaf kissing.

He'd been a fool to fall asleep. Had he remained alert, he might have prevented their embrace by calling forth another gust of wind through the chimney. In the end, he'd managed to pull his wits together enough to cause the skies to hurl pea-sized hail upon the cottage. That had put an end to the kissing, thank the gods.

He plucked a feather from his breast and spat it toward the fire. It was a waste of time to feel as unsettled as he did about a simple kiss. He could not afford to squander his strength on tantrums.

Perhaps his fever had returned, for Ansgar was stricken by a sharp pang of longing for all he'd lost when he'd betrayed Truda. He tore out another feather in a useless attempt to distract himself from the unwelcome emotion.

Concentrate. Plan for the future and forget the past. When he regained his human form, he could woo and win whomever he chose. Yet he knew he'd never find another woman like Truda. She had been the very heart of his crooked heart.

Gretel stirred the potion over the fire, wearing a half-smile. She had the audacity to look like a woman in love. Wide swathes of magic encircled her body, glowing and twinkling like bands of constellations. She was beautiful. Glorious. And he hated her for it.

Why should she have everything when he would never again hold his true love in his arms?

He'd help her become the witch-queen because the forest magic compelled him to do so—but he'd be hanged if he helped her to be happy.

The duck stared into the flames and plotted treachery.

Twenty-Three

Marga stood outside the cottage. The hens she'd brought from Eschlinsdorf cooed and strutted around her ankles as she watched Lukas work to secure the wished-for horse to a small wagon. He fumbled with the straps, apologizing to the horse for his limited experience with bridles and reins. Marga smiled, pleased by his patience, tenacity, and gentle way with the animal.

Task done, he patted the mare's side and said, "Good girl."

Marga stepped closer and handed the baker the last pear she'd picked from the witch's tree. Several cups of chamomile tea had helped to soothe her nerves after the horse's sudden appearance, but the drink had not altered her feelings for Lukas.

She adored the baker, body and soul.

"We'll have good bread when I return," he said as he pocketed the pear.

"It won't be good if I make it," Marga replied.

He laughed and leaned down to kiss her forehead. "Never will I ask you to."

"I consider that a sacred promise, Herr Beckmann."

Lukas climbed onto the wagon seat. It was barely wide enough for a man of his stature. Indeed, the wagon's bed looked too small to contain the flour and supplies they'd abandoned at the lake. She dismissed that particular worry. Lukas would know which things were essential and which things could be left for the forest creatures to consume.

"I'll return as quickly as I can," he said, as if he sensed that she already missed him.

"You have the map I drew?"

"Right here." He patted the pocket of his jacket. "Take good care of Felix."

The horse set off as if confident of a successful journey. Marga hadn't wished for an extraordinarily intelligent horse, but the magic seemed to have provided one. As clever as the horse might be, it would probably not bring Lukas home before nightfall. Already, the sun hovered at its zenith. Few hours lay between noon and dusk this time of year.

If she'd been willing to risk making more wishes, she would have wished for Lukas's safety.

As Lukas and the wagon disappeared among the trees, she tried not to think about him spending the night in the wild woods, at the mercy of roving faeries and fierce boars. It was frightening enough to imagine him out there in daylight hours.

Marga brushed a dried leaf off her shirt and took note of its filthiness. Her trousers were in a worse state. Indeed, nothing about her was tidy or clean. She'd been so occupied in taking care of Felix when they'd arrived at the cottage that she had never taken the time to change out of her travel-stained garments. It was astounding that Lukas had wanted to kiss someone arrayed in soot and dried mud.

Then again, his clothing was hardly much cleaner and she'd wanted to kiss him. Very, very much.

Their kiss seemed like a wondrous dream. The urge to wish aloud that Lukas would kiss her again fluttered in her stomach. No, she would not use magic to manipulate him. What kind of person would that make her?

The answer came to her without delay: *a witch*. A true witch would wish boldly for Lukas's affection, and for many other selfish gains as well. She vowed in her heart to do all she could to resist becoming a full-fledged, evil-minded sorceress. There was a chance her power came from the house or some force residing within it. As soon as the duck and Felix were well, she'd test that theory. She'd go away from the gingerbread cottage and never return. She'd swim to America before she'd choose to live here again.

Even as she pondered leaving, her heart said *no*.

Her heart said *stay*. It was only her mind that still objected to living in the cottage. Something within her had shifted. The cottage's cinnamon-and-clove-scented walls had become home. It felt like her place in the world, which was a terrible irony. For on this property, she'd cowered under the witch's cruelty, watched Hansel suffer in a cage, and then murdered their captor.

What would Lukas say if she told him she wanted to dwell in the gingerbread cottage? Would he ever consider living deep in the enchanted forest with her?

Now that Lukas was well and truly gone, there was a chill in the air she'd not noticed before. Time to stop daydreaming and speculating. She'd go back inside, check on Felix, and find clean clothes to wear. After that, she'd tend to the duck and make a hot drink for herself.

When she opened the door, warmth welcomed her. Lukas had stocked the hearth well before he'd left. The kettle of water steamed, ready for tea-making. The duck slept in its basket. If Lukas had been there, the scene would have been close to faultless. But then Felix moaned, summoning her to the bedchamber and setting her nerves on edge. All was not well, she could feel it.

She rushed into the bedchamber. Felix lay still among the tangled quilts. He looked younger and more fragile than the boy she'd first met behind the bakery in Eschlinsdorf. Marga tiptoed to his side and bent to examine his wound.

"Oh, no," she said when she saw the swollen, greenish-black flesh and the dark streaks running up and down his arm. Without touching him, she could feel heat radiating from his body. A fever, and a dangerously high one at that.

All thoughts of clean clothes and tea fled her mind. She sank to her knees and prayed for help from above. Felix whimpered like an injured animal as she got to her feet and paced the room. She had to do something fast. But what? Bloodletting? Different medicine? A salve or plaster? She was no doctor, and Felix needed one without delay. If only Lukas had not taken the horse and wagon...

The horse. She'd wished for it, and it had come. Perhaps she could wish Felix well. The idea appalled her, souring her stomach and chilling her so that she shivered like a frightened dog. She didn't want to meddle with magic, but she couldn't stand idly by and watch the boy die.

She knelt again, placed her hands on Felix's arm, closed her eyes, and wished aloud for his healing. She wished and wished, again and again, but his skin only grew warmer and more riddled with streaks. Wishing had done nothing. She'd have to try something else, and quickly.

Marga sprang to her feet and ran to the shelf in the kitchen where the witch's books lay in a dusty pile. Until today, she'd used only the thin volume of herbal recipes to make the various treatments she'd given to Felix and the duck. She'd avoided touching the books she'd thought contained actual spells.

But now, desperation drove her to seek help from wherever it might be found.

Twenty-Four

Marga's back ached as she transferred the big pile of dust-coated books from the shelf to the table. She dropped them with a thud, then spread them out, trying to ignore the vague buzzing in her fingertips that happened when she touched them. The smallest book would fit in her pocket, but the largest took up almost half of the table. Some were covered in plain, brown leather, but others had covers dyed scarlet, blue, or green. They all looked like relics of a past age.

Thee Longue and Varied Historie of Magick would be of no help, and neither would *Curses: Common and Rare*, or *Mirandola's Treatise on Moon Spells*. She flipped through the stiff, stained pages of *The Goodly Receipts of Truda Eichel* and found instructions for cookery. A bookmark made from braided hair marked a recipe for "a nice peppered stew of young boy with wine and currants." She shut the book and shuddered, remembering little, cage-bound Hansel.

One book remained, a hefty volume bound in crimson leather, with the simple title *Potions*.

Marga shoved the other books aside. She pulled up a chair and sat down to read. The thin, yellowed pages crinkled like the delicate skin of onions. A musty, old book smell tickled her nose as she turned page after page, searching and scanning. Many different hands had scribed the words, some more legibly than others.

There were recipes for potions to change flax cloth to silk, to make a cow fertile, to improve eyesight, and to keep deer out of a vegetable patch. Someone had scribbled instructions for a concoction to win a suitor's heart, and another for turning a rival's fancy to disdain. There were ten different recipes for potions to transform one's enemies into flocks of chickens. Marga's head started to pound. Felix might die before she found anything helpful inside the disorganized behemoth of a book.

She turned several more pages. A clumsy illustration of a swollen, streaked arm caught her attention. Below it, scrawled in dark brown ink, was the heading, "A cure for a woond which did come from a byte of a creechur of ill-will and powerfull vennum, when such a woond festerates and casts forth menny deathly strippes." Under the title, the author had listed at least twenty ingredients. She ran her finger down the page, whispering the words as she read. Her heart pounded fast with excitement. Here, finally, was something that might save Lukas's brother from death.

"Sweet wormwood, salt from the sea, powder of white willow bark, root of blackthorn, cloves, petals of yarrow, wolf's bane..." She stopped reading near the end of the list.

The witch's stores held many of the ingredients—she'd seen them on the bottle-laden shelves and in the crammed cupboards. But nowhere in the house were there "live lake snails, gathered by thine hand from the goodly mud near water's eastern shore."

An inscription below the entry discouraged her further. Dated 24 March, 1627, it read, "Mine poore husband did perish of a black woond of his leg when I made do with common snails from mine garden, being large with childe and unfitted to journey to the lake. Mine heart is rent and shall nevermore heal."

"Lake snails from the eastern shore's mud," Marga said aloud. Felix was so ill, the lake so far away and so wide. If she managed to reach the lake, she'd have to build another raft or beg the nixes for aid in order to cross to the eastern shore. The nixes had deferred to her before, but they were changeable creatures. This time, they might drown her. And if she perished, so would Felix.

She crossed the room, mulling over the situation and nibbling her thumbnail. The duck lifted its head and quacked at her from the hearthside. She kept pacing, pondering.

A few minutes later, the duck nipped her calf.

She exclaimed in surprise and glared down at the duck, ready to scold it for leaving its basket. The fowl dipped its bill to the floor and pantomimed digging.

"You can help me find the snails," Marga said, translating the duck's signs."

The duck nodded.

"But are you well enough to travel? Your wing..."

The duck nodded again. Marga knelt and kissed the top of its feathered head.

"Thank you, thank you," she said, full of hope. But her optimism faded when she realized that leaving the cottage meant leaving poor Felix alone.

If she had to temporarily abandon Felix—and what choice did she have if she were going to save him—she'd need to return quickly. She'd have to try wishing for help again. Perhaps her earlier wish for Felix's healing had been against some rule of wishing. Maybe she could only wish for certain things, or at certain times.

Her stomach tightened. Her mouth went dry. Everything within her revolted at the thought of using magic. It was bad enough that she intended to brew a potion from the old witch's book. But surely this was different than that evil woman's use of magic. This was a good deed, not a selfish act. She wasn't conjuring rats to vex the townsfolk or cursing the waters of an enemy's well to turn sulfurous. Her desire was to save a young man and to spare his family from grief.

She closed her eyes and clenched her cold, trembling hands over her heart. "I wish for the greatest deer of the Igelwald, the wisest and swiftest buck of all, to come with great haste to carry me."

It might have taken hours for a horse to navigate the forest and find the cottage, and hours more for it to bear her to the lake. The deer she needed was close by; she felt it in her bones. It would bear her to her destination on deft hooves. As the magic awoke and obeyed her, the sensation of a thousand needles pricking her skin spread from her scalp to her toes.

The duck quacked as if in approval.

Shaking off the magic's effects, Marga rushed back to the bedchamber to check on Felix. He slept peacefully now, thanks be to *Gott*. She returned to the kitchen and set an empty jar in her basket to hold the snails. It was then that she heard antlers scraping the door. Not five minutes had passed since her wish.

She threw on a cloak. With the basket in the crook of her elbow, she gathered the duck under her other arm. She hurried across the kitchen, reached for the door latch, and then hesitated. If she left the cottage fires untended for hours, the rooms would become cold. A chill might be enough to finish Felix off. Like it or not, she had to make one more quick wish. "I wish for the fires of the hearth and stove to warm the cottage well until my return," she said.

The magic sent tiny sparks through her veins. The feeling was closer to pleasure than pain. The duck under her arm sighed contentedly, but Marga felt far from serene as she opened the door.

She'd willfully employed magic twice within minutes. How many times could she do so before she became, irrevocably and completely, a witch? Perhaps it was already too late.

That was a worry for another day. Holding the duck firmly against her side, she stepped out onto the frost-covered doorstep to meet the buck.

Twenty-Five

Ansgar snuggled against Gretel's side as she strode toward the majestic buck. The chestnut brown animal was almost a foot taller than the girl, antlers aside, and its muscular legs promised a swift journey to the lake.

If he'd possessed his human voice, Ansgar would have shouted for joy. The day of his liberation had finally arrived. He would convince Gretel through his clever use of pantomime that to find the snails she wanted, she'd need to ride his back over the water. Because all he had to do was ferry the girl across the lake once more, and he would be free of the worst part of the curse.

He would be a man.

Oh, the glory of it! To once more be featherless and tall, to have hands that grasped, two steady feet instead of hideous webbed extremities, and to have the full use of his brilliant mind—a mind unclouded by base thoughts of minnows and nest-building...

Once he'd regained all his human faculties, he expected to

have no problem shepherding the new witch-queen onto her proverbial throne. With that, his suffering would cease. He would be completely free of the enchantment and able to leave the Igelwald forever.

Why, the girl had already started to yield to her fate. Summoning the Great Buck as she had, wielding her power over one of the forest's most revered inhabitants—this was queenly behavior indeed. And then little Gretel had exerted her wishing power over the household fires! If he had not despised her so keenly, he would have been proud of her.

Naturally, she'd failed to heal the injured boy with a wish, ignorant of that power's rules and limitations. Wishes for healing or killing were never granted, nor were wishes for food or love. She would learn these things, but not today.

The huge buck knelt to allow Gretel to mount. She swung her leg over and half fell, half sat upon its wide back. Jolted and squeezed beneath her arm, Ansgar quacked with dismay. His wing smarted. It was not completely healed, as he'd led her to believe. But he knew his chance had come, and he would not waste it or wait for another.

"Pardon my clumsiness," Gretel said to the buck. Ansgar sneered as much as his stiff bill would allow. The very idea of the future witch-queen apologizing to an animal under her rule was preposterous. Well, if he was to be fair, how was she to know, when she'd been raised by unmagical, undereducated commoners in a tiny town pressed up against the mountains?

He would enlighten her, that he would. Before he left for France—for he'd decided to settle in that splendid land of fine food and superior wine—he'd make certain Gretel knew her place. If she was to reign in Truda's stead, she'd need to learn to hold her head high and dominate her subjects. A few brief but stern lectures ought to suffice to set her on the proper path. She could take notes to consult later, perhaps. Thank the gods that her inferior upbringing had gifted her with literacy.

The stately buck took a few steps. Gretel grabbed onto the thick hairs of its neck to steady herself. Ansgar felt her muscles tense as she sought balance. And then the buck bounded forward, out of Truda's garden and into the forest.

Safe beneath the girl's arm, he relished the rush of pine-scented air against his face. The trees around them were blurs of greens, browns, and grays. The buck charged through the landscape, vaulting fallen trunks and darting over ditches. Its hooves found purchase, impossibly, on rocky upward slopes, and they never faltered on steep, stone-strewn descents. Sometimes, Gretel gasped in surprise or fear, but the buck neither hesitated nor slowed until they approached the lake's northwestern edge.

A sly honking laugh burst from Ansgar's bill as the buck strode onto the shore. The girl could have ordered the buck to transport them directly to the eastern shore, but she had not. Her inanity would work in his favor. He would not have to lie to get her onto his back after all. She needed him to ferry her to the eastern shore and the correct snails.

His freedom was at hand. *At hand!* Ha! Soon, he would possess hands!

The buck halted a few yards short of the water. Ansgar breathed in the scents of his longtime home: algae and mud, decay and reeds. He'd missed the place, or at least the duck part of him had. The sound of the sloshing water beckoned him like a saucy nix. He wriggled until the girl loosened her grip, and then he leapt to the ground. His webbed feet sank into the cold mud, but the sensation was not one that bothered him. He turned to watch Gretel.

The girl dismounted clumsily, dropping her basket and almost tumbling onto the black pebbled beach. She righted herself, blushing as she did too often. She would have to stop coloring up like a radish at every turn; it was not at all regal.

"Thank you for helping us," Gretel said to the great buck. "You are most kind."

It bowed to her, its black nose touching the ground. She reached out and patted its forehead as if it were a pet pony. "I would be grateful if you would return in an hour or two. We must return to the cottage before nightfall."

The buck replied with a submissive nod. It knew its place, even if the future queen did not.

After the buck sprang away, Gretel set her basket on the ground. She crouched down and started to take out the jar she'd brought. Ansgar poked her shin with his bill and quacked, forming a sound as close to the word "no" as he could.

The girl eyed him. "Is something wrong?"

With his head, he motioned toward the sky and the sun, and then he pointed to the east with his good wing. After a moment, she frowned.

"Oh. This isn't the right place, is it?" She grunted with exasperation, then asked, "Can you take me to the eastern shore? Are you certain you're strong enough?"

Ansgar nodded. He closed his eyes and summoned all the

magic within his feathered breast. He willed his duck bones to lengthen and his duck flesh to expand slowly, slowly. He had learned to neither grow nor reduce in size too quickly. Pain had been a harsh and merciless teacher.

Once he'd become as large as his enchanted body allowed, he opened his eyes. The girl stared at him with wonder, as if she'd not seen the feat before. This was yet another example of unqueenly behavior, but far be it from him to despise a little admiration. Ducks didn't receive many adoring glances, not even from other ducks.

He waded into the shallows and waited for her to climb onto his feathered back. She muttered as she splashed toward him, reassuring herself that she could do what had to be done to save Felix, and that she would be safe. Ansgar rolled his eyes. Queen Truda had never needed to scrounge up courage like a poor man rummaging under his bed for enough coins to pay the landlord.

Gretel stopped muttering when she reached him. She swung her leg over his back, weighing him down only a little. An intoxicating feeling of power and domination spread through his body. She was, after all, trusting him with her very life. He knew the perfect place to drown her, where the water formed a black whirlpool that would suck her under no matter how she flailed. If he chose, he could summon the cullberfish, or awaken the lake dragon from its centuries-long slumber. These dark thoughts sent a thrill down his spine, but he would not act upon them.

He focused on his three goals: to escape duck form, to enthrone Gretel, and to leave the Igelwald. If only Truda could see him now, confidently swimming toward victory.

Undaunted by his inconvenient shape. Embracing every opportunity to accomplish the goals she and the Igelwald had cruelly set before him.

That woman. He hated his late wife as much as he loved her. The two emotions scrapped like mad dogs inside his heart, snapping and snarling for dominance. It took all of his will to still them so he could concentrate on his present mission.

Gretel adjusted her body, gripping his sides with her thighs. She trembled a little, obviously unused to the touch of cold water. “The eastern shore, please,” she said, as if he were brainless enough to have forgotten.

Ansgar paddled his webbed feet, propelling himself and his passenger forward. He felt the eyes of many upon them, but the water folk dared not move a fin or flipper to hinder Gretel’s journey, as if they, too, sensed the invisible ribbons of magic that encircled the girl.

She posed little danger to them, scared and meek as she was at the moment. But soon, very soon, everything would change.

* * *

Marga shivered from head to foot as she glided across the lake astride the white duck. The cloud-obscured sky offered little light and no warmth. Frigid water had soaked through her shoes, stockings, and the legs of the breeches she wore. For this, she blamed herself. If only she’d had the presence of mind to ask the deer to carry them directly to the lake’s eastern side, she would have stayed dry for longer.

The duck sailed along with the assurance of one familiar with the route, giving no indication of discomfort. Still, she wondered if the barely healed wing continued to pain the bird. The second the reedy shore came into view, she readied herself to jump off its back.

The duck stopped paddling a few yards short of land. Marga dismounted clumsily, with a splash that soaked her face. She wiped her eyes with her soggy sleeve, then settled her basket into the crook of her left arm. Here, in knee-deep water, was as good a place as any to look for snails. Bending at the waist, she peered downward. She reached into the lake and fished out something gray—an ordinary stone. Again and again, for what seemed like hours, she harvested bits of broken shell and round rocks that looked like snails from above.

"Darnation!" She flung a pebble hard toward the shore. She'd told the duck to rest after their journey. It occurred to her now that she should have asked it to help with the snail hunt, or at least to point out the best place to search.

She turned a slow circle, looking for its white form in the shallows and along the strip of beach. But the duck was nowhere to be seen. With a huff of frustration, she waded a few yards closer to the beach and resumed the hunt.

Cold water slapped against the backs of her calves as she dug numb fingers deep into sandy mud. The smooth curve of a shell met her fingertips. She pried it loose and held it aloft like the prize it was. Finally, a lake snail to put into her jar. Her smile grew as she found another, and then another, each one larger than the last. The recipe had been vague about the number needed, so she kept harvesting until she'd filled the jar to its brim.

She straightened her aching back and hurried toward the shore. The search had taken longer than expected. Felix needed medicine she had yet to concoct, and judging from the color of the sky, twilight would fall soon. Her chest ached with anxiety. She called out for the duck, more than ready for quick transport back to the place where the buck would meet her.

The duck did not come.

Where was that bird? Had it returned to its old nest before she could bid it farewell? She couldn't fault the creature for that. She missed her home, her bed, her dead father, and even her selfish brother Hansel. And most of all, she missed a certain tall baker.

"Lukas!" she cried, in case he was still in the vicinity of the lake. Her voice reverberated over the water. No answer came. He might already be traveling back to the cottage with the supplies. Or perhaps he was too busy working to notice her voice amidst the croaking, buzzing, and sloshing. She had been foolish to call for him. Impractical. Whether he answered her or not, the horse and small wagon could not bear them and the supplies to the cottage swiftly. For speed, she needed the duck and the big deer.

"Duck!" she shouted again. "Please come back, white duck!" She turned slowly, squinting hard and scanning the lake and its shores, but she could see neither the duck nor the princely deer.

If the duck was gone, would the buck know to come to

this side of the lake to find her? Ought she to wish again? She couldn't stand idle and wait, not with Felix's life at stake.

Marga filled her lungs with algae-scented air and shouted for the buck. Her voice echoed through the Igelwald. Surely every inhabitant of the forest, natural and unnatural, heard her cry. She prayed for the buck to arrive before something claimed her as prey.

Her clothes dripped as she walked along the shore. She shouted again. Behind her, twigs snapped. An animal whimpered in pain. Her heart urged her to seek out the poor thing, but her mind advised against it. This was the wild Igelwald. There was no knowing if something was making the sound to lure her into danger.

From nearby came the deep, trumpeting bellow of a buck. The sound of rescue—for her, and if *Himmel* favored, for Felix. Marga grabbed the basket and made sure the jar of snails sat securely within it.

The buck leapt over a wall of brambles and pranced to her side. It knelt to permit her to climb onto its back.

"Please take me back to the gingerbread cottage as fast as you can," she said. Her hands grasped onto the thick fur at its neck, and an instant later, the great buck bounded into the trees.

Twenty-Six

Again, Ansgar vomited onto the slick, dead leaves that surrounded his naked body.

He'd never felt so ill in all his life. That thankless wretch of a girl had ridden off astride the buck, leaving him weak as a newborn kitten and miles from shelter.

Curse Gretel.

And curse Truda, the merciless cow. Could she not have commanded the magic to make his change back into human form pleasant, or at least tolerable? His stomach cramped as if it meant to twist him into a permanent knot. Vertigo and muscle spasms conspired to keep him on the damp ground, unable to escape his own malodorous spewage.

After a while, he managed to roll onto his belly. A nap and an hour later, he started to creep along the damp forest floor on hands and knees. He moved away from the lake; he'd never be able to swim across in his enfeebled state. Besides, he didn't trust the nixes now that he'd transformed. His magic had all but deserted him when he'd shifted shapes, so they'd likely drown him before they'd help him.

It might take weeks for his powers to return in full, but return they would. This sure knowledge gave him the will to fight through his current suffering.

Ansgar crawled along the ground as if he were still an undignified animal. Briars scratched his tender, newly reborn skin. Decayed matter and mud from the forest floor besmirched his long-missed, manly limbs. He stopped to nap again, curling into a ball on a patch of soft moss. When he awoke, the vertigo had lessened but his hunger and his anger had grown. His mind simmered with schemes.

He slept once more, and awoke feeling stronger. He reached for the lowest branches of a young pine and used them to pull himself to a standing position. He took a few halting, clumsy steps, grabbing at other trees for support. How ironic it was to take aid from trees! It was a tree's fault he'd been trapped in the shape of a duck for years as much as it was his. Or Truda's.

By the gods, he detested trees. He scowled at the slender bole of silvery beech his fingers encircled. The faerie within the bark sighed in response to his touch. He tore his hand away as if burned.

Finally, he found he could walk on his own—albeit with a slow, uneven gait. A humiliating, almost duck-like waddle.

He hated ducks with even a greater passion than he hated trees. In the future, he'd endeavor to eat roasted waterfowl often. His mouth flooded with saliva at the thought of a forkful of hot duck breast slathered with plum sauce.

Time passed slowly. His loathing for the forest multiplied

as he staggered onward. Never again did he want to see another squirrel, boulder, or mountain slope. He glanced upward to take stock of the stars studding the darkening heavens. He found the North Star and altered his course a little, for he had a fixed destination in mind: Eschlinsdorf, the closest town, and the very one he'd heard the baker and Gretel speak of as home.

The place where he'd set his newest plans into motion.

Ansgar ambled through a meadow of dead grass. His bare toes squelched into a mushy pile of animal droppings. He swore aloud and wiped his foot on a patch of moss. The sound of his voice startled him, so unfamiliar had it become. A red squirrel paused on the path and stared at him with beady, questioning eyes. He lunged for it, but the animal darted away and up a tree.

No great loss. He was hungry but not quite hungry enough to want to consume a rodent. He could wait for bread. Surely the mother of the two bakers would offer him fresh, warm *Brötchen* when he called upon her to tell the distressing tale of her stolen sons. The tale of an Eschlinsdorf girl turned witch who'd lured her darling boys into the enchanted forest to despoil their immortal souls with her depravity.

"But do not worry, dear woman," Ansgar imagined himself saying to the tearful mother. "For I shall venture into the perilous woods to rescue the lads. If I do not return within a week, you must send all the men of the town, well-armed, to help me defeat the witch. For if we do not destroy her now, her power will grow. She will come to steal the town's children in the night, as the witches of old did. She will pluck them from their beds like plump fruit; she will cook and eat them, skin, bones, and all."

The baker woman would believe him, of course, and with that, his plot to coerce the new witch-queen into assuming her Fate-given role would take a great leap toward its glorious climax.

* * *

Marga lifted the big copper pot from the hook over the fire and set in on the hearthstones to cool, as the recipe directed. Snail shells bobbed atop the sputtering brew. The aroma rising from the mud-colored mixture brought to mind the fetid alley behind Eschlinsdorf's tannery, a lane she'd sneaked down often to avoid the other townsfolk. Even the rats steered clear of Tanners' Alley. No doubt she'd have to pinch Felix's nostrils shut to get him to swallow the stuff.

She wiped her brow with the edge of her apron—rather, the witch's old apron. The witch's possessions were not hers—would never be hers. She wore them out of necessity only. As she moved across the overheated room to pour a cup of water, the skirts of the gray linen gown she'd borrowed from the wardrobe dragged along the floor, collecting dust and duck feathers. She needed to take up the hem, and she needed to sweep out the cottage, but not until after she gave Felix a dose. First things first, as her mother used to say long ago when they'd been a poor woodcutter's family, back when Marga had been happy to be called Gretel.

So much had changed since then. Every day, it seemed, things shifted by some degree, for good or for ill.

After gulping down two cups of tepid water, she opened the shutters and peeked into the side yard. A few lazy snowflakes tumbled down and stuck to brown blades of grass. The sky, a gray expanse of dull clouds, promised much more snow. She hoped Lukas would return soon. She missed him, and worse—she feared Felix might yield to death's invitation if his brother did not come back to forbid it. The boy had the air of someone who'd grown weary of fighting.

Before her worries could lead her mind farther down that dark path, the clopping of hooves reached her ears. She rushed to the door and yanked it open. Her stomach did somersaults as she stood on the doorstep and waited for the cart to roll to a stop.

"Whoa there," Lukas said to the horse.

He set down the reins, stood, and leapt to the ground. He patted the horse and said, "Well done, girl." Finally, he turned to face her. He spoke her name and a smile lit up his round face. For a moment, overcome with bliss, she couldn't move.

And then she ran. And she tripped over the too-long skirt and fell hard onto the frozen ground.

"Are you hurt?" Lukas helped her to her feet. Worry creased his brow.

"I'm fine." Her face grew hot with embarrassment. Looking down at her bodice, she tried to brush off the dirty snow. Her efforts only crushed it into a layer of grimy slush. *Stupid, too-long dress. So much for looking clean and comely.*

"Good. And Felix? How does he fare?"

"No better, I'm sorry to say. I've made more medicine, but it's cooling still. Come inside. He's sleeping, but your presence will be a comfort." She took his hand and led him toward the house.

"I regret that my return took so long," he said as they walked. "Some sort of creature was stalking us for a time. I heard it creeping through the brush, and the horse seemed to sense it as well. After a while, the horse made a long detour through a vast grove of silver trees with leaves like glass, which evidently made the thing give up the hunt."

"Thank *Himmel* you are safe," Marga said. She refused to entertain thoughts of what might have happened in the wild forest if the horse had been less canny, but a chill ran down her spine nonetheless.

Lukas opened the door, allowed her to enter first, and then followed. She stumbled over the excess fabric of her hem again. This time, his strong, certain grip kept her from falling onto the kitchen floor.

"That dress could use some altering, maybe," he said.

"I'm paying the price for my vanity with bruises. I wanted to look nice when you returned. If I'd been wise, I would have worn the filthy breeches until I had a chance to take this skirt up properly."

Near the door of the bedchamber, Lukas tugged her closer. He put his arms around her. "To me, you would look nice even if you wore a dusty flour sack."

"I could say the same of you." It was a silly reply, but it became hard to think when he held her so near. He smelled of the forest, flour, and faintly of cinnamon. She rested her hands on his back. The fabric of his cloak remained cool from the long journey. She glanced past him to the pot of steaming medicine. This was a good way to spend the waiting time.

Now that Lukas had returned, she felt even more at home in the gingerbread cottage. Like she could bide with him forever inside its walls, in spite of all that had happened there when she was a girl. How strange that was. But she would not spoil the moment by thinking on that. He looked down at her with his blue, blue eyes and made her heartbeat race.

"I thank you for the compliment, Fraulein Holzfäller." He leaned to kiss her smiling mouth. She stood on her toes to meet him. The press of his lips was gentle, comforting at first, but as the kiss continued, his hand slid up to cradle the back of her head and his mouth grew more eager.

Marga's knees weakened as she clutched the back of his cloak. Little stars exploded behind her closed eyes and her stomach fluttered, even as alarm bells sounded in her mind. Was the tingling she felt from magic? Had she somehow lured him to kiss her through enchantment, like one of the shameless, hungry nixes? By all the angels, she hoped not, for she didn't want to stop him from kissing her. She wanted to melt into him, to forget where she ended and he began.

Questions continued to intrude. How much danger was there in kissing Lukas? Could her desire for him destroy him and his pureness of heart?

Might she consume Lukas's soul, like the old witch had consumed the flesh of children?

She shoved him away and stepped back. He looked as if he'd been slapped.

"Forgive me," Lukas said. "I fear I forgot my manners." Shamefaced, he bowed his head.

Her whole body shook. She gripped handfuls of fabric at the sides of her skirt as she tried to gain control of her feelings. "You need not apologize. It is only that I do not trust myself. These powers that course within me ...they're growing. What if I harm you or cause you to act against your will? I do not know who or what I am anymore, Lukas. If I bring ruin upon my own soul, so be it. But to ruin a good man like you? That would be an unforgivable transgression."

"I kissed you because I wanted to. I chose to," Lukas said with conviction.

"How can you be certain?"

He closed the space between them, then took her hand and laid it on his chest. His heartbeat reverberated against her palm.

"I know it here. It is as true and real as every pulse of my heart, *Liebling*. It is love that draws me to you, not magic. Love that is good and full of light. Love that will make us better and stronger, not bring us to ruin."

From the bedchamber came the sound of Felix groaning.

"Come." Marga took Lukas by the hand and led him to his brother's side. Felix's skin was as white as snow but dotted with a scarlet rash. His cheeks were sunken so that his face looked almost skeletal.

Lukas gasped. He fell to his knees. "Dear *Gott* in heaven. He looks nigh unto death. I should have taken him back to town, to the doctor. If he dies, I will never forgive myself. And our *Mutti*..."

Marga rested a hand on his shoulder. Her chest ached

with sorrow. “I’m sorry. I’ve done everything I could think of. One minute, he was improving, and the next…”

“But you are not a doctor, Margarethe. Please do not blame yourself for not being able to heal him.”

“You could fetch the doctor now. The horse is still in the yard.” She could call the great buck again, if Lukas wanted, or wish for a dragon. A giant bat. Anything that might help Lukas bring the doctor quickly.

He shook his head and glanced up at her. “The doctor would never come here. You know this as well as I.”

She could not disagree with him. “We must keep trying to help him ourselves, then. I made new medicine. It should be ready now.”

“Hurry and bring it, please.” Still on his knees beside the bed, Lukas gently enfolded Felix’s hand between his own and closed his eyes.

Marga fled the room to the sound of Lukas’s fervent prayers. She hastened to the copper pot and scooped out half a teacup of the potion she’d brewed, the dose recommended by the book. Mindful not to spill a drop, she lifted her too-long skirt and hurried back into the bedchamber.

“Here. He must drink this as I say—oh, drat. I cannot remember the words.” She pressed the teacup into Lukas’s big hand. “Wait while I fetch the book.”

In seconds, she returned with the heavy red volume. She set it on the edge of the bed and knelt. Magic hummed under her skin like a swarm of tiny gnats that could not be swatted away. She wanted to read the strange poem because it might heal Felix—and she dreaded reading it because in doing so, she’d become more like the witch.

Lukas stood bent over his brother. Felix's eyelids were only half open, but when he saw the cup in Lukas's hand, he turned his head away.

"Felix," Lukas said sternly, "If you don't take this, you'll die. And if that is not threat enough to inspire you to swallow it, I promise you that I will thrash you soundly if you spit one drop onto the bedclothes."

Felix scowled. He said in a raspy voice, "I hate you. And witch or no, that woman is a dreadful cook."

"We cannot all be good cooks, brother." Lukas used one arm to help Felix sit up, and then he pressed the cup to Felix's lips.

Marga nodded to indicate her readiness to read, and Lukas said to his brother, "Drink."

Felix downed the liquid in a few slurps. While he drank, Marga whispered the words from the book. Someday soon, Felix might go before the town council and cite this incident as evidence of her wickedness, but the boy's life meant more to her than her reputation.

"Well done," Lukas said. "Now rest."

"You're bossier than *Mutti*. Give me water, I beg you."

Marga ran to the kitchen and brought back water, but Felix had already settled back against the pillows. He snored.

Lukas clutched his brother's hand while Marga watched his face for signs of improvement. The recipe claimed the potion worked "faste as a hare runneth," yet he remained moon-pale and red-speckled. Had she forgotten an ingredient? Had she misspoken the words of the poem? She cast a glance at Lukas. The worry she felt in her gut was the same worry she saw etched upon his face.

The baker took a step back from the bed and wrung his hands. "We must wait now, I suppose?"

Marga nodded. It felt like lying. The magic under her skin had ceased its prickling before Felix had swallowed the draught. She felt certain that she'd done something to make the medicine ineffective.

Lukas reached down and pulled her to her feet. He said, "I cannot bide here and do nothing. Give me a task, whatever is most urgent. I will pray as I work, but I cannot sit here helpless and watch."

"The horse needs attention, if it's still in the garden," Marga said. "And then perhaps you could put the flour into the shed to protect it from the weather."

"Thank you. Yes, these things I can do." He left the room quickly, as if prompt completion of the tasks might impress heaven and earn his brother's healing.

Marga stared at Felix as he slept. He looked ten years old, dangerously thin, and completely vulnerable. With all her might, she willed him to be well. But wishing for his healing had not worked before, and it would not work now.

Somehow, she had to save him. Not only for Lukas, whom she loved—*Himmel* help her, she could not deny it—but because Felix would be healthy and at home with his mother had she not led him to a danger-filled lake.

There had to be a way.

Perhaps the witch had left more books or journals somewhere in the cottage. Maybe, tucked away in a hiding place, there was some magical object with the power to end illness. Marga rushed from dresser to wardrobe, from chest to cupboard, turning out clothes and shoes, trinkets and tools, and leaving them scattered on floors and tables. She rifled through drawers and looked under the bed while Felix's breath rattled in his chest.

Far beneath the bed, pressed into the corner, a rectangular object sat swathed in shadows. On her belly, Marga inched across the floorboards until her fingers could grab the black wooden box. She slid it toward her. The wood vibrated in her grasp as if it contained a swarm of bees.

Magic. Strong, dangerous, and alluring. Magic within her connecting with the magic of the box.

Her pulse galloped and her stomach threatened to expel its contents—for she knew that to open the box meant to run headlong down the path toward becoming the very thing she did not want to be: the true witch of the gingerbread cottage. And there might be no turning back.

Twenty-Seven

Ansgar rested his stocking feet on a finely embroidered, cushioned footstool in front of a blazing fire. How he loved well-made stockings! And toes to wriggle inside them! Never again would he take any of his appendages for granted.

The widow Waldemar, a drab, frizzy-haired, fortyish matron, waddled to his side to present him with a tray holding a mug of soup and a thick slice of brown bread.

"You poor dear," she said for the tenth time.

If she said it once more, he'd nip her with his bill. But oh! He had teeth now. Never mind, then. He did not fancy tasting her saggy flesh.

She perched on the armchair facing his and eyed him with motherly concern. "I do wish you would let me summon the doctor."

When he'd arrived at her door after nightfall, nearly naked and oozing blood from countless abrasions, the woman had readily believed his tale of being attacked and robbed on the road between Eschlinsdorf and Hunzelfeld.

Thanks be to the gods, years of speaking only in quacks and hisses had not damaged his ability to charm and deceive.

Now, the woman prattled on about her past dealings with the town physician. Swirls of steam rose from the mug, and Ansgar inhaled the intoxicating scent of beef, onions, and potatoes. The grainy bread, slick with bacon fat, was a work of art. It seemed a century since he'd eaten well-cooked human fare. It was all he could do not to gobble it down like an animal. He gripped the spoon and forced himself to lift it to his lips in a gentlemanly fashion. The soup slipped down his throat like swallowed sunshine.

Belly warmed, he glanced at the woman. "You are too kind, Frau Waldemar. I assure you that I am on the mend and shall not require the physician's services. Why, I do believe that your healthful soup is curing the remainder of my ills as we speak." He offered a small, wobbly smile. He didn't want to look too recovered before he'd had a chance to fully abuse her hospitality.

"What good news! And how fortuitous that my late husband's clothes fit you so perfectly." Her droopy, hound-dog cheeks reddened as she gazed into the fire. Ansgar assumed she was remembering how he'd shown up on her doorstep wearing nothing but a pitiful look and a pine bough.

"As am I, dear woman. I only wish that the brigands had not taken my purse, so that I might pay you for your trouble and reimburse you for this fine suit." In truth, the brown ensemble was as unfashionable and plain as the widow. At least the moths had not nibbled holes into it.

"Well, I'm happy for some company, so I am," she said,

twisting the thin gold band on her finger. "Since my son ran off to join the army last spring, I have only myself to talk to most days."

"A fine young woman like you should consider marrying again."

She waved away the suggestion as if it were a fly. "Ach. I'm not so young. And there are few unmarried men of my age in Eschlinsdorf."

"Perhaps you'll meet a stranger from afar." Ansgar eyed her over the edge of the mug as he sipped the remaining broth, amused that with his steady gaze, he was able to make her blush deepen and spread from her cheeks to her throat.

He licked his lips and placed the mug back onto the tray. He poured out the full measure of his charm, moving from mild compliments to vigorous flirtation. Her caution melted like butter on a hot griddle. If he'd had a timepiece, he would have kept track of the number of minutes it took to lure the widow into his embrace. And to think, he'd had so little practice wooing women, having wed Truda when he was hardly more than a boy. It felt good to wield a power of which he'd been previously unaware.

It felt most excellent to inhabit the skin of a man.

He'd enjoy a brief lark with the widow and then turn his attention to more serious matters, like starting a rumor about the odd, almost simultaneous disappearances of a suspected witch and two of the town's virtuous young bakers.

* * *

A long, tense night of watching and praying over Felix gave way to morning—and Marga saw that the boy still breathed. His face remained ashen and gaunt, yet his sleep seemed more peaceful than before. For a moment, hope sprang up in her heart. If Felix's health was improving, she could leave the powerful book in its box under the bed. She had put it back where she'd found it, fully expecting to need to retrieve it before daybreak. Fully expecting to have to wield the strong magic that would be his salvation and her sure ruin. Now, perhaps she'd never have to touch the box again—other than to toss it into a bonfire.

But then, with Lukas standing close beside her, she drew the bedclothes back from Felix's arm. She gasped and grabbed onto Lukas's arm. The cullberfish's poison had etched dark stripes on Felix's skin. Like thin vines, they snaked from his wrist to his shoulder.

Lukas cringed. "This is bad. Very bad. I must take him home without delay. The doctor might be able to amputate the arm and save him. If not, if he's going to die, he should die at home. Our mother should have the chance to say goodbye to him."

"I found something," Marga confessed. "A box with a special book inside. I think I can cure him with it."

He turned toward her. "There is something you're not saying."

Unable to bear the intensity of his searching gaze, she stared down at her frayed hem. "This magic is different. More potent. It would mean—"

"It would mean you'd endanger your immortal soul. No, Margarethe. You cannot." Gently, he placed his fingers under her chin and coaxed her to look up at him once more. "You must not."

"It is probably already too late for me to escape that fate. If I am doomed to slip into wickedness, let me do this one last good thing for Felix, and for you. For your mother." She offered without reservation. This, she thought, must be what it means to truly love someone—to be willing to plunge into calamity in order to save them from suffering. While Lukas might grieve the loss of her for a brief time, he'd mourn for his little brother, blood of his blood, for the rest of his earthly life.

Lukas shook his head. "No. A thousand times *no*. Help me wrap him in the blankets and get him onto the wagon."

"The trip would be too much for him, I think, with all the jostling and bumping. And how will you cross the lake? The nixes will tempt you, and there's the cullberfish, and who knows what else—"

"Good *Himmel*!" Lukas threw his hands into the air in frustration. "What am I to do then, woman? I cannot, I will not allow you to sacrifice yourself!"

Tears filled Marga's eyes. She wrapped her arms tightly about herself as if the gesture might help contain her emotions.

"I'm sorry, *Liebling*. I should not have shouted," Lukas said softly. "Forgive me?"

"Take. The arm. Off," Felix muttered, eyes shut. "Get. The axe."

Marga and Lukas locked eyes. An unspoken question passed between them. Lukas nodded almost imperceptibly.

"No, Lukas. I don't think I can do such a thing," Marga said in a shaky voice.

Lukas's face went almost as pale as his brother's. "I think we must. I saw it done once, when I was twelve or thirteen. The doctor grabbed me off the street. He was in urgent need of help with a patient, and I was too shy to refuse."

Marga felt like all her bones had turned to jelly. She wanted to beg him to reconsider. If she could do the magic properly, Felix would keep both arms. Within days, he could be back at the bakery, living as if he'd never been bitten by a lake monster.

"Lukas, please let me try the magic." She reached out to grasp his wrist. "Please."

"Axe," croaked Felix. "Not magic. Hurry."

"We should do as he wishes. It is his life, his arm," Lukas said.

"You, Lukas. Do it," Felix said.

Outvoted and weary, Marga surrendered to the brothers' request. "Tell me what you need from me."

"Towels. Rags. Hot water. Herbs that staunch bleeding," Lukas said, covering his brother up to the neck again. "I'll fetch the axe."

He rushed out of the bedchamber. Marga started to follow, but hesitated. She turned and eyed the black wooden box she'd left on the dresser. Her heart beat so hard she thought it might burst.

Although Felix despised the idea, she had to try the magic. To permit Lukas to chop off his brother's arm would be too terrible—and would probably result in the boy's demise. She ran to the box and opened the hinged lid. The wood felt warm, like a living thing. On top of its contents, as evidence that the old witch had known the future, sat a piece of creased parchment with Felix's name scrawled upon it. Inside were the words of a spell to eradicate the monster's poison from his body.

According to the note, all she had to do was recite what was written. Her innate power would complete the task. It seemed too simple, really. Still, she shuddered with fear and her stomach clenched. Was this the right thing to do? Was it not said that the easy path was always paved with destruction?

"Hurry, brother," Felix mumbled. "I hear wings. Death's wings. He comes."

She had no more time to hesitate.

Marga lifted the parchment from the box and began to read aloud. The bedchamber swirled with magic, palpable as a breeze. The candles flickered. Her ears rang. A loud buzzing filled her body, the room. Felix cried out as if stabbed, and then everything went dark as midnight as Marga's knees gave out and she collapsed onto the floor.

The last thing she heard was Lukas calling her name.

Twenty-Eight

Ansgar ran his hands through his freshly trimmed, white-blond hair as he stood on the front doorstep of a three-story, brick house. The scent of fresh bread emanated from the bakery next door, making his stomach rumble. He tapped his foot as he waited for someone to respond to his violent use of the brass doorknocker. In spite of the blue sky overhead and the cheerful chirping of birds in the well-tended shrubberies, the lengthy delay was souring his fine mood.

He'd spent a leisurely morning in the company of Frau Waldemar before strolling across town to the Beckmann residence. Frau W. had proved to be a woman of myriad talents, including barbering skills. He almost wished he might have stayed with her longer. Alas, his obligations to the Igelwald were not yet fulfilled. Work first, pleasure after, as a wise and boring sage once said.

A servant girl no older than ten opened the door and

stared at him as if he were a trespassing leper. "What do you want?"

Chin held high, Ansgar asked, "Have you no manners, child?"

She sneered, undaunted. "Housekeeper's on an errand. Everyone else is at the bakery. I'm here to clean, not answer doors for the likes of you."

He stalked away without thanking the brat.

Above the door of the shop next door hung a painted sign: BÄCKEREI HORST BECKMANN. A stout woman wearing a ruffled cap and a dress of somber blue stepped outside. She paused as the door shut behind her, and with a lace-edged handkerchief, she dabbed her nose. She might have been pretty in her youth. Now, her face bore countless creases and her figure resembled a lumpy sculpture made from over-risen dough. Her shoulders slumped as if she'd carried too much for too long, burdens both physical and spiritual in nature.

"I beg your pardon, but might you be Frau Beckmann?" Ansgar asked as he strode toward the woman.

With a nod, she confirmed his suspicion. "Is it bread you've come for, sir? We're out of cake for the day."

"Your wares smell delightful, and I am indeed tempted, but I regret to say that I have come to speak to you about something far less pleasant than bread. I bear tidings of your sons, Frau Beckmann."

The woman's face betrayed no emotion as she summoned him to follow. He trailed behind her, mentally modifying the speech he'd composed. He'd imagined that his announcement would provoke sobbing or swooning, but this mother of bakers was as hard-crusted as a cheap loaf. He could only hope that Frau Beckmann's crust concealed either strong maternal possessiveness or strict religiosity—traits he could play upon easily.

She marched him into the house and through the spotless entrance hall, not pausing for him to remove his overcoat. When they entered a parlor full of heavy, dark furniture, she pointed to a dull brown horsehair sofa.

"Take a seat, Herr...?"

"Steuben. Ansgar Steuben." His true name felt like a lie. It had been ages since he'd been simply Ansgar Steuben. Too long since he'd been a boy smitten with a beautiful young woman in an apothecary's shop. How many years had passed between then and now? As a duck, he'd quite lost track of time. None of that mattered at the moment. He focused on the task at hand.

The woman settled into a green velvet armchair, her back straight as a board. She rang a brass bell and called for coffee to be served.

Folding her hands in her wide lap, Frau Beckmann said, "I am a busy woman, Herr Steuben, and I loathe idle chatter. Say what you've come to say and let us be done with it."

"I arrived in town yesterday after being robbed on the road by a band of brigands," he began, in case the widow repeated his earlier tale. "I fell to the mercy of good Frau Waldemar. It was she who sent me to your door. She begged me to speak to you of what I have witnessed. You know of her, do you not?"

"Yes, yes. Luisa's a cousin of mine. Get on with it, please."

"Yes, well. While lost in the forest, I happened upon a most peculiar sight: a cottage built of cake and candy. Yet that is not the strangest thing I beheld. No, indeed. As I watched from a distance, I saw a woman emerge. Two young men followed her, faces dazed as if they'd been ensorcelled. The woman, a diminutive, dark-haired creature, tugged the men along on a silver chain, and commanded them to cut up firewood and hang her washing. They obeyed without hesitation, moving like sleepwalkers to complete their tasks."

Frau Beckmann leaned forward in her chair. The color drained from her face. "My sons left word that they were going to aid a cousin in Hezenbruch. Nevertheless, would you describe the men you saw?"

"I took them for brothers, although one was much taller than the other. Unusually tall, in fact. Both were blond and fair skinned. The shorter one, who could not yet have attained twenty years of age, looked most unwell. And the witch—for I do not doubt for a moment that the creature was a witch—said lewd and terrible things to the tall man, things which I shall not repeat to a lady."

Her face scrunched up as if she'd swallowed a nasty dose of castor oil. "Margarethe Holzfäller. The little trollop."

"You know this woman?"

"She lived here in Eschlinsdorf until recently. I'm not one for gossip, but there were rumors about her aplenty. Too many to ignore. They say she'd been apprenticed to the witch of the woods when she was a tiny *Mädchen*, until one day she burned the old hag alive to steal her power. Her brother claimed the girl had repented, but no one in town trusted her. She had an air about her, something not right.

Wandered about at night, especially at the full of the moon. I suppose she's been scheming all along, waiting to lure my boys away. Oh, *Gott*, have mercy." A tear glinted in the corner of her left eye. The woman's crust appeared to be cracking.

Ansgar stood and laid a hand over his heart. "Something must be done, Frau Beckmann. Your sons must be brought home, rescued without delay. And this Holzfäller woman cannot be allowed to continue to dwell in the Igelwald—for I do not doubt that she'll return to steal more innocent young men to beguile and ruin. After that, who knows? She might develop an appetite for children, as witches do."

Hands folded as if in prayer, the woman fixed her gaze on her guest. Her staid demeanor had vanished. She quaked like a frightened pup. Ansgar half expected her to fall to her knees and weep upon his shoes. "Can you help, Herr Steuben? Can you save my sons?"

He paced with slow steps, like the question's gravity encumbered his movement. "Perhaps. I have studied a number of books on the subject of eradicating witches. But it would put me in grave danger. Why, my own dear mother would take to her bed in despair if she knew I gave a moment's thought to undertaking such a perilous errand." Gods above, he enjoyed crafting a good lie.

"I'll pay you well. Your mother need never know, may *Himmel* bless her soul. You'd surely succeed, a clever fellow like you. Margarethe Holzfäller is just a small thing. A mere gnat."

"A gnat armed with magic is as dangerous as a fire-breathing dragon, my good woman. No, now that I have considered it, I do not think it prudent for me to challenge this witch. Is there not a minister in town you might send?"

The woman scowled. "Pastor Günter is as skittish as a calf and too frail to walk a mile. He's in no way fit to bring down Satan's mistress."

Ansgar gazed up at a portrait above the mantel, a well-executed oil painting of the family and a fat dog. Among the many siblings, he recognized Lukas and Felix.

"These are your children? Ah, my family was large once. My mother still mourns the loss of my four brothers. The pain of losing one's children is worse than death, she says. Poor *Mutti* is but a shadow of her former self now."

Frau Beckmann's face paled. Her chin wobbled. "Please. You must help me. I beg you. I will give you all I have saved, and all of the family jewelry. The jewels are old. Worth a fortune."

Ansgar returned to his seat. "You're too generous. I would not think of robbing you of your money and heirlooms. Allow me a few hours to think upon it. The road to suffering is paved with rash decisions, as dear *Mutti* used to say."

A uniformed, gray-haired maid brought in a tray of coffee and rolls and set it on the small table between Ansgar and Frau Beckmann. The bakers' mother poured some of the dark brew into a cup. It rattled on its saucer as she handed it to her guest. He'd done well preying on her secret fears.

Frau Beckmann smiled feebly. "Take refreshment, Herr Steuben, and then, if it pleases you, you may go upstairs to my late husband's library. It is a good, quiet place to think and pray."

"Thank you, madam." Ansgar sipped the bitter liquid. The bakers must be wealthy indeed to be able to afford coffee of such high quality. He wondered exactly how much money the Frau might offer him if he continued to hesitate—not that he needed it. There were chests of gems hidden under the floors of the gingerbread cottage and buried beneath Truda's shed, enough treasure to sustain even a wastrel three hundred years or more.

He constructed yet another plan. He would go to the husband's library, take a brief nap, and then inform Frau Beckmann that her motherly pleas had moved his heart. He would vow to attempt to rescue her sons. She'd weep, of course, and praise him for his kindness and courage. She'd order the cook to make his favorite foods for dinner, and once sated, he'd appropriate the Beckmann family's finest horse.

Into the Igelwald he'd ride, proud and princely, toward the nixes' lake. And why should he not be proud? Was he not a history-maker? Because of his clever machinations, the reign of Queen Gretel was about to begin.

Twenty-Nine

Marga lay on the hard floor, unable to speak or move. The back of her head throbbed, and she hadn't the strength to open her eyes. She must have fallen, but could not recall how or why.

"What have you done, *Liebling*?" she heard Lukas say.

She felt the baker's arms slide beneath her body, felt herself lifted up. His bread and wood smoke scent made her feel safe. She hovered between unconsciousness and awareness as he lowered her onto the bed and tucked blankets around her.

"Brother," she heard Felix say from nearby. "Where am I?"

"I'm here, Felix. How are you?" Lukas replied.

"I feel...I feel better. Much better," Felix said slowly. "Dear *Gott*! My arm! It's vanished!" A strange keening filled the room.

"It cannot be possible," Lukas said.

Marga tried harder to open her eyes and sit up, but weakness overpowered her. All she could do was panic inside her mind. She remembered trying to heal Felix's arm. What had happened? How had the magic gone so awry?

"The witch! She took it with her foul spells! She must pay for this!"

"Calm yourself, brother. It was the axe or magic—or death. If Margarethe chose magic, it was because she saw no other way to save you." He paused for a moment, and then she heard him say, "No bleeding at all. Not even a scar. Surely this was for the best."

"You only say that because she has bewitched you. Where is that axe? Give it to me. You didn't save me from her wickedness, but I'll save you, by *Gott*. I'll fell her like a tree."

"Lie down, brother. You need rest. We will speak of this later."

"Later? After she takes my other arm? After she tires of toying with you and changes you into a toad? No, I will deal with her now, before she has the chance to ruin anyone else's life with her deviltry." Felix sounded frantic. Unhinged.

"Felix, please—"

"I need the axe and my clothes."

"Sit down and I will fetch them."

"I will not sit!"

"Then fetch them yourself. They're on the clothesline in the garden. I don't know where the axe is. I was just searching for it—at your request, if you do not remember—so *I* could chop off the arm."

"Fine. I'll find it. You stay here and make sure the witch doesn't get away. Prove to me she hasn't already made you her pet."

Felix's uneven footsteps resounded and then faded.

"Margarethe, wake up," Lukas said, shaking her by the shoulders. "Get up. You must find somewhere to hide, quickly. Felix is out of his mind with rage. He means to kill you."

With great effort, Marga forced her eyes open. Lukas put his arm around her back and helped her sit up.

"Margarethe, you have to go now. He thinks you've bewitched me. I must pretend to help him or he might come after me as well, mad as he is. If he doesn't find the axe, he'll find something to use as a weapon."

She tried to move her legs to the edge of the bed, but they felt leaden. She blamed the use of magic more than the bump to her head. "I'm so weak. I don't think I can walk."

Lukas stepped away from her bedside, toward the damaged wall he'd clumsily boarded up with planks torn from the shed. With a grunt, he shoved the dresser aside that helped hold the planks in place, and then he tossed the boards to the floor.

"I'll take you out this way. Less chance that Felix will see us," he said as he returned to the bed and scooped her into his arms. Clutching her to his chest, he climbed over the low ledge of crumbling gingerbread. Once outside, he took off running.

Swiftly, Lukas bore Marga across the herb garden and through the back gate. As the forest closed around them, the scent of pines and moldering leaves filled Marga's nose. Her body jostled against Lukas's midsection as he charged onward. She clung with both hands to the fabric of the cloak he still wore. The events of the last few hours blurred together: his return, the kiss, the spell, Felix's arm disappearing and his vengeful rage...

Lukas charged through the woods, moving almost as swiftly as the great buck had. After five or ten minutes, he stopped. Before them, partly obscured by vines and brush, gaped the mouth of a cave.

"This could do as a hiding place," Lukas said as he set her on her feet. He breathed hard, his exhalations forming miniature clouds.

Marga swayed a little and grabbed his arm for support. Their eyes met. Fear and regret mingled in his gaze.

"I'm sorry. I should not have tried the magic," Marga said.

"You saved him. The axe would have been the death of him, no matter who did the cutting."

"But I have ruined us. All of us. His arm is gone. He'll go and tell—"

Lukas cupped her cheek with his palm. "Nothing is ruined. You acted out of mercy. Now, please, you must hide here until I calm Felix. Do not go far inside." He shrugged out of the jacket he wore under his cloak and draped it over her shoulders. "If you must flee, this won't trip you at least. Now, try to stay warm. And don't worry, *Liebling*, I'll talk sense into the boy. If all else fails, I could beat him in a fight —although I do not wish to harm him."

Marga nodded. His compassion was one of the things that had won her heart. Felix had already suffered too much. The boy was scared, not a monster.

"Take this, too," Lukas said. He took a pocketknife out

of the pocket of his trousers and pressed it into her hand. "Not much protection against wild beasts, but something."

Impulsively, she pulled Lukas close. Answering her unspoken plea, he leaned down and claimed her mouth with his. She encircled his waist with her arms as his hands pressed firmly against her shoulder blades and brought her closer. Heat spread throughout her body. Her knees trembled behind her skirts. She would have wanted this moment to last forever, were it not for the trouble with Felix.

Felix's voice echoed through the woods. "Lukas! Brother! Are you there?"

Lukas stepped out of Marga's embrace and shouted into the trees, "I'm here! Looking for the girl. She ran off when I turned my back, and now I've lost her trail."

"Go," Marga said, pushing him away. "I'll be fine." Already, she felt the loss of him. Already, she missed him.

Lukas nodded. He hurried in the direction from which Felix's voice had come.

Marga pushed decayed branches and dried vines away from the cave's mouth. Now, her smallness proved to be a blessing, for she was able to climb into the narrow hole with ease. The air inside the cave was damp, heavy with the scent of earth and mushrooms. She ran her fingertips along the dark walls and took a few cautious steps. She prayed she'd not meet any wild animals as she crept deeper into the blackness.

Finally, she stopped and sat on a little ledge of rock that jutted from the wall. She buttoned Lukas's jacket, and in the stillness, took account of her weary body. Her head hurt from her fall, as did one elbow. The dull buzz of power still reverberated within her bones, reminding her of the path she had chosen, the destiny she had stepped into.

Her heartbeat skipped as she remembered Lukas's kiss. Her mouth still tasted of his. Her hands ached to touch him again.

Lukas had forgiven her for working the magic that took Felix's arm. He loved her. Of these two things, she was sure. Everything else—her identity, her future, her place in the world—seemed as unpredictable as next month's weather.

She wrapped her arms around herself and waited for her beloved baker's strong voice to call her out into the daylight. Hours passed. She dozed and awoke a dozen times. Outside the cave, an owl hooted mournfully, and then, in time, the twittering of birds replaced the owl's cries.

She waited, and as she waited, she used Lukas's knife to hack three inches of excess fabric from the bottom of her skirt. The job was not well done, but she wouldn't trip over her hem anymore once she emerged from the cave.

She waited more. Slept. Prayed.

The owl called out again, and then the day birds sang.

Nausea rose from her stomach to her throat.

Lukas was not coming back.

Willingly or unwillingly, he'd left her to her own devices. Like Hansel had.

As she inched her way out of the mine, an image formed in her head: the picture of a hideous old hag bent over a blackened kettle, alone in a cottage made of crumbling gingerbread. A picture of herself, doomed to spend the rest of her life in the company of mice and spiders, apart from the man she loved.

Lukas *could not* come back. She had always known that his family needed him, and now that Felix had only one arm, they'd need him all the more to keep the bakery running. He was a good man, and he had made the best choice. She could not forgive him, for he had done nothing wrong.

She walked back to the cottage slowly, hardly noticing the squirrels and birds that crept close to watch her with reverent, curious gazes.

Thirty

In the shifting shadows of late afternoon, Ansgar stood on the lakeshore and shook his head like a sodden sheepdog. He picked water weeds off his coat, and swore profusely when he observed the state of his fine leather shoes. If only he'd had enough remaining magic to command his clothes to dry...but he had not an iota to spare. Days or weeks might pass before he'd be strong enough to move even a wisp of steam.

Upon his recent arrival at the lake, the nixes had instantly sensed his vulnerability. His jaw clenched as he remembered their wide-eyed duplicity. He hated them almost as much as he hated little Gretel.

The selfish wenches had bargained hard. During his years as a duck, he'd observed their antics daily, and therefore knew better than to yield to their requests for kisses. Death by drowning did not appeal in the least to a former waterfowl. Instead, in exchange for safe passage across the lake, he was forced to give them a year of his life *and* the exquisite gold watch Frau Beckmann had tucked into his waistcoat pocket.

Much use the asinine water faeries would have for a well-crafted timepiece.

At least they'd made quick work of tugging him across the water, warding off the cullberfish, fire-frogs, and fanged turtles.

Now, Ansgar plodded across the squishy sand in his squelchy shoes. He passed an old, abandoned boat swathed with weeds, its oars neatly crossed in its bow. He'd spent many nights there as a duck, snuggled down and hidden from predators, but he'd forgotten its existence until now. It might prove useful if ever he needed to cross the lake again.

He walked onward, fury at the nixes giving way to brooding. Eager to avoid faerie traps and hungry wild animals, he paid attention to every sound and scent as he left the shore and entered a stand of old oaks.

He hadn't walked a quarter mile when he heard the snap of twigs and the swish of branches. Someone was approaching at a rapid pace. Someone stupid enough to barrel through the dangerous Igelwald with all the grace of a bee-stung bull.

The incautious traveler spoke and was answered. So, there were two ignoramuses. Grand. They'd make fine sport for the faerie-blooded boars or lusty tree nymphs. He almost wished he had time to watch their demises.

"Slow down, Felix," one of them said as Ansgar ducked behind a broad tree trunk. "You never move so fast when it's time to make the bread."

"Well, we'd be home already if you hadn't spooked the horse and made it run off, brother," another man replied.

Then Ansgar's depraved heart sang. These voices he knew.

The Beckmann brothers had come to him. What good fortune! He reworked his plans in light of this stroke of luck. His new strategy brought a wicked smile to his lips.

"Hello there," Ansgar called as he stepped out of his hiding place. "Are you good gentlemen lost?"

"Perhaps," Felix said.

"No," Lukas said at the same time.

Ansgar strode toward the brothers, stopping when within an arm's length of them. He gave a courteous bow, and hoped the forest shadows concealed his damp state. "Ansgar Steuben, dauntless surveyor of the Igelwald, at your service. Might I be of assistance, gentleman? You seem to be in some distress."

Young Felix's smile was welcoming. Trusting. "We're Felix and Lukas Beckmann. We're going home to Eschlinsdorf, or trying to. You wouldn't happen to know if we're headed in the right direction?"

"I know where we are," Lukas said crossly. "The lake is just over the next hill."

"Your estimation is correct, sir," Ansgar said. "Have you a boat waiting? To attempt to swim across that particular lake would be the worst sort of folly. Its waters teem with deadly creatures. But you have the look of seasoned travelers, so of course you must already be aware of the forest's many dangers."

Felix rolled his eyes. "We know, believe me."

"Nevertheless, perhaps I might offer you some guidance," Ansgar said.

"No need, thank you. We'll find a way to cross," Lukas said.

"Why must you be so stubborn?" Felix said to his brother before angling his body toward Ansgar. "Do you have a boat, sir? I'd be grateful for the use of it, even if my dolt of a brother would rather swim. Some of us have only one arm, you see." He moved the edge of his cloak to reveal a blood-stained shirt missing a sleeve.

Ansgar laid a hand on his heart and widened his eyes in mock surprise. "Gracious *Himmel*! How did this happen? Let me hazard a guess. You ran away to war, seeking adventure and riches, and lost your limb in a fierce battle."

"More like I was bitten by a vicious lake monster and then bespelled by a cunning witch," Felix said.

Ansgar's pretend gasp of astonishment came out too much like a quack. "Surely not here in the Igelwald! The witch of this forest has been dead these last thirteen years. Destroyed by fire, or so the tale says."

Felix leaned close as if confiding a secret. "A new one's taken her place. She's been living in the old hag's gingerbread house. She's more evil than—"

Lukas grabbed Felix's shoulder from behind. "Felix, stop. That isn't true. She—"

"You poor boy," Ansgar interrupted, shaking his head sympathetically. "Please. You simply must take my boat. You have suffered enough. You need home and hearth, as soon as possible. The care of a wife or sweetheart."

"You see, brother? This gentleman insists," Felix said. "I need to get home. I haven't much strength left."

Lukas threw his hands up in surrender. "Fine. Thank you for your offer, sir. We cannot pay you now, but if you call at the bakery in Eschlinsdorf at your convenience—"

"Do not fret over such trivialities," Ansgar said in a saintly tone. "I will reap my rewards in the next life. Now, follow me. Hurry, for night falls fast in the forest."

Ansgar led the brothers to the abandoned boat. "I covered it with weeds to safeguard it from thieves," he lied. Arms crossed and damp shoes planted firmly, he spent a few minutes watching the brothers tear vines and weeds off the boat. The last thing he wanted was to further sully his clothes. Finally, he said, "Well, I'll leave you to your task, as I must return to my camp before dark. Good fortune to you both."

"Thank you," the brothers replied.

"A word of advice," Ansgar said as he started to walk away. "The nixes of the lake will try to entice you into the water. Stuff your ears with cattail fluff so you cannot hear their songs and wheedling. Be thankful that the boat is made of rare silver oak wood. They cannot touch it and live. Indeed, none of the creatures of the lake will dare to come near this vessel."

As much as it served his plans, Ansgar cringed inside at the thought of giving the priceless, magic-infused boat to the dimwitted bakers. Alas, it had to be done in order to advance his grand scheme. He smiled, imagining how Frau Beckmann would react when her maimed son returned home with his tale of the Igelwald's newest witch. She'd have the townsfolk up in arms before the clock in the square tolled midnight.

Praising his favorite gods, Ansgar hurried into the trees, away from the sound of Lukas and Felix arguing about the best way to transport the heavy boat to the water's edge. He took note of the sun's position, using it as a compass, and then directed his feet toward the gingerbread cottage.

Thirty-One

Morning light trickled through the cottage's candy windowpanes. If Lukas had been sitting beside her at the table, Marga would have pointed out the pale puddles of color, and he would have called them pretty. But she was alone, so she wept.

She mourned for everything she had lost: her comfortable home in Eschlinsdorf, her father, and even her exasperating, runaway brother Hansel. She wept for the loss of her blamelessness, and for the loss of the virtuous baker she'd had the audacity to love. She even shed a tear or two for the strange white duck who'd been her sole companion for a time.

When she sensed that it was midday, she dried her face with her sleeve, and then rose and stoked the fire. A sudden, raw hunger gripped her belly, so she filled the copper pot with water and poured in some dried beans from a sack she'd found stuffed behind the witch's many bottles of spices. She tossed in pinches of herbs and kept watch until the mixture bubbled. The place behind her breastbone, so recently full of joy and love for Lukas, felt vacant and sore. At least cooking occupied some of her time.

So much empty time loomed in front of her.

She did not dare to believe Lukas would ever return.

The knock on the door came as a thud on the thick cake. Dull as it was, the sound startled her. Hope leapt in her heart. Could it be Lukas?

"Is anyone at home?" a man said from outside. The voice was not the baker's. She ought to have known better than to have imagined it might be, even for a second. The visitor continued, "Hello? I mean no harm, I assure you. I've been lost in the forest and saw the smoke from your chimney."

"Please go away," Marga shouted toward the door. She had no desire to play hostess, especially not to a stranger. She couldn't even be sure the caller was human. Many kinds of faerie folk loved to trick, trap, or eat humans. Surely some of that ilk called the Igelwald home.

"I would go elsewhere, but I cannot walk another step. I fear I ate some poisonous mushrooms. My stomach pains me terribly, Fraulein." The man moaned before adding in a hoarse voice, "Have mercy, I beg you."

Too well did she remember her childhood experience of being lost in the forest and in dire need of help. Empathy overshadowed fear, and she rose from her chair to go to the door. If she did perish at the stranger's hand, at least she would die doing what was right and good—before her dealings with magic had a chance to render her forever cold and heartless.

She lifted the latch and pulled the door open. A well-dressed gentleman crouched on the doorstep. His ashen face glistened with sweat as he clutched his belly.

"You are…an angel of *Gott*," he said, peering up at her.

It was impossible to guess his age. He was older than she, but not yet elderly. His abundant, straight hair was the color of the palest corn silk, except for a streak of black growing from his widow's peak.

Marga bent and put an arm around the man, thankful he was of average size. With a grunt, she hauled him to his feet. Together, they hobbled to the settle. He lay down upon it and half sighed, half sobbed.

"I will find something to counteract the poison and settle your stomach," she said as she removed his damp shoes. The weedy, muddy smell of the lakeside wafted up from them. "In the meantime, try to remain still and rest."

The man shut his eyes. "You are indeed an angel, Fraulein."

There was something familiar about this visitor, Marga thought as she consulted the herbal remedy book. His dark, beady eyes and that tuft of black hair reminded her of…she could not think who. If he had eaten poisonous mushrooms, she hadn't time to speculate. She flipped through the book's thin pages until she found "tisane aginst poisonus mushroomes eaten."

In accordance with the recipe, she grabbed bottles of dried milk thistle, peony root, thyme, and something labeled "foxbone." She measured the leaves and powders into a bowl and added hot water. Her hands tingled as she mixed everything together. The magic. It was always with her now. She felt it in the air and her bones, like tiny pricks of pins but almost pleasant.

She did not want it. After the man left, she'd search the books for a way to rid herself of it. But as surely as she knew her name, she knew she'd never find a way to purge herself of the magic. She and it were wed, joined together until death. Or longer.

While the tea steeped and filled the air with a spicy, herbaceous aroma, Marga eyed the man across the room. His high-quality clothing and fine leather shoes were not new, but must have once cost a fortune. He spoke like a gentleman of intelligence, yet he was unwise in the ways of the wood—or he would not have eaten poisonous mushrooms and wandered to her door.

Who was he, and what could have driven him into a forest everyone knew was dangerous? An irresistible lover's tryst? A faerie's call? Enemies in pursuit?

The man groaned as she strained the tea through a piece of cloth, into a mug. When the task was done, she hastened to his side, set the steaming drink on the floor, and helped him sit up.

"This is quite hot, but try to take little sips." She picked up the mug and handed it to him, careful not to spill its contents.

"Thank you." His nose wrinkled as he sampled the tisane, but soon he'd gulped down half.

"Is it bitter?" Marga asked.

"Not so bad...if you have a fondness for imbibing horse liniment." Pinching his nostrils closed, he swallowed what remained.

"I'll add a little honey to the next dose. I should have thought of it before." She had so much honey now. Jars and jars of honey that Lukas had brought, for the gingerbread he'd never bake.

The man smiled faintly. "I must say, I feel better already, Fraulein."

Marga lifted the mug from his grasp. "I don't know if you're being truthful or lying to avoid another dose. You should try to sleep now."

"Sleep is the best medicine. That is what my dear grandmother used to say, may *Gott* rest her soul. You do remind me of her."

With a sinking feeling, Marga remembered how her hair had changed since she'd come to live in the gingerbread cottage. Absently, she touched the unraveling bun of hair on the back of her head. Had the magic she'd done for Felix whitened her hair completely? Did she look a hundred years old now?

The man cleared his throat. "Not that you resemble her in appearance. But in kindness, wisdom, and skill."

"You hardly know me, sir."

"Nonsense. I am a great judge of character. Now, I shall endeavor to be an exemplary patient and take the rest you prescribed." He lay back down on the settle and crossed his long, white hands on his chest.

Soon, he snored lightly. Marga stirred the pot of beans over the crackling fire. She wished she'd asked his name. Perhaps then she could have figured out if they'd met on another occasion. *Himmel*, she hoped he wasn't one of Hansel's disreputable acquaintances. It would not have surprised her. What was the old saying? *Polished brass can shine brighter than tarnished gold*. The man seemed a little too shiny to be trusted.

Night fell. Marga ladled soup into a bowl and sat at the hearthside. The beans were still crunchy and she'd over-seasoned the broth, but she ate every bit of it. She was hungry, so hungry since she'd worked the magic that had "cured" Felix. She did not want to consider what it might mean. Or what it could lead to.

She set the bowl on the floor and leafed through the remedy book. Not ten minutes passed before she nodded off in the chair. Her sleep brought vivid dreams. In them, she feasted on fresh bread. She danced with Lukas, a wedding dance under a starry sky. Next, she dreamed of the duck she'd nursed back to health. The white bird waddled onto the doorstep and pecked at the cake door until crumbs covered its webbed feet like shoes. When she opened the door, it made its way to the hearth and settled down to sleep. This time, she knew, the duck would stay.

Ansgar awoke with an aching back and cramped legs. A rickety old wooden settle was no place for a grown man to sleep. He considered moving to the bedchamber. He remembered well the soft, thick mattresses of Truda's beds. No, he couldn't be so bold in a "stranger's" house. This game required cautious and calculated moves.

Gretel slept slouched down in the chair beside the dying fire. How young and small she looked there, in spite of her silver-streaked hair and wrinkled visage. How vulnerable. Her appearance in no way alluded to the fact that she was the powerful sorceress who'd soon rule the Igelwald.

Ansgar stood and stretched. He crept to the hanging pot and helped himself to the soup, mindful not to wake Gretel. His magic, infinitesimal as it was, had protected him from any harm the girl's remedy might have wrought, and now he longed for food, even rustic peasant food such as she'd prepared from her limited resources. Almost anything would be better than the fare he'd eaten as a duck. How had he ever found grubs and tadpoles delicious?

Cradling the bowl in one hand, he spooned a scorching bite into his mouth and sat back down on the settle. The soup was atrocious, but he forced himself to swallow it. One had to keep up one's strength when one was steering the course of history.

The oafish baker Lukas would come back sooner or later, for he was a lovesick fool. He'd charge in like a flour-covered hero, determined to save a girl more than capable of saving herself. The question was whether Lukas would reach the cottage before or after the arrival of an angry mob bent on killing the witch who'd maimed Felix. In either case, there would be heartbreak, magic, fighting, and all sorts of dramatics.

By the gods, this was going to be fun. He only wished Truda were by his side to witness the spectacle.

Truda, whom he had betrayed.

Truda, who had turned him into a miserable duck for his sins.

As black as his heart was, he would never stop loving that witch.

Thirty-Two

Marga dried a crockery bowl as she stared through the candy pane. The snow was falling fast, in flakes as big as acorns. At the edges of the garden, the trees were garbed in the cold, white garments of winter. Had Christmas already come and gone? She knew neither the day of the week nor the name of the month. She had not thought to ask her visitor, who called himself Herr Steuben, for the date.

Although he'd come to the cottage wracked with illness, Herr Steuben had declared himself fit after one day's rest. He'd insisted on helping with chores, fetching water and shoveling ashes out of the fireplace. Even knocking cobwebs down from the ceiling.

Now, he stamped his feet in the doorway. He staggered in with his arms full of cut firewood. A gust of wind carried snowflakes into the kitchen. Marga rushed to shut the door.

"This should keep us through the night at least," he said as he crouched down to arrange the wood in a tidy pile near the fireplace. "Beech wood. Well-seasoned."

Marga wiped her hands on her apron. "Thank you. Your help has been a great blessing to me."

"You saved my life, Fraulein. I must repay you with the work of my hands, since I lost my purse in the woods. But I'm sure you manage splendidly on your own, a resourceful young woman like you." Herr Steuben finished stacking the wood and held his damp, reddened hands close to the fire.

Marga turned her back on him and resumed drying the plates and mugs. "That is something I shall find out soon, I imagine."

"Yes, regretfully, I cannot stay much longer. Much as I enjoy sharing your hearth and company, I must return home to my dear little daughter. Gretel loves visiting her grandmother, but she always misses her papa after a day or two. She suffers terrible nightmares since her mother died, and I am best at soothing her."

"Your child's name is Gretel? I was called Gretel when I was small." A pang of grief pierced her chest as she remembered her own mother. How kind and loving she'd been before hardship and famine had befallen the family. Hunger had driven her to madness and then death, poor *Mutti*.

"It is a good name. Sweet yet strong. It suits you, even now. Perhaps you should consider taking it up anew."

Marga shook her head and set the towel on the counter. She faced Herr Steuben again. "No, I prefer Margarethe."

"I surmise there is a story behind that choice, Fraulein." Herr Steuben left the hearth to hang up the cloak he'd borrowed—the one she had worn when masquerading as a man. The cloak fit him as if tailored for his body. Was it some trick of the old witch's lingering magic or a mere coincidence? The witch's clothes had certainly not conformed to her shape and height.

"There is a story, but I prefer not to tell it. It is...an unpleasant tale," Marga said. The very thought of sharing the terrors of her childhood made her heartbeat flutter with anxiety.

The man settled into the chair by the fire and held his feet toward the flames. He had a fatherly, wholesome look as he sat there. Ever since he'd arrived, she'd lived in dread of being asked how she'd come to live all alone in the strange gingerbread house, but he had never broached the subject. Now, she felt oddly tempted to tell him the story of her life—in its entirety. But caution bade her to hold her tongue. She'd committed murder and used the witch's magic. Why should he not turn against her?

"By all means, keep your story to yourself, if it disquiets you to share it," Herr Steuben said amiably. "Come, sit beside me and I will tell you of my Gretel, and of my darling, departed wife. The pretty house we built near the river. The gardens we planted, and our clever cats."

"I would like that." Marga pulled a wooden chair out from the table and carried it to the hearth. The visitor smiled at her as she arranged her skirts and sank into the chair. How sleepy she was all of a sudden—in a comfortable, winter afternoon way.

Herr Steuben spoke of romance and joy, marriage and heartbreak. He told of his beloved child, who was the image of her dead mother and the sweetest creature ever born to mortals. His voice cracked with deep emotion as he described little Gretel's recent illness.

"I have traveled far and wide, Fraulein, searching for the cure. Indeed, that is how I came to be passing through this forest. I have consulted doctors and priests, herbalists and scholars. I believe—and forgive me if this notion offends you —I believe that only strong magic can make her well."

Marga's contentment dissolved as she stared at the black, owl-shaped andirons in the fireplace. The mention of magic caused her stomach to churn, even as her hands tingled to remind her of magic's presence.

Her cheeks burned with secret shame. "I do not think anyone should meddle with magic. I have seen it worked, and the harm it causes surely outweighs any benefits."

Herr Steuben leaned toward her. His face shone with eagerness. "You know a worker of magic? A wise woman? Please, tell me. In truth, I do not believe they are wicked, as some testify, but that they are women with rare and mighty gifts. In my heart of hearts, I believe they should be revered rather than persecuted." He lowered his voice and confided, "My grandmother was a witch, you see. Sadly, I did not inherit her gifts."

Marga said nothing, but clenched her hands together into a tight ball on her lap. She bit the inside of her lip and hoped he would soon change the subject of conversation.

Instead, he gasped. He pointed a finger toward the ceiling and shook it excitedly. "Ah! I think I understand now why you remind me of Grandmother Hette. You have the same—what shall I call it—energy about your person. It is magic. I am certain of it!"

Hot tears gathered in Marga's eyes. She willed them to stop, but to no avail. She was unsettled and angry, guilt-stricken and remorseful, all at once. She wanted to run out into the snow, to run and run and never stop running until she escaped both herself and the magic. But she sat still and bit her quivering lower lip instead.

Herr Steuben launched himself to the floor and crouched before her. He took her clasped hands between his, offering a benevolent smile.

"Why do you weep, Fraulein? To be a witch is to be a wonder in a dull world. Think of what you might do—things ordinary mortals could never dream of doing. You have the power to change things, perhaps to reign and rule. You could even...No, I cannot ask it of you. I will not, for I see the pain in your pretty eyes at the mention of your gift."

Marga looked past Herr Steuben and into the flames. "You do not understand. I cannot save your child. I have already done great harm while attempting to use magic. The man I tried to help...I used a spell from an old book, but it did not heal him from the lake monster's bite as it was meant to. Instead, it...*I*...I took his arm. I ruined his life."

"But this was not your intention, to harm the man. Perhaps the spell was poorly written, a word left out. You cannot throw away your power and neglect your calling because of one mistake. You did not kill him, after all. Indeed, one might argue that you saved him from imminent death."

Marga sniffled. Herr Steuben released her hands and fished a handkerchief from his pocket. She accepted it and dabbed her eyes and cheeks.

"Even so, I don't want to be a witch. I hope to never

practice magic again." Her words were true, but as ineffectual as a dead man's promise.

He stood and then returned to his chair. Hands on knees, he eyed her with grave sincerity. "Forgive my boldness in saying so, dear *Mädchen*, but you are already a witch. You have testified that the power runs within your veins, and that you have made use of it. Yet far be it from me to force you to take up a role you despise. Live as you choose. You are a free woman."

"But I am not free, am I? This 'gift,' as you call it, holds me hostage." The memory of little Hansel shut inside the bars of the witch's wooden cage played in her mind. She felt as trapped and wretched as he must have, caught by the same witch.

"That is untrue. A reversal of truth. The gift is your servant, yours to command. Think of it as a child. A poorly trained child will do all the mischief he can. He'll run wild and cause destruction. But a disciplined child works hard to please his parent. He will obey, and grow stronger and better as his parent guides him."

Marga closed her eyes and breathed out a long sigh. Inside her, all was turmoil. Nothing seemed right anymore. Herr Steuben made magic sound useful and good, but magic had surely made the old witch what she was—heartless and evil. How could both things be true?

"I have wearied you with all my talk. For this, I beg your pardon." Herr Steuben stood and plucked the cloak from its peg. With a flourish, he draped it about his slim shoulders. He pulled a woolen cap onto his head. "This winter promises to be colder than usual. It is good that I shored up the bedchamber wall with the boards before this storm came. I'll go cut what wood I can before the weather worsens. I owe you that, and much more, in exchange for the kindness you have shown me."

Wrapping a scarf around his face, he opened the door and plunged into the swirling snowflakes.

Marga could not sit still with her tangled, vexing thoughts a moment longer. She got up and grabbed the broom from the corner. With broad, rough strokes, she swept the floor, wishing it were as easy to bring order to her life.

But she had already learned that some wishes did not come true.

* * *

Ansgar reveled in the strength of his human muscles as he drove the axe into the fallen elm tree.

His true age eluded him. His duck brain had been useless for judging time. But, by the gods, today he felt young. Not as young as when he'd wed Truda but still young enough to wage and win the war at hand.

Indeed, he'd already won a great battle or two.

Gretel's profound gullibility had surprised him. Her bruised heart left her vulnerable to his suggestions. He'd been right to move slowly, to coax her along with crafty half-truths and emotion-laden fabrications. The invented witch-grandmother had been a stroke of genius. With the depiction of the sick little daughter, Ansgar had almost brought himself to tears.

He was so close now to achieving his goals. He felt almost giddy with anticipation.

The trunk split. The tree's invisible faerie whimpered as she slipped free of the wood. Stupid faerie. By the old edicts of the forest, she ought to have left the dead tree long ago, but in Truda's absence, no one had enforced the rules of the Igelwald.

A bit of lawlessness could be entertaining, but no one liked chaos.

The sound of heavy boots tromping on snow caught Ansgar's ear.

"So soon?" he said, pivoting. He chuckled with dark amusement as he beheld a tall, brawny baker charging pell-mell into the yard.

Thirty-Three

The needle pierced her finger. Marga was tempted to throw it into the fire beside her—not for the first time that afternoon. Instead, she sighed and let her hands and the needle fall into her lap with the dress she'd been repairing.

How she loathed all tasks requiring needles and thread. Who had decided that sewing was supposed to be one of the joys of a woman's life? She spent more time stabbing her fingers than she did stitching. Nevertheless, she was stuck hiding in the forest for the winter with few garments to wear. Torn seams demanded attention. If she ignored them, they'd only grow larger and harder to mend.

A single wish might have been enough to repair her entire wardrobe, but she would not try the magic, not even to avoid the worst of household tasks.

She snipped the thread with the witch's tiny, crane-shaped scissors. Lifting the witch's gray work dress from her lap, she examined the repair she'd done to the sleeve. It would hold, and that was what mattered. Once Herr Steuben left, no one but spiders and mice would lay eyes upon her anyway.

When the door opened behind her, Marga was busy folding the dress. She didn't turn her head to welcome Herr Steuben back into the cottage, hesitant to start another conversation with him about witches or magic or dying children. She was still irritated by their last discussion, riled up by his zealous attempts to direct her decisions. Silence was preferable.

A blast of icy wind assaulted her bare neck. She shivered. It might be prudent to start wearing her hair loose. When the full brunt of winter came, she'd have to use whatever means she could to stay warm while being conservative with the stores of firewood Herr Steuben had amassed. Otherwise, a time might come when she'd have to choose between freezing to death and employing magic.

Meanwhile, why had Herr Steuben not yet closed the door?

"Do you require help?" she asked crossly, tossing the scissors into the sewing basket at her feet. She brushed a few snippets of thread off her lap. If only she could curse as carelessly as Hansel.

"Margarethe," Herr Steuben said in a muffled voice. The door closed with a thud.

He'd never addressed her by that name, and he was panting as if he'd run a mile. Something was wrong.

Marga stood and turned.

The snow-encrusted man wore a knitted hat and a thick woolen scarf that obscured most of his face, but she knew those sky-blue eyes—and they did not belong to Herr Steuben.

"Lukas," she exclaimed. The dress fell from her hands and she ran to him. She embraced him, snow and all, and pressed her cheek against his chest. "I thought you'd left me forever."

His arms held her so tightly it almost hurt. "I'm sorry, *Liebling*. I had to lead Felix away from your hiding place and ended up escorting him all the way home. It wasn't an easy thing to talk him out of hunting you down and killing you, but I managed it. I knew that once I took him back to *Mutti*, she would never allow him to return to the forest. And then the weather turned, and the snow fell ...But I came back as soon as I could. Tell me, who is that strange man in the garden? Is he to be trusted?"

"His name is Steuben. He collapsed on the doorstep, ill from mushroom poisoning. He's been cutting firewood to pay me for medicine and lodging. No need to be jealous." She rose on her tiptoes and kissed his wool-covered chin.

Lukas gently removed himself from Marga's arms, then unwound his scarf to reveal a look of desperation she'd seen only when Felix was close to death. "Perhaps he can help us," Lukas said. "We must not delay."

She tilted her head quizzically. Had the cold addled his mind? Something was amiss with him. "Help with repairs to the cottage? Herr Steuben just did some work on the wall in the bedchamber. I think the rest can wait."

"No, *Liebling*. I mean that perhaps he can help protect you. I tried to prevent them, but Felix and *Mutti* have roused the men of the town. They're coming soon to burn the cottage. And you, with it."

Shock eclipsed Marga's bright happiness. Her knees buckled. Lukas caught her under the arms and escorted her to the hearthside chair.

Kneeling close, he enfolded her hand in his. "The snow at the edge of the forest is waist deep. That will stop some of the older men, at least. And then, if they make it to the lake, they will have to find a way to cross it. Unfortunately, it was half frozen when I crossed by boat last night, so they may be able to walk over it. The nixes were nowhere to be seen. Perhaps they hibernate in winter. If Felix remembers the way here, and they're moving at a decent pace...Well, we cannot afford to wait to leave this place. The sooner we go, the better our chance to elude them."

"If I run, they'll track me through the snow, or I'll die from the cold." Already she felt chilled, as if her blood carried crystals of ice through her veins.

"I'll be with you. We'll find a way to get through the Igelwald. We can go north to Hussenberg, then make our way to the coast. Find a ship to board. Start a new life in America, or wherever you wish."

His hopefulness, the earnestness in his eyes...these things broke her heart. Best to speak the truth and not to entertain foolish fantasies of a happily-ever-after story. "The weather is against us, Lukas. The snow is piling up as we speak. There is no horse or any other beast I could wish for that could carry us through such deep and heavy snow. We must be reasonable. Let them come, and I will surrender. You can say I bewitched you for a time, and they'll have mercy on you. You're a good man. They know this."

Had it not been for another strong draft, Marga might not have noticed Herr Steuben's entrance. Lukas stood and nodded in greeting, well-mannered as usual.

"You look distressed, Fraulein. Might I be of some assistance?" Herr Steuben said as he approached her.

Lukas stepped forward to form a wall between her and Steuben. "You should leave now, sir. Men are coming from the town. Hateful men who wish to take Margarethe's life."

"No, Herr Steuben. You should not try to flee in this weather, in such deep snow," Marga said wearily. "You might hide. Or claim that I bewitched you, as I've told Lukas to."

"*Liebling*, please," Lukas said, turning toward her again. He clasped his hands as if praying.

Herr Steuben moved past Lukas to stand before her. Snow capped his shoulders like epaulets, and little flakes sparkled as they melted atop his white-blond hair. On his face, he wore an expression of grim sincerity. "Fraulein, you must not surrender. I sense the love you share with this man, and it is a rare and wondrous thing. A miracle. It emanates from you like starlight. Would you have him mourn you for the rest of his days? True love cannot be cast aside like an old garment. It is as much a part of him as his flesh and bones. You must fight for him, for love. You have the power within you to conquer any foe. Now is the time to embrace it."

"I don't want to kill people with magic," Marga said. "I will not." She clenched her hands in her lap.

Herr Steuben removed his snow-coated gloves and laid

them on the mantel. "You need not kill anyone, Fraulein. There are other ways to defend yourself with your power."

Lukas eyed the man suspiciously. "How do you know such things? Are you a wizard, sir?"

Herr Steuben lifted his chin haughtily. "I am the grandson of a most talented wise woman, one you would call a witch. I did not inherit her gifts, but I did inherit her writings. I recall every word of them. Together, with her instructions and this magic, we can overcome your foes, Fraulein. I am certain of it."

Lukas crouched again beside Marga's chair and gazed steadily into her eyes. She wished they would have met in another time and place, one without witches and angry mobs and agonizing choices. She wished for the mob and Herr Steuben to disappear, knowing it was futile.

Lukas said, "This is your choice, *Liebling*. You must follow your own heart now, and do what you think is best. I will respect your decision. Know that I love you, and have loved you since boyhood, and that I will continue to love you no matter what happens here today."

A sound of derision, rather like a quack, came from Herr Steuben's throat. He picked a twig off his cloak and tossed it into the flames. "Come now. You insult this woman by fawning over her so. If you loved her as you say you do, if you knew her true power, you would encourage her to fulfill her potential for greatness. You would take up her banner and gladly charge into battle under her command."

Lukas stood and balled his fists at his sides. "I know her strength, sir. I've witnessed it for years. You hardly know her at all."

"Stop, I beg you," Marga said. "I do not need to hear arguments. I need to think. Alone." She rose and walked toward the bedchamber. "Drink something warm. Read books. Polish your boots. Only keep quiet, please."

Herr Steuben nodded. "Yes, go and think, Fraulein. Seek the wisdom that lies within you."

Marga glanced at Lukas to see him roll his eyes at the mystical advice.

"If you need me, I will be right here, *Liebling*," Lukas said.

She closed the bedchamber door and sat on the edge of the bed. After a moment, she got up and paced. The choice was impossible. Her heart urged her to do whatever it took to stay alive and to protect Lukas, but her mind argued that wielding magic was wrong and risky.

Light reflected off the oval looking glass that hung on the wall between the beds. Curiosity drew her to the gold-framed, murky mirror—as did the desire for a momentary distraction. After all she'd done and been through, did she look different than she had back in the bakers' shed? What did Lukas see when he looked at her?

She stood on tiptoe and tried to catch sight of her face.

Instead, she beheld the face of the witch she'd shoved into the oven—only years younger and strangely beautiful. Held in thrall by an unseen force, Marga was forced to continue staring at the image before her.

Thirty-Four

"There you are," said the witch's shadowy, youthful face in the mirror. Her hair streamed in golden ringlets that writhed like snakes. She gazed, unblinking, at Marga with huge, dark eyes. "Not as vain as I'd thought, my little Gretel. I expected you to return to my looking glass much sooner."

"Let me go," Marga demanded. She wanted nothing to do with the dead, especially not the evil dead. Nor did she wish to speak with the witch who had caused her misery of one kind or another for over thirteen years. But Marga could not escape. Her limbs refused to obey her will.

"Listen well, *Mädchen*. The time has come for you to reign. Long ago, jealous of your unspoiled beauty, I betrayed us both. I let hunger rule me and forgot to heed the order set in place by the Igelwald. The forest chose you to be the next witch-queen, and witch-queen you shall be."

"No," Marga said. "Not I." Her feet ached from being stuck on tiptoe, and her immovable arms felt as if they were sculpted of ice-cold marble. If only she could shut her eyes, perhaps she could escape the mirror-witch's power. But her eyelids refused to even flutter.

The witch laughed, then said, "You're a brazen one, thinking you can refuse the forest's edict. It is older and stronger than you can possibly imagine. It chose me once, and drew me here to reign. If I could not deny its will and its calling, neither can a snippet of a girl like you. Did you never wonder why your father could work as a woodcutter in the Igelwald when many before him tried, only to die horrible deaths or disappeared? You family lived here unharmed only because of you. Your inborn magic and your vocation."

"No," Marga said again, although what the witch said made sense. For as long as her family had lived in Eschlinsdorf, and before her father's brief time as a woodsman, no one had harvested timber from the Igelwald. The townsfolk knew the risks far outweighed the convenience. They hauled their firewood over many miles, from the mountains to the south, where the trees were only trees and faeries were never seen.

"Ansgar Steuben is here, is he not?" the witch continued. "Back in his human form, for I have heard his voice. He made a comely fowl, but a better husband—when he behaved, that is. I have greatly regretted turning him into a duck for his unfaithfulness, but the spell I cast was potent and complex, and the Igelwald added to its conditions. As powerful as I was, I could not change him back."

"Herr Steuben was a duck? And your husband?" Nausea roiled within Marga's gut as she recognized the similarity between Herr Steuben's black shock of hair and the black feathers atop the duck's head. Man and duck also shared the same dark, beady eyes and proud demeanor. If she were so magically gifted, how had she not sensed the connection between the two?

"You're as slow-witted as December treacle," the witch said as if she'd read Marga's mind. "Some fresh red meat and a dose of powdered she-bear claw would set you to rights. But back to the matter at hand. I shall tell you what my inner sight shows me. Your enemies are on their way. Three feet of snow is no match for their vengeful fury. They slide across the ice-covered lake as I speak, unmolested by the nixes who slumber deep below the surface. The men are armed with rifles, muskets, axes, and swords. Silver shot rattles in their pockets. Some of them bear torches aflame. I see them, and I see the future that rides upon their backs like a dark ghost."

"Why should I believe you?" With all her strength, Marga fought to get away, but her limbs remained inflexible. She wished, calling upon her magic, but nothing happened.

"If I possessed hands, I would smack your pretty face. Show some respect, child. Attend to my instructions—unless you wish to see your beloved baker hacked in two by a pig farmer. Fetch the key hidden in the back of the wardrobe and use it to unlock the drawer in the table under this glass. Take my brown book from the drawer. Read the words aloud. It is as simple as that. No lengthy ceremony, no incense or offerings, just strong, ancient words combined with the gift you already bear."

"But—"

The witch's dark eyes narrowed. "They're bringing hounds too. Ropes, chains, holy water. Knives forged by faerie folk. They'll try every way they can think of to destroy you, but you will live. You'll live, though barely for a time, but the baker will die a dreadful death. I see so much blood. It shall melt all the snow from my gardens."

"No," Marga shouted. Everything within her objected to the witch's words while affirming the truth in them. Marga could see the future too, in dim bursts of smeared color. *Oh, Lukas. No one deserves to die so violently. And not for my sake.*

"Marga?" Lukas's voice said outside the bedchamber door. "I thought I heard voices. Are you well?"

"Fine, Lukas," Marga replied firmly. She hated to lie to him, but what might the mirror witch do to him if he entered the room?

The witch grinned coldly. "You *are* fine. Yes, pretty little Gretel is as fine as fine can be. Now, hesitate no more. Get the book. Gather your wits and your power before the mob arrives. Then say the words. Be the queen. Save your young man. Marry him. Plant gardens with him, run barefoot through the flowered meadows, ride the backs of bucks in the moonlight, swim together in the hidden mountain pools. Have a dozen delectably plump babies...Or watch him die. You choose."

Marga's heart beat hard in her chest, aching with love for Lukas and with fear of what might befall him. He was the best man in the world, and she would give anything to save him. Anything. "I'll do as you say. To save Lukas, not because it pleases you."

"I am beyond seeking pleasure, child," the witch said with a toss of her golden curls.

Abruptly, the witch's magic released Marga from her

frozen state. She turned, stumbled toward the wardrobe, and retrieved from inside it a small black key. She returned to the table and inserted the key. It turned in the lock with a click. The drawer slid open, and there, waiting for her, was a brown book the size of Marga's palm. Its leather cover bore neither title nor embellishment.

With a trembling hand, she picked it up and opened it to the first page.

She read silently. Merely passing her eyes over the text stirred up stinging sparks of magic within her. There was no denying that the words held great power. She stopped reading and dropped the thin volume into the pocket of her apron. If she was going to do as the witch said she must, she wanted to speak to Lukas first.

Surely there was enough time to say goodbye to the man she loved—in case the witch had lied, things went badly, or she botched the spell and brought disaster upon them all.

* * *

Ansgar hid a sneer of derision behind the mug of rosehip tea he'd been sipping as he lurked near the bedchamber door. The big baker's pacing and hand-wringing were beginning to annoy him.

Herr Beckmann was far less stalwart than his rugged outward appearance suggested. The sort that dies with a knife in his hand because he can't bear to slip it into a neighbor's belly. The sort who'd be eulogized as "too good for this earth." Which was another way of saying someone had lacked ambition and had lived a boring, forgettable existence.

Voices seeped through the cracks around the bedchamber door. Ansgar's chest burned with sudden longing as he recognized Truda's voice. Had she somehow appeared to the girl in spirit form? He could hardly restrain himself from rushing into the room. *Truda, my love...*

"I remember you," the baker said as he tossed a log onto the fire. Orange sparks flew up into the chimney. "It took me a while to place you, but now I'm sure of it. My brother and I met you near the lake. You lent us a boat."

"You are correct," Ansgar said. "The boat served you well, or you would not have lived to tell the tale."

Lukas faced him, eyeing him with unconcealed suspicion. "What are you doing here?"

Ansgar maintained a calm demeanor. He playacted the role of a meek, honest laborer. "As I told you when last we met, I am a surveyor. As I plied my trade not far from here, I mistakenly ate poisonous mushrooms. I became deathly ill, but thanks to Providence, stumbled upon this cottage. Fraulein Holzfäller took pity upon me and nursed me back to health. In return for her kindness, I've been helping with household tasks. Fetching water, replacing cracked chair legs...I even did my best to reinforce the wall in the bedchamber. Still, I have advised the Fraulein that she'd be better off sleeping in the kitchen as winter progresses." He crossed the room to set his mug on the table, casually, as if he owned the place. "I did plan to leave tomorrow, upon supplying her with enough firewood to see her through the next few months. Of course, none of that matters now that the townsmen are coming."

At the mention of the advancing mob, the baker's face

darkened. He approached Ansgar like a scudding storm cloud. "You and I must convince her to flee. I could take her one way, and you could go another, disguised as Marga to lead them astray."

Ansgar sneered. He couldn't help it. "What appeals to you about perishing from the cold? Where do you think you and she could safely hide in an enchanted forest full of chest-deep snow and malicious, hungry creatures? The only way she can save herself is through the use of magic."

The conversation was clearly deteriorating into an argument. No matter. Ansgar knew how to dominate a verbal battle. Strong, clever words felt good on his tongue, so much better than quacking.

"You have an agenda," Lukas accused. "A secret reason for pushing her to do something she opposes. What do you hope to gain from this?"

Ansgar smirked. "Everyone has an agenda, dear baker. Your own springs from your simplistic desire for a bride. Mine is none of your concern. But our goal is one and the same, I assure you: to see Fraulein Holzfäller live and flourish."

The bedchamber door opened with a squeal of its candy hinges.

"I asked you not to quarrel," Gretel said with the air of a weary mother. Dark circles ringed her eyes, but the eddying magic that surrounded her had grown in intensity. Ansgar could almost hear it snap and sizzle.

"I'm sorry, *Liebling*." Lukas looked contrite. For such a large man, he did a fine job of impersonating a guilty toddler.

Gretel addressed Ansgar firmly. Scornfully. "I need to speak to Lukas alone."

"Of course," Ansgar said. He rushed past her and into the bedchamber, eager to see if his true love existed there in some form—although he also dearly wanted to stay to shake little Gretel. To implore her to get on with the inevitable.

As he shut the bedchamber door behind him, he felt a presence. Its essence was fading, flickering like a spent candle, but it beckoned him.

She beckoned him.

Truda.

Thirty-Five

Ansgar's all-too-human heartbeat thundered in his ears as a dozen strong emotions fought for supremacy. He knew well whom he had heard. His wife's voice was not one he would forget for as long as he lived.

He subverted the impulse to run, and instead walked toward the mirror that seemed to be summoning him. What if Truda wasn't there? What if the cottage was playing a cruel trick on him? Still a few steps away, he caught sight of the faint outlines of a female face. Coiled locks of golden hair. It was she. Everything within him testified to it. His bones warmed with wanting. A hundred wild birds flapped savage wings within his belly.

Through a haze like churning steam, he saw her as she'd looked when they'd first met. A wealth of flaxen curls, a red cupid's bow of a mouth that begged to be kissed, cheekbones worthy of a Norse warrior woman, a regal nose. Beholding her image, he fell in love with her again, and then again.

Ansgar pressed his fingertips to the cold oval of glass. "My love. How I have missed you."

"Have you?" Truda asked with a cynical glare. "You're not in love with young Gretel? Or besotted with another tree, perhaps? A shapely gooseberry bush?"

"If you had given me five more minutes as a man, I would have thrown myself at your feet and repented. Every day, every hour since, when I had any presence of mind at all, I have regretted my infidelity. I have carried my remorse like leaden chains."

The expression on her cloudy face shifted from smug to sad to apologetic. "I acted in haste. But the magic I'd wielded over the years had cost me my beauty. I feared you would betray me again and again as I shriveled and decayed, and I could not bear the thought. My temper—"

"I loved your temper. Can you not come out of the mirror, my love?" The bliss of seeing her tangled with the agony of being unable to touch her skin.

"Here I must bide, though not for much longer. When the child pushed me into the oven's flames, I had little chance to react. The only spell I could think to speak was one to send my spirit into this glass. The moment Gretel becomes queen, the spell will break, and I will meet the devil, I suppose. These years of imprisonment have seemed an eternity. So much waiting. But the vision of your handsome face, Ansgar Steuben, has been worth waiting for."

"Slip into another body, Truda. Reside within a doe, a tree, anything. Only do not leave me again." He regretted mentioning the tree option, seeing her cringe at the word. He awaited her wry rebuke, but received a melancholy smile instead.

"You're a fool, Ansgar. Still and always. My magic days are finished. The small measure of power I still possess will soon pass to Gretel. But I would stay with you if I could. I would be a vine to twine about your leg, a breeze to kiss your throat, or a dog to nip your heels and sleep nestled beneath your arm. But I cannot. I cannot."

Tears all but obscured Ansgar's view of his shadowy wife. He forgave her for making him a duck. He would have spent the next century enrobed in feathers if it meant they could be reunited to live as husband and wife for a single week. A day.

"Why did you not speak to me before, my heart? I have been in this house, this room, so close to you for weeks..."

"The spell would not allow me to converse with you when you were a duck."

Ansgar groaned. The spell! The blasted spell!

Mirror Truda gestured with a ghostly hand. "Go now, my husband. Gretel will speak the oath soon. You should witness her assumption of power. You have worked hard and suffered long to bring her to it, have you not?"

Ansgar nodded, too overcome with love and despair to reply with words. No one had ever been able to undo him like Truda could. If he lived a thousand years, he would not permit anyone to do so again.

"Dry your eyes and stand tall, Ansgar Steuben. Give me a picture of you worthy of carrying in my heart for eternity."

He squared his shoulders, straightened his cravat, and did his best to form the semblance of a smile with his mouth. His lower lip quivered in rebellion.

"Better," Truda said. "Ah, but you're a fine figure of a man. I chose well." A weary but proud smile flitted over her spectral mouth. Her image rippled and grew faint. "I must rest. All that I am is nearly spent. Go now, and see that the girl yields to her fate."

"Goodbye, my love, my heart." The words scalded like a mouthful of acid.

"Goodbye, Ansgar." Her face flickered and faded away.

Ansgar was alone. Alone and torn in two by grief.

He closed his eyes and summoned his meager power. With all that he had, he stirred up a wind strong enough to rattle the candy panes and howl down the chimney.

The wind mingled with the sounds of the storm and almost concealed his cries of anguish.

* * *

As the sudden wind diminished, Marga pushed against Lukas's chest to end their embrace. Still, he gripped her hands in his as he looked down at her with an expression of grave concern. She wished she could kiss that look away, but if he loved her—and she believed he did—he was right to worry. The person he loved might cease to exist once she spoke the words from the witch's brown book.

"You're certain this is what you want to do? You trust the advice of a ghost-witch and her deceitful husband?" he asked.

"I trust what I feel in my heart and I sense in my bones."

"Then I will trust as well." Lukas released her hands. He moved to the window and peered out into the darkening yard. "Do you hear that? I thought it was more wind coming in from afar, but—"

"It's singing. An old song for marching into battle. They're coming." She'd expected this, yet her heart sank. Her hands trembled as fear washed over her in an icy wave.

Lukas's face blanched. "Already? How could it be?"

"They found a shortcut or some forest faerie guided them. It doesn't matter."

"*Liebling*." Lukas started toward her. She'd take one last kiss from him. Perhaps it would strengthen her. But the bedchamber door opened, stopping Lukas in his tracks.

Herr Steuben emerged, handkerchief in hand. His cheeks were damp. "The townsfolk approach," he said flatly. He seemed different, deflated. "I expect they'll be at the door in minutes."

Marga shut her eyes for a moment and gathered her courage. She would do this for Lukas. For love.

She thrust her hand into her pocket and drew out the small book. "Stand back. I don't know what will happen when I read this."

Herr Steuben lifted a hand. "Wait. Better to read it outside, Fraulein. Better to make your declaration to the trees and sky and every creature with ears to hear. The storm has stopped and a bright moon is rising."

Lukas grabbed a cloak and wrapped it around Marga. His fingers fumbled as he fastened the button under her chin. She inhaled his ever-present bread and wood smoke scent and felt the press of his mouth on the top of her head like a blessing.

Herr Steuben opened the front door. "The time has come."

Thirty-Six

The storm had moved on, and with it, most of the clouds. The night sky was speckled with winking stars, and the full moon poured pure white light all over the landscape. The world seemed to hold its breath as Marga stepped outside and waded through knee-deep snow to the center of the buried herb garden.

She forced herself to breathe in slow, even doses of frosty air and to exhale lingering doubts. The task set before her was simple enough, really, just a bit of reading. The magic would do the rest. Inside her belly and chest, it was stirring. Fluttering and sparking, like tiny butterflies made of lightning performing jigs and reels.

"Read now," Herr Steuben said from somewhere behind her. She would not obey the scheming former duck. The magic would tell her when the moment was right. Of this she was certain.

"I believe in you, *Liebling*," Lukas said.

Love, the truest magic, filled her heart to overflowing.

This, I willingly do for Lukas, she reminded herself. *To save him.*

She opened the book and recited the old words in a loud, confident voice. In the manner of a queen.

As she spoke, the townsfolk trudged out from beyond the trees, like trained wolves that had awaited her call. Some raised torches overhead. Others brandished swords or readied rifles. They chanted, "Death to the witch. Death to the witch." A dozen growling dogs with bared teeth tugged on ropes or chains, causing their masters to stumble forward.

The final words glowed on the page before Marga, and she read them boldly. "I take my place as the witch-queen of the Igelwald. From this moment on, I shall reign over tree and root, beast, bird, and faerie. Bow before me, one and all."

A flash of light illuminated the entire forest. Thunder rumbled through the sky and the ground, shaking snow from the branches. Some of the townsfolk cried out in fear, but a few were not cowed by the magic's spectacle. With a shout, they charged forth, weapons ready for war.

"Kill the witch!" they yelled. Amidst the chaos, Marga thought she recognized the tailor and the innkeeper. The candlemaker's youngest son. Hansel's friends.

She raised both hands heavenward. "Stop!"

The men stopped. They laughed.

"Not a very good witch, are you?" the tailor said. "Come on, boys. Whoever gets to her first shall have a new coat and a keg of Georg's finest!"

The men surged forward.

"Concentrate, Gretel!" Ansgar shouted from behind her. "Believe your words. Be the queen and vanquish your foes!"

Marga filled her lungs anew. She stretched her arms higher and drew upon the magic in her marrow. "I am queen. You will bow!"

The townsfolk bent at the waist like reeds snapped by a tempest.

Herr Steuben's hot breath slithered across her earlobe as he spoke over her shoulder. "Kill them all. You need only say the word. Finish this. Let the world know who reigns in the Igelwald now."

Her lifted hands vibrated with unspent energy. Darkness bubbled in her soul, urging her to kill the men who'd come to kill her. *Repay hatred with hatred*, the darkness said. *Never have you harmed a hair of their heads, yet they have despised and vilified you for years. They sentence you to death without cause; it is justice to give them death in return.*

The darkness spread through her slowly, like a serpent slipping through her veins. *Yes*, it said. *Kill them. Kill.*

She wanted to see their blood staining the snow. For all their cruelty, for all their abuse and gossip. For shaming her from innocent girlhood until today. She spread her fingers and let the darkness whisper the words of a new spell into her mind.

Such simple words. She'd speak them, and her attackers would never vex her again. They'd turn to ash and mingle with the snow.

"Long live Witch-Queen Gretel!" Herr Steuben cried.

Her childhood name took her by surprise, like a sudden blow to the head. Her hands fell to her sides. The darkness within her hissed, dismayed by her hesitation. The mob continued to bow before her, moaning and praying with terror.

Witch-Queen Gretel? Is that who she would become now, as the gossipmongers of Eschlinsdorf had foretold? Did she wish to rule cruelly, to use violence and torture as weapons?

"No," Marga whispered.

She was not that girl. She would never be little Gretel again—one forced to fear and to murder.

For many years, she'd striven to leave behind Gretel and everything that had happened to her. Now, Margarethe Holzfäller wanted nothing but a life of love. A peaceful life with Lukas the baker, eating good bread, and laughing at crumbs.

The queen of darkness was neither who she was nor who she'd become.

If she was to be the witch-queen, she would rule with grace. She would use her magic to beautify the Igelwald, to make a sanctuary for the flora, fauna, and faeries. She could do it.

She straightened her spine and stood as tall as her small frame allowed. With all her might, she declared, "This power does not own me. I own it."

Once more, she lifted her hands. Sparks of magic swirled inside and outside her body like fireflies, chasing away the darkness that had tempted her. The trees waved their branches. Flock after flock of birds appeared, circling overhead. Unseen foxes and wolves snarled within the brush. Hundreds of other creatures—faeries and mice, hedgehogs and pixies, rabbits and martens, deer and boar—scurried out of the woods to surround her.

"Witch!" someone shouted. "See how the wild things come to do her bidding!"

The animals and faerie folk peered up at her with adoration, and Marga smiled at them, pleased to be their sovereign.

Head held high, she said to the townsfolk, "I am Queen Margarethe. The Igelwald is my kingdom, and upon my land, all are obliged to obey my voice. Go home, folk of Eschlinsdorf, I command you. Forget your hatred. Never again enter this forest, for the creatures of this place shall guard its borders well. If you trespass, you will find them without mercy."

The men straightened, released by the enchantment that had held them. They drew back without a word and scrambled into the cover of the creaking trees. The clouds rolled in, stealing the starlight and muffling the moonlight, promising to add more snow.

"You should have killed them," Herr Steuben said as the animals and faeries dispersed. He still stood close behind her, like a shadow formed from wickedness. "The forest needs a strong and fearsome queen. The faerie tribes are capricious, the animals unruly. You will fail if you do not inspire terror in your subjects."

"That is my concern, not yours," Marga said, spinning to face him. In the dimness, he looked older and smaller. Humbled, perhaps. Nevertheless, she would not allow him to remain among her subjects to sow discord and strife. "At first light, I expect you to leave this forest and never return."

"That, my dear *Mädchen*, is what I have desired all

along," the former duck replied, eyeing her as if she were a filthy peasant. "Besides, I would not stay and watch you waste the gift my Truda bestowed upon you."

"I waste nothing. I only choose to rule in a new and better way," Marga said in a tone befitting her station.

Herr Steuben sniffed but said no more. He trudged back into the house as tiny snowflakes drifted down from the heavens.

Marga's queenly feelings failed her as she cast a glance toward Lukas. He stood in front of the cottage, his expression unreadable. Snow, like a dusting of flour, settled upon his broad shoulders and his wind-tossed hair.

Somehow, facing him now, alone, frightened her as much as confronting the mob of angry townsfolk. He owned her heart, but what if he no longer wanted it?

She walked toward him on the path she'd trodden through the snow, stopping when at arm's length. She gathered up her courage and forced herself to meet his gaze.

"You may leave as well, if you like," she said. The words pricked her heart like daggers. "I will not beseech you to stay with me. If you dislike the idea of being wed to a witch-queen, I understand."

"You're different," Lukas stepped closer, looking more astounded than afraid. At least he hadn't run away. Yet. But the odd intensity of his gaze unsettled her.

"My hair's turned pure white and my face is shriveled as a prune, I imagine." She steeled herself for the heartbreak to come. Every second brought it closer.

Lukas took another step forward. She tried not to flinch as he tucked a lock of her hair behind her ear. "No. You look exactly as you did before you fled the town. As lovely as you did that night we met in the graveyard."

"Truly?"

Finally, he smiled. "Oh, Margarethe. It would not have mattered to me if you'd become prune-faced and gray. Now, say again what you said before, about me wedding the witch-queen. I believe you might have offered me a proposal of marriage. I would hate to be wrong about a thing such as that."

Her stomach fluttered, not with magic but with hope. "If I asked you, what would you say, Herr Beckmann? Lukas?"

"I would say yes, a thousand times yes. And then I would kiss you."

Marga took both Lukas's hands and gazed up into his kind, adoring face—the face she wanted to look upon every day for as long as she lived. "But...you would leave your family and the bakery? Can they do without you? Can you live without them?"

"I have already left them for your sake. The bakery has survived for a hundred years. It will go on in the care of my siblings, and pass into the hands of their children and grandchildren, I do not doubt."

"Then, will you be my husband?"

A mischievous smile played upon his lips. "You are sure you want to be wed to a baker? I cannot promise there will be no crumbs." Lukas tugged her closer and encircled her with his arms.

"I will tolerate as many crumbs as I must, and I will love you faithfully and always," Marga said.

"*Ja*, I will be your husband, Queen Margarethe."

She stood on tiptoe and kissed him as snowflakes whirled around them.

"Long live our good queen and her true love!" a high-pitched faerie voice cried out from the branches of a nearby tree. Joyous shouts rang out from all around the yard. Not all the forest creatures had dispersed, after all.

Marga did not know the proper etiquette for the situation. She probably owed her subjects a fine speech or a week-long feast in return for their support. It was something she'd have to research later. Nothing seemed more important at that moment than kissing the baker who'd accepted her bold proposal.

And so she kissed him, again and again.

Every snowflake that lighted upon them evaporated into a glittering wisp of silver.

Thirty-Seven

Defeated.

Ansgar stood alone in the gingerbread cottage and stared at the fire, attempting to rub warmth back into his long white fingers.

Why did he feel so weighed down with defeat? Had he not achieved everything he'd set out to? He'd shed his feathers and reclaimed his manly form. Through his efforts, the new witch-queen of the Igelwald had been enthroned. Yet these things did not feel like victory.

Banishment did not feel like winning.

Ansgar had no personal possessions to gather. On the day she'd turned him into a duck, Truda had burned every object he'd owned, save for the clothes Gretel had chanced upon, worn, and sullied.

He found a burlap sack inside a cabinet and tossed in a few things for his journey: flint and steel, a blanket Truda had knitted, several candles, a water skin, and a bottle of powder designed to ward off wild beasts and dangerous fae. On a whim, he snatched Beckmann's tattered-edged journal from the mantel. Who knew when a recipe for magical gingerbread might prove useful? Before he set out in earnest, he would top off the sack with gems and coins from the hoard hidden in the shed.

In spite of the bitter cold and the falling snow, Gretel and the baker were taking an eternity to come inside. Ansgar glanced out the candy windowpane as he passed. Of course they were kissing. Of course they'd get the happy ending he'd thrown away by indulging his lust like some stupid animal.

He averted his eyes, sighed, and moved into the bedchamber, hoping to find Truda's old velvet cloak. It wasn't heavy, but it would help him preserve a measure of warmth as he traveled through the forest. Was it too much, too sentimental to hope the garment might have retained her scent? She'd always smelled of roses, thyme, and wood smoke. Magical, indeed.

When he opened the wardrobe's doors, he found nothing but a nest of newborn mouselings and a thin shawl. With a grunt, he snatched up the shawl and then shut the doors. He wished the mice long lives and many progeny. Perhaps they'd vex the new queen with their endless nibbling and nightly gifts of droppings. The gods knew she wouldn't have the heart to kill the wee vermin with her words.

The mirror in which Truda had appeared had become nothing but an ordinary mirror. It lay on the bed where he'd left it. Speckled and hazy with age, it was an object for which no one would pay a quarter hour's wages. Nevertheless, he wanted it with a visceral longing. He could not leave it behind, no matter that its weight would slow his journey. No matter that nothing of Truda remained within the mottled glass.

Ansgar picked up the mirror and tucked it under his arm. His heart swelled with memories as his eyes scanned the room he'd shared with his bride. His eyes brimmed with tears. By the gods, he was becoming sentimental in his old age.

He was old, he felt it now. Something had gone out of him when Gretel had banished him. His joints creaked and complained as he hefted the sack and let it settle over his bony shoulder.

When he crept across the yard to the shed, Gretel and the baker paid him no mind, consumed with their kissing. He might have been as noisy as a herd of cattle and they would have ignored him. He was tempted to stir up a gale or pummel them with hailstones just to see if they'd end their embrace, but the experiment was not worth the energy it would cost. He had a long walk ahead of him.

Inside the shed, as he stuffed the sack with jewels, he pictured the cottage by the sea where he'd spend the rest of his days in peace. He'd cast away his earlier plans of living in luxury amidst fawning French servants. He'd dwell simply and let his magic rest.

He laughed aloud at the thought of abandoning his magic. How utterly ridiculous! He envisioned the first traveling peddler who dared to annoy him as he tossed crusts to circling, squawking gulls. Would he curse the fellow with huge warts to repulse the housewives, or bestow upon him an itchy, fiery rash to make him wriggle upon his wagon seat? Why not both?

"Oh, Truda," he said as he left the shed with the full sack slung over his shoulder. "I shall find pleasure enough for us both in the days that remain for me. This I vow, my love. My true queen."

He trudged through the snow, heading west.

Thirty-Eight

"No one will marry us," Marga said, setting the teapot on the table. She sat across from Lukas and watched him transfer a griddle cake from the platter to the pile on his plate. In the midst of this tranquil, domestic scene, it seemed impossible that yesterday she'd fought off an enraged mob, exiled her enemy, and become the queen of the Igelwald.

Lukas lifted his fork and poked at the air. "Pastor Günter would burn himself at the stake before he'd agree to perform the ceremony, it is true. I saw him among the townsfolk yesterday, you know. Cowering at the edge of the woods with a hoe in his hand."

"Even if he wanted to wed us, Pastor Günter would never get consent from the town councilors. Without that, our marriage would be void."

"Who needs them?" Lukas said, spearing a bite. "You are the queen of this forest, *Liebling*. Surely a queen can perform a legally binding wedding ceremony."

Marga's face brightened as she pondered his point. "Yes.

And since I am bound by magic to remain in the Igelwald for the rest of my life, it does seem to me that what the rest of the world considers legal is of no consequence."

"There. Queen Margarethe has solved the problem." Lukas reached for Marga's hand and lifted it to kiss her knuckles.

A blush warmed her cheeks. Queens were not immune to blushing, apparently. "Well, then. As queen, I declare that Lukas Beckmann and Margarethe Holzfäller shall marry under the pines, by starlight, this very evening."

His eyes widened with surprise. "Tonight? You don't need time to sew a dress or some such thing?"

"You object?"

"I would never oppose the edict of my queen." He kissed her knuckles again, worshipping her with a gaze that made her insides feel like melting candle wax.

She smiled and slipped her hand out of his. "You would, and you will, when I am your wife and you are my husband. We will disagree, and we will fight, and I will love you more and more each day."

"Such wisdom in one so small," Lukas said.

She pushed the platter of griddle cakes toward him. "Have more. You'll need your strength. You have a wedding cake to bake before sunset, one large enough to feed all the faerie guests and forest creatures who might happen by."

"I will bake the very best cake I have ever made," Lukas vowed. "And after that, if the weather allows, I will bake gingerbread to repair the bedchamber wall, and biscuits to fix the roof properly."

"You still want to risk trying your old family recipe? I

don't mind staying in the kitchen. Only a little snow sifts through the roof, and it's no trouble to sweep up." She'd come to terms with using magic herself, but she did not want him to endanger himself by meddling with magical recipes. "Why not wait until spring to work on repairs?"

"I am not afraid. My bride holds more power than paper, ink, flour, and spices. But we should speak of this later, or our breakfast will go cold."

Marga smiled as he poured honey onto his cakes. It was a good thing the man knew how to bake, because his love for food was becoming more and more obvious. The Holzfällers of Eschlinsdorf had always employed a cook, so her knowledge of food preparation was limited. Griddle cakes and tea were her only specialties. But she would try, and she would learn to put palatable food onto their table. If all else failed, they'd have bread—or great stacks of toast slathered with wild berry jam.

In comfortable silence, they ate. After Lukas swallowed the last morsel of griddle cake, he patted his belly. Marga poured the rest of the lavender tea into his mug. "When spring comes," she said, "I want us to build a new house on the hill beyond the meadow. One made of wood and stone."

Lukas nodded. "I've glimpsed the spot from the far edge of the garden. The perfect place."

"We'll grow wheat and barley in the meadow, and build a big oven for you behind the house," Marga added.

"Our children will grow fat on my good bread."

"They'll climb trees and befriend faeries and fawns."

"And they will be cherished always."

"And afraid of nothing."

"They will be brave like their mother...but taller, perhaps."

Marga laughed. "Well, they'll never nibble a magic-tainted gingerbread cottage as I did. I will make sure of that." A memory came to her mind, a vision of little Hansel feasting on a piece of gingerbread he'd torn from a windowsill. She missed that boy, her brother. She doubted she would ever see Hansel again. But she would not allow thoughts of her foolish brother to impinge upon her present happiness.

Lukas pulled Marga out of her chair and onto his lap.

"May I have the queen's leave to kiss her?"

She brushed a crumb off his chest with only the slightest cringe. The day would come when crumbs no longer bothered her, this she knew. A crumb would be only a crumb and not a memory of darker days.

She was the ruler of the Igelwald and everything in it, after all. The past could hurt her no more.

"You have the queen's permission to kiss her often and well," she said. And then she kissed him before he had a chance.

* * *

The day had been endless.

Ansgar stumbled up another slippery hill, stubbing his toes on rocks concealed by deep snow. He'd run out of curse words, or he would have uttered a string of them. He was beginning to wonder if the forest magic was playing tricks, adding hours to the day to spite him. It *was* on the new witch-queen's side now, the Igelwald. It likely abhorred him as it abhorred the beetles that ate the hearts of its trees. Truly, he would have counted it a favor if the forest had spat him out into some village beyond its bounds.

After plodding through the snow for mile after mile, Ansgar's feet felt as if a hundred hornets were ceaselessly stinging them. Eventually, his toes grew numb. He knew no spell to warm them while he walked, and besides, his magic now felt weaker and more sluggish than ever. He would have to stop to build a fire before frostbite took his extremities.

Dusk fell about him in a purplish gray haze as he filled his arms with dry kindling and branches snapped from dead trees. Next, with reddened, chapped hands, he cleared snow off a large, flat boulder and started to arrange pine needles and sticks as his mother had taught him long, long ago. He had not the mental capacity to calculate the number of years that had passed since then.

Overhead, flocks of birds and faeries whooshed toward the east. Their many wings stirred a mighty breeze. They twittered and chattered as they flew. Along the ground, wingless types of faeries ran, followed by squirrels and rabbits, and trailed by ambling hedgehogs. Through the trees, he spied deer and bears traveling the same direction. He heard the grunting of wild boar charging through the brush. He did not smell smoke, but for what other reason would creatures that hid or hibernated in winter be galloping through the Igelwald?

"Is the forest on fire?" Ansgar asked an old hedgehog that lagged behind the rest.

The hedgehog grumbled a few sentences in its own

language, but Ansgar understood its meaning. At least that part of his magic remained.

According to the hedgehog, the animals and faerie folk of the forest were hurrying to witness the moonrise wedding of the new witch-queen. After the ceremony, the faeries would provide three days of feasts. The birds would offer music for dancing. Had he not heard of the new queen? She was young and good, with a heart full of love for the Igelwald's inhabitants. Things would be different now. The woods would be greener in the spring and less frigid in the winter. From now on, there would be greater peace among them—and more food. The hedgehog fancied fattening up on grubs and berries.

"Of course. Of course," Ansgar said. He ought to have suspected as much.

The hedgehog waddled away, complaining under its breath about the agony of having short, age-weakened legs.

For most of his life, Ansgar had been proud of his black heart and wicked ways. Truda had helped to make him that man—a spouse fit for a cruel witch-queen. Yet here he stood, wishing he could see little Gretel marry oafish Herr Beckmann. Well, Truda had always said he had a romantic soul.

If he was honest—and it made him cringe to be, in this instance—the brawny baker was a suitable match for Margarethe Holzfäller. He was thoroughly wholesome, and she was good as good could be.

Ansgar returned to fire-building as the commotion died down. His frozen fingers fumbled with the small sticks. Ah, the minute tasks of daily life. How tedious and yet how essential. When done for oneself, they meant little beyond survival. But if he could have made a fire to warm Truda, to bring her comfort, to please her—that would have meant everything to him. The task would have been a sacred act. But what did he know of sacred things? He'd been a villain for so, so long. And Truda was gone.

When the fire finally sparked to life, he lifted his gaze to the eastern sky, where a golden glow hovered above the treetops. Cheers and howls echoed through the woods. It was done, then. The witch-queen had married the baker.

He picked up the old, frost-glazed mirror and hugged it to his chest.

"All of this is your fault," he said to his vanished wife. "But I must tell you, my dark and dreadful love, that you have failed most beautifully."

From the glass, he thought he heard the faintest of whispers.

Ansgar.

Also by Carrie Anne Noble

The Gingerbread Queen

The Mermaid's Sister

The Gold-Son

Gretchen and the Bear

The Peddler's Reward

About the Author

In the wake of her thrilling past as a theater student, restaurant hostess, nurse aide, and newspaper writer, Carrie Anne Noble now crafts enchanting fiction for teens and adults. Her debut novel *The Mermaid's Sister* won the 2014 Amazon Breakthrough Novel Award for Young Adult Fiction and the 2016 Realm Award for Book of the Year. Her other books include YA fantasies entitled *The Gold-Son* and *Gretchen and the Bear*. Carrie lives in the Pennsylvania mountains, where she enjoys taking walks, frolicking with her half-Corgi, and hosting the occasional mad tea party. Connect with Carrie online at www.carrienoble.com.

Printed in the USA
CPSIA information can be obtained
at www.ICGtesting.com
CBHW031156110624
9887CB00009BA/231